I stood in the cell door and watched her, the fingers still in her ears. Useless. She was not even aware that I had stood up and was now leaving.

Beside her on the table was my peace offering, the cup of coffee, now cold.

For the first time during that long afternoon, I saw her lift her head and look directly at me through the bars, her eyes black and fearful. And still looking at me, as though she was trying hard to conquer her fear, she lifted the cup of cold coffee to her lips and drank it.

It is difficult to describe my feelings at that moment. Her gift to me, the simple act of drinking the coffee, I still consider one of the most treasured I have ever received . . .

HATTER FOX

MARILYN HARRIS

BALLANTINE BOOKS • NEW YORK

Library of Congress Catalog Card Number: 73-5057

ISBN 0-345-30026-2

This edition published by arrangement with Random House

Manufactured in the United States of America

First Ballantine Books Edition: January 1983

For Judge,
for reasons too numerous
and personal to list . . .

We cannot live for ourselves alone. Our lives are connected by a thousand invisible threads, and along these sympathetic fibers, our actions run as causes and return to us as results . . .

Herman Melville

HATTER FOX

The Notebooks
of Doctor Teague Summer
Concerning Hatter Fox

I had heard of Hatter Fox, but I had never seen her.

You can't live in Santa Fe and not have heard of Hatter Fox. Name it, and Hatter's been accused of it. Someone who should know better once called her "the worst of all possible bitches, an intelligent Navajo." Hatter, the renegade, the prostitute, the drug addict, the thief. In the year since I've been here, I have heard her blamed for the bad water, the economy, President Nixon, the tourists, the hippies, and the traffic lights around the Plaza that never work.

The first time I saw Hatter Fox, she was standing in the middle of a crowded jail cell directing traffic. There were about twenty other kids, all drug offenders, in the cell with her. Hatter had organized the twenty into two groups of ten each. One group marched from the north wall to the south wall, then halted, permitting her to direct the other group to march from east to west.

When I arrived on the second floor of the jail, I saw about half a dozen of Santa Fe's finest standing outside the locked cell, yelling for Hatter to cut it out or else. But the curious marching ritual proceeded with military precision, Hatter standing directly at the center, holding back one group while waving the other on in the opposite direction. She was wearing a battered policeman's helmet that she had picked up from God knows where, well-worn bell-bottoms, and a shirt that probably had been white once but was now covered with splotchy brown stains. Nothing about her appearance was very unique. You could find several like her within five blocks of the jail. She was doing a pretty fair job of ignoring the cops outside the cell, and an equally fair job of completely controlling the kids inside the cell. There was no sound at all except for the shuffle of bare feet following the movement of her hands, and a groan or two from the Indian boy in the far corner who had cut his wrists and was now bleeding to death. The marchers moved back and forth across the cell floor, leaving red footprints in the areas where the blood had not yet spread.

As a new doctor with the Bureau of Indian Affairs, I'm frequently called to the jail when Indians are involved. My job, as I was informed before I entered the cell, was to see if anything could be done for the kid bleeding to death. From the amount of blood already spilled, my snap judgment was no. In addition, I was to see if I could find the sharp object he'd used. The kids had all been picked up the night before in the Plaza, stoned out of their heads, running toward the Palace of Governors with enough dynamite to make a noticeable change in the Santa Fe landscape. They had all been searched, yes. But obviously someone had overlooked something.

During this briefing, I watched Hatter, who was watching no one. Her eyes were closed. She looked to be about seventeen. She had long straight black hair and the delicate lips, nose, face, and large slanted Oriental eyes of the more unusual type of Navajo. She was slender to the point of emaciation, and at that point her own feet were covered with the boy's blood.

Suddenly the marching stopped. I watched her slowly extend a toe as though to block a new stream of blood as it flowed toward the front of the cell. The other kids halted and watched her closely as she stooped to touch the blood, immerse her hands in it, taste it, rub it over her face and down over her breasts. The most incredible aspect of the spectacle, besides the actual and grisly fact of what she was doing, was the flowing quality of her movements. She gestured with sustained, circular, ritualistic motions.

Someone behind me cursed, "Goddamn Indian kook."

A police officer opened the cell door for me. I've never seen anyone look at me as Hatter Fox did while I finally entered the cell and passed behind her on my way to the dying or dead boy; there was a degree of terror in her eyes which seemed to suggest that I was all of the world's curses and plagues rolled into one. I have never seen such an expression on the human face. And, I swear it, I have never seen anyone draw a knife as quickly as Hatter Fox did at that moment; she planted it into the area of my back directly beneath the left shoulder joint, the blade penetrating the scapula and parting the deltoid muscle.

The pain was not as bad as you might think. I suppose the suddenness of the attack caught my nerves off guard along with everyone else. The initial penetration was a burning sensation, sharp and stinging. But it was over soon, followed by a blessed numbness, as though my entire back had gone to sleep.

The last thing I remember was falling forward and down. The blood-covered floor was coming up very fast, and the side of my face was resting finally in the boy's blood. And I remember something else. I remember Hatter Fox kneeling beside my head, her fingers making blood drawings on the side of my face—the terror still in her eyes, but mixed now with relief and satisfaction, as though she had just rid the world of all curses, all plagues. I remember the delicate nose and mouth, the slanted Oriental eyes, that stupid policeman's helmet. And I remember that she was smiling.

After that, the whole scene became incredibly foolish, and I viewed it all as though underwater. There seemed to be mass confusion in the cell. Some idiot leaned very close to my ear and said, "Hang in there, buddy." I saw through underwater eyes that two cops had pinned Hatter against the wall close to the boy's body and were at that moment stripping her. The humiliation and fear on her face pleased me, but at the same time I thought it was a stupid thing to do; obviously I had found the sharp object.

St. Vincent's Hospital is only a short distance from the jail, and I was taken there in a melodramatic fuss of screeching sirens. Viewing the world from a semiconscious state isn't half bad. You're still a part of everything, but you feel no responsibility. You are happy to be nothing, to belong to yourself no longer, to let someone else play the hand for you. What foolish vanity it is to always demand the leading role! There was the usual glut of tourists gawking at every intersection, and a pleasant colorful blur of treetops and high blue sky, and the stately and at that moment ominous hulk of St. Francis of Assisi Cathedral. Predictably, last rites passed through my head, and I cursed Hatter Fox and the new twinges of discomfort jumping across my back.

I made the AP Wire Service—*Medic Stabbed in Jail Cell*. There were a few frantic parental calls from Lowell, Massachusetts, three potted plants from the guys at the jail, a visit from the District Attorney urging me to press charges, a visit from a Father Duval urging me not to press charges.

Four days and twenty-one stitches later, I stood in the sun on the porch of St. Vincent's and promised the doctor that I wouldn't drive until all the numbness was gone from my left arm, that I'd take a few days off from my rounds and rest, and that I'd check back with him in about a week. He started to pat me on the back, but caught himself in time.

The world is beautiful when you've been flat on your stomach and haven't been able to look at it for a few days. The blue of a really blue sky is something to see after you've had one vivid thought that you may not see it again. I moved very slowly down the hospital steps, as though I were carrying on my back a dozen fresh eggs. A half a block later, I went in the side door of the cathedral and made my way through a group of tourists to a front pew. I got on my knees in spite of the objection coming from my back, and I did something I haven't done for twenty years, since I was a kid.

I gave thanks.

The boy with cut wrists died. In fact he was dead before I'd ever entered the cell. Hatter Fox knew he was dead—knew, I think, the exact moment he died. Navajos have an interesting conception of death: the act of dying is worthy of ritual, but death itself is something to be ignored.

After I left the cathedral, I went over to the jail and learned from a very sympathetic desk sergeant that most of the twenty young drug offenders had been released on bail, but the two older men who had been carrying the dynamite had been held over for trials and would probably be given prison sentences. I learned that some of the kids were from the commune outside town, others were street people, and the rest were Indians.

And Hatter Fox?

She was still upstairs, locked up. She was only seventeen, too young for prison. The judge had refused to release her, and apparently no one had come forward with bail, or to claim her in any way. An indeterminate sentence at the State Reformatory for Girls was about the best they could come up with unless I had other ideas.

Fresh from praying, there was no accounting for the rush of barbaric feelings I had at that moment. It seemed perverse somehow that the knife-wielder was still sitting upstairs with only a few months in the reformatory facing her. Someone asked if I wanted to see her. I said no. Several other cops had gathered by then; I accepted their condolences, permitted them to examine the wound, and told them I walked stooped over because it was easier than standing up straight; then I started to leave. I'd gotten as far as the door when I realized—and it was quite a surprise—that I wanted very much to see Hatter Fox. I wanted to see her behind bars, even if they were only county-jail bars. I wanted her to see me and the new stoop in my back, and I must confess that I wanted very much to see the humiliation and fear that I'd seen in her face as the cops were stripping her that day in the cell.

The matron came, a fat, bored-looking Mexican woman with a mouth full of gold teeth. She jerked her head at me, indication that I was to follow her. A few good-natured obscenities were shouted after me by the gaping cops, generally concerned with what I could and could not do to Hatter Fox within the limits of the law.

There was a silent elevator ride up, countless clankings of doors, a walk past cells with male prisoners staring blankly out, more clankings, and finally a long corridor with a dim cubicle at the end, and the muttered advice of the matron to stay away from the bars, as the devil had long fangs—her words, not mine.

I knew the cell. It was the isolation unit. Only a few months before, I had been called there to treat an old Indian in the last stages of VD. Such an end is noisy, beyond mere pain. The hospital didn't have room for him, so they kept him isolated in the jail, and sedated with daily injections. To the best of my knowledge the cell hadn't been used since the death of the old man.

After giving her advice, the matron stopped at the last door making it clear that I was to proceed alone in my lunacy. Somehow I felt I owed her an explanation, but how could I possible make clear to her that we all are irresistibly drawn toward that which tries to destroy us. For at that moment I felt a pull toward the cubicle that was as strong, as certain, as if there were a magnet behind the bars.

Four paths of sun were filtering in through the high barred windows. There was no movement in the cell that I could see. The stool was visible from my vantage point at the end of the hall, and the corner of the cot on which the old man had died, and a blanket in disarray. It pleased me somehow to think that Hatter Fox was locked up in that place of death.

Halfway down the hall, and still I'd caught no glimpse of life or movement. One stark thought flashed across my mind: she had escaped, and was at that moment hiding behind a door close by, waiting, knife in hand. But then I saw the unmistakable lump of feet beneath the blanket, then the whole of her stretched out on the cot.

I stopped a few feet from the cell door. She was not merely lying on the cot. She had arranged herself into a kind of royal pose. The ceremony of a Navajo Sing came to mind. Her toes were aligned and pointed beneath the blanket, her legs straight, her bare arms uncovered, and her hands clasped across her breasts. The long black hair was arranged too perfectly, fanlike beneath her head, and the head itself was lifted slightly, the chin pointing upward, the large, slanted Oriental eyes were opened and fixed on the ceiling. From where I stood I saw no sign of chest movement. Suicide, I thought.

I called back to the matron, "Is she sick?"

"Stubborn," came the reply. "She won't put on the dress."

"Dress?" With the question I turned too rapidly from the matron and felt an imaginary knife in the fresh wound. Then I saw it, the gray heap of material thrown in the corner of the cell, in color and shape not unlike the one the matron was wearing. So! That was good, even worth the dull turn of the imaginary knife, the thought that Hatter Fox was crouching naked beneath the soiled blanket. The only trouble was, she wasn't crouching. There was no way that the word "crouching" could be used to describe her position on the cot. She had assumed a position, a state of mind which was strong enough to literally transform the barren, ugly isolation unit into a royal chamber. She turned her head in my direction, and her eyes widened. There it was again—the incredible fear and terror that I'd first seen in the cell downstairs. Suddenly she closed her eyes and opened them again, focusing on a spot on the ceiling. I watched her profile more closely and thought of one or two things to say to her. I wanted in the worst way for her to know what I'd been through at her hands. But for one of a very few times in my life, I could not bring myself to speak.

I noticed other specifics about her. There was what appeared to be a raw scraped place on the right side of her forehead which I had not noticed the first time I had seen her in the cell downstairs. On the floor to one side of the door was a tray of uneaten food. Several flies were buzzing over it; they made the only noise. It was hot, and the air smelled of old urine and vomit. But if any of this mattered very much to her, she had learned somehow to live with it. Her forehead glistened slightly from the heat of the blanket, and once I noticed a fly land on the raw place on her forehead. But no irritated hand moved to brush it away. No movement at all. No sign of life. Nothing.

When you've lost blood and been flat on your stomach for several days, your knees have a tendency not to support you in their customary manner. I felt myself becoming nauseated at the sight, the flies, the heat, the smells. Hatter had somehow managed to remove herself from these minor agonies. I stood for a while longer, trying to ignore the most persistent questions in my head. Why? Why everything? Why the need for such a room? Why the need for emergency calls to jail cells where kids have cut their wrists? Why Hatter Fox? Why the human waste beyond redemption, beyond help? And finally, why in the hell was I standing there, apparently transfixed by a young girl who had tried hard to kill me?

There were no answers. Just the heat, the smells, and the fearful yet victorious outline of Hatter Fox, naked beneath the blanket. I turned to leave, using the corridor wall for support. I got about halfway to the door and the bored matron when I heard it: a low chant of sorts, a hum with a rapid pulsing movement, a restless, beautiful melody limited to no more than four or five notes—plaintive, of minor tonality, yet somehow, I swear it, victorious sounding. No recognizable words accompanied the chant, only sounds and the music itself, no more than a humming.

I did not turn back to look. I had seen enough, but I stopped to listen. Only an American Indian can take a minor key and make it sound victorious. The chant continued, the rhythmic pattern became more complicated than the tonal pattern—her way, I supposed, of letting me know she knew I had been there.

The matron had the door unlocked for me. I moved slowly down the line of gaping male prisoners. At the elevator, the matron opened the door and closed it behind me, and I was alone in the descent. My back hurt; it felt like the stitches had broken. The meager hospital breakfast kept trying to rise in my throat, the elevator was making a peculiar sound like Hatter's chant, sweat was pouring off my forehead, and the image of Hatter Fox was burning itself indelibly into the center of my brain.

Somehow I got past the desk and the curious cops to the door and outside, where the sun was gone and the air was cool and rain was falling. There seems to be an unnecessary amount of theatrics in New Mexico rainstorms. The trees dip and quake, and everyone seems to run a little faster for shelter than they do in ordinary rainstorms.

I remember I didn't run at all that day. I walked very deliberately down the middle of an empty sidewalk toward the Plaza, where I stopped at the first bar and got bombed out of my head. Drinking to excess generally doesn't appeal to me, but to my surprise I discovered that I was a hero to the barflies. They seemed to know who I was, and what had been done, and that I'd just come from the hospital. They viewed the whole thing as legitimate reason for celebration. I was given the seat of honor and all the free booze I could drink in exchange for a look at the knife wound and a firsthand account of what had "really happened." The "Indian bitch" was verbally raped, crucified, drawn and quartered. The bottle was always within easy reach, and I discovered that the more I drank, the less I could hear the chant and see her form stretched out on the cot. When the bar closed, I was lovingly placed in the back seat of a taxi, and driven free of charge, in drunken splendor, to my trailer.

A voice left over from med school told me not to lie down because I might choke on my own vomit. So I passed the night sitting up in a chair, covered with my own sickness, the drunken hero, listening to Hatter Fox's chant, vowing to leave Santa Fe for a change of scenery when the sun came out.

As bad luck would have it, the sun didn't come out for three days. It rained constantly, and I stayed inside and cleaned myself up and wrote a few letters to Lowell, Massachusetts, and tried a few tricks of physical therapy to get rid of the numbness in my left arm, and got bored as hell.

On the fourth day, I decided to drive up to Taos to see a friend of mine, an artist who makes erotic sculpture out of remnants of junkyards. The barflies at La Cocina stood up and applauded when I came in, and at one time I counted an audience of seventeen strangers listening intently to my account of what had "actually happened" that day in the jail cell. All the screwed-up artists who come to the bar to talk about their unwritten plays and unpainted paintings were my pawns. And once again Hatter Fox was verbally assaulted, the imagined brutality slightly kinkier, and the "Indian problem" became all but intolerable in the mere act of talking about it. I drank too much again, and was carried out on someone's shoulders, and spent a lost number of days and nights watching my friend sculpt a nude female Mexican with a great body, and feeling the stitches dissolve in my back.

As a rule, drunken stupors run their course. I wanted very much to preside again over the ritual of birth and death. I wanted equally as much to forget about my itching back, and Hatter Fox, and the chant, and Hatter Fox, her forehead bruised, stretched out beneath the blanket, and Hatter Fox washing herself in the boy's blood. So, freshly washed, shaved, and standing erect, I left the great Mexican female body, the lost artists of La Cocina Bar, the junkyard erotica, the enchilada dinners, and drove back to Santa Fe.

I don't remember who told me that Hatter Fox had been taken to the Girls' Reformatory outside Albuquerque; at best it was useless information. I had reached the point where I only heard her chant as I dropped off to sleep at night. The knife wound had completely healed except for a slight itching beyond my reach. And Santa Fe was in the process of settling down for the winter.

For the most part, the town and I seemed to be in a comatose state. I still made my rounds and took the overflow calls from the clinic, and delivered 4.2 babies per week and assisted in an equal number of deaths. Somehow it balances out. Even life at the commune had settled down as most of the city-kids-turned-frontiersmen predictably opted for the comforts of city life. Only the dedicated freaks remained behind, and they knew how to take care of themselves.

In prolonged periods of extreme boredom the mind elects mundane things to anticipate. Mail. I would frequently break speed limits driving home in the afternoon to see what the mailman had left. Bills, mostly; reminders of payments due on the stereo; cheap paper booklets on tax breaks for those making $50,000 a year or more; medical journals; letters primly printed from Lowell, Massachusetts; bulletins from the church reminding me of God's needs. And one day a starched, all-business-looking letter from the State Reformatory for Girls outside Albuquerque.

I knew before I opened the envelope that it concerned Hatter Fox. Part of me, the most honest part, was very pleased to receive word. The letter was an inquiry from a social worker named Miss Joan Valdez. She stated in brand-new master's-degree English that she had been assigned to a few of the new cases at the reformatory, and she was conducting personal-file investigations on the following names. There followed four female names. The only one that interested me was number three—Hatter Fox. She concluded by saying that if I could assist her in any way with any of the names, I was to place a collect call to the following number, and an appointment would be arranged.

Admittedly my reaction was all out of proportion to the simple content of the letter. I think in a way I was hoping for news, not a request for assistance. There was nothing I could tell Miss Valdez about Hatter Fox, and nothing, I suspected, that anyone else could tell her. The puzzle was theirs.

A week passed. The letter from Miss Valdez had been ignored, but not destroyed. It rested to one side of the general clutter on my desk. I looked at it now and then and recalled the skinny, delicate-featured Indian, the marchers walking through blood, and the initial sensation of burning on my back. And I remembered too the low, motionless, and proud outline beneath the blanket.

About a week later, I received another letter from the State Reformatory. This time they had hauled out the big guns. It was from a Dr. Thomas Levering, head psychiatrist at the school. He didn't beat around the bush in the polite, official language of Miss Valdez. The first line bluntly stated that this letter concerned an inmate at the reformatory named Hatter Fox. He went on to list her "activities" of the last several weeks. She had managed to set fire to her dormitory once, had stuffed a toilet with Kotex and flooded an entire floor, had tried to escape twice, and had only recently attacked a girl with a knife. No amount or measure of disciplinary action seemed to make the slightest difference. He went on to say that he had learned from a local agency that I had once come in contact with Hatter Fox.

In short, Dr. Levering sounded like a desperate man. He somehow felt that they were missing a vital clue as to what made Hatter tick. They had searched the Navajo reservation and other Indian communities within the area and could find no one who would claim her, or even claim that they knew her. He surmised that she seemed to be dedicated to the proposition of destroying everyone and everything around her, and then herself—in that order. He pleaded that if there was any way at all I felt I could help, I should contact him immediately. There followed a phone number and a backward-slanting personal signature that renewed my distrust of all shrinks.

Help Hatter Fox! The suggestion seemed merely insane. As long as I had been in Santa Fe I had made exactly one trip into Albuquerque. Why should I make a second? I hated cities and insoluble problems, and knife-wielding, hate-ridden females. Change the world? No one could do that.

Except me.

Albuquerque is about a sixty-mile drive from Santa Fe. You come down out of the high, crisp air and dazzling colors of the Sangre de Cristo Mountains into the flat brown doldrums of desert New Mexico, and with every mile, you feel like asking yourself, "Why in hell am I doing this?"

It was a Thursday, I remember, in early December. I felt snow in the air, and I thought it would be just my luck to get snowed out. I had ignored Dr. Levering's letter for two weeks and had worked overtime in an attempt to get caught up on my cases. I had neither forgotten nor ignored Hatter Fox; I had not forgotten her for a moment since the first time I had seen her. And I wanted to see her again, I'll admit it—to see for myself the young Indian who apparently had completely upset the bureaucratic machinery of the State Reformatory for Girls. "No amount or measure of disciplinary action seems to make the slightest difference." That, too, stuck in my mind. It seemed an awesome confession coming from one of the strictest disciplinary institutions in the state.

There is no adequate way to describe my feelings as I was driving down to Albuquerque that day. Part of me saw myself as a kind of army-surplus Don Quixote. Another part of me saw the world's all-time sucker, and still a third part refused to see myself as anything at all, a kind of physical vacuum, as if no one was driving the jeep, as if the jeep wasn't even moving, as if the highway and the passing cars and scenery were all figments of my imagination. This multiplicity of personal visions was compounded by the fact that no matter how hard I tried to project an image of what I might find when I arrived, I could produce nothing of reality or substance. It was as if Hatter Fox had become for me an essence, an airy representation of all my past failures.

But something prevented me from turning the steering wheel and going back. Whatever the something was, it wasn't strong enough to prevent me from pulling off onto the shoulder, three, four, five times.

It took me three hours to go sixty miles. On an adequate highway. With little traffic.

There is no such thing as a good state reformatory. My apologies to all those states who are making sincere efforts to reform their reformatories. But it seems to me that a reformatory is a perfect symbol of a society's failure to understand and incorporate its young, a kind of Grand Canyon between what we think we are and what we are afraid we might become. Too young for prison, too incorrigible for hearth and home, these kids are mirror-image reflections of our failures; and like all failures, they are an embarrassment. So we hide them away behind bricks and bars in places staffed for the most part by people who with only a slight twist of fate might have been the inmates instead of the keepers. The primary tenet of all reform authority is first instill fear, then with the remaining energy and little money, try to rehabilitate. In state budgets, the reformatory's place comes somewhere after the graft, between campaign debts and payoffs. I knew all this before I arrived at the reformatory that day. Why, then, was I in no way prepared for what I found?

What I found was a barren complex of red-brick buildings surrounded entirely by high barbed-wire fences; at the gate were two guardhouses, and chained outside, four dogs. Admittedly the day was bleak and cold, and my own mood, as I have stated, was at best unaccountable. But the flat, empty landscape surrounding the institution seemed unduly sterile after the natural variety of the area around Santa Fe, and I confess that I experienced a small twinge of actual apprehension as I stood outside the gate in a bitter wind, trying to explain to a sullen-faced Mexican guard who I was and why I had come. He looked at me as though he were accustomed to lies and liars, asked again for the name of Dr. Levering, and finally, without a word, went inside his sentry booth where I could see him, still keeping his eye on me, pick up a telephone.

I hopped on one foot and then the other in an attempt to keep warm, and pulled my jacket tighter around me, and tried not to look at the red-brick façade, and tried not to imagine what went on behind the barred windows. The most interesting experiment was my attempt to imagine what a young girl would think and feel as she was being driven up to this gate.

Apparently the guard was having some difficulty. I saw him dial a series of numbers, obviously with no success. Finally he must have made contact with someone because I saw him cup his hand around the receiver, and for the first time take his eyes off me and turn away. It was all very secretive and might have been threatening if it hadn't been so melodramatic. The whole ritual seemed designed to intimidate. I began to walk in a brisk circle around the jeep, trying to explain to myself why I was walking in a brisk circle around the jeep, why I had driven sixty miles on a miserable day to talk to a shrink with neurotic handwriting about an Indian girl who had tried to kill me.

No answers. Finally I crawled into the jeep, slouched down behind the wheel, and watched the little one-man drama being played out for my benefit in the sentry box. The guard was looking at me again, perhaps describing me to someone. Once he leaned out of the door and studied the front of the jeep closely. License number? Good God.

I remember I'd gripped the wheel at an angle to make a broad turnabout when suddenly the Mexican reappeared at the gate, begrudgingly unlocked it, swung it open just wide enough for the passage of a small car, and with a clearly hostile and still-suspicious jerk of his head, motioned me through.

Too late. Having put him to so much trouble, I couldn't very well refuse. The next dilemma was to determine which of the forked gravel driveways led to the one red-brick building where I would find the alleged Dr. Thomas Levering.

A perfectly logical solution occurred. Which one did I feel like taking? I stopped the jeep to examine my feelings on the matter, and spied a small white sign close to the ground, almost invisible: on it was a black hand pointing to the right and the words "Administration Building." True absurdity has no signposts. It had begun to sleet If the icy rain kept up, in a few hours the highways would be slick and dangerous. I would be trapped.

All institutions have the same odor. State buildings, federal buildings, schools, prisons, reformatories —they all smell the same, a curious blend of floor wax and old coffee, and strong detergents, a necessary odor when dealing with humanity en masse. In the foyer of the administration building, I found this odor, a coke machine with an out-of-order sign hung on the front, two plastic-covered sofas, a motley assortment of worn tables, two benches, and slack-jawed, one-eyed custodian who seemed to resent the fact that I was alive. I stated the name of the man I was looking for. I might as well have been speaking a foreign language. He glared at me with his good eye while I tried to figure out how he got the puckered, drawn, brown, and very useless eyelid, and decided on a slingshot accident or a firecracker. His good eye seemed concerned only with the fact that I was tracking up his floor. I was sorry about the floor and the sleet outside and the slingshot accident, but there wasn't a hell of a lot I could do about any of it. Finally he shook his head, a gesture of resignation he'd probably been born with, and went on about his business of old tile floors and hate.

At the end of the foyer, I saw what looked like the spill of a fluorescent lamp, very efficient compared to the dismal line of fifty-watt bulbs hanging at the end of long, frayed cords overhead. I moved toward the fluorescent spill, and around the corner found an empty chair behind a desk covered with what appeared to be invoices. To one side on the desk I saw a half-eaten apple turning brown and an ashtray filled with old butts. The signs of life were encouraging, but the life itself had not yet materialized.

And then it did, in the form of a mannish-looking, middle-aged woman with graying, close-cropped hair, no make-up, and a foolishly tight skirt—foolish for her. She had emerged from what probably was a ladies' room, still adjusting her garter belt, girdle, or whatever, and thus revealing the upper part of her leg. When she saw me, her expression seemed to suggest that I had been lurking there for some time waiting for a glimpse.

I identified myself as quickly as possible, stated my business and the name of the man I'd come to see, and tried to be pleasant and reassuring about the whole thing.

"Generally," she said curtly, slipping quickly behind the desk, "visitors ring the bell." From beneath the clutter of invoices she unearthed a small brass bell similar to the ones used by desk clerks in old-fashioned hotels.

I apologized for the oversight, and again asked about Dr. Thomas Levering. Now her whole attitude was a mindless attempt to reduce me to a ten-year-old child. Of course she knew who I was. Whom did I think the guard at the gate had called? But I really should have phoned for an appointment. But since I had failed to do that, why was I just standing there when Dr. Levering was at that moment waiting for me in his office?

I had known this woman for less than three minutes, and I hated her. She had looked at me and seen the worst. In everyone's childhood there is the memory of a grade-school teacher who had this same questionable talent, this perverse ability to shatter with a look the frailty of an uncertain personality.

I'm moving slowly here because I feel it's important that I re-create the institution exactly as I first saw it. These institutions belong to the taxpayer. Ideally every citizen in the country should conduct his own investigative visit, but I realize this is a dreary way to pass a Sunday afternoon. Still, certain things should be known. I had been on the grounds and in the building for less than fifteen minutes. I had come into direct contact with three people, staff members of one sort or another, and I had yet to be treated in any manner other than a subhuman one. There is the school of thought which holds that since these institutions deal with subhumans, a like manner is good enough. I don't know. If the criminal lies latent in all of us—and I believe that it does—the treatment I received that day did nothing but bring my latent criminality perilously close to the surface. I wanted to smash that sterile woman's face, but when she told me again, in the manner of an annoyed and overbearing third-grade teacher, that I must not keep Dr. Levering waiting, I turned obediently to face the dilemma of two staircases going in different directions.

"Room 214," she snapped. "Right stairs. You can't miss it if you open your eyes."

I thanked her for her kindness and tried to feel compassion for her gray, empty life and boring job.

On the second floor I found another long corridor, heard a typewriter and a phone ringing somewhere, but saw no sign of life. The whole afternoon had taken on a spectral quality, my own private twilight zone: empty rooms and corridors, high, cracked ceilings, hissing radiators, phones ringing, but no life. From the top of the stairs, I saw the men's room and took refuge for a few minutes in the solitary comfort of a locked stall. Then I was back in the corridor on my way to Room 214 and Thomas Levering. The burning question of why I had come seemed to have faded at some point. I was here, and hidden away someplace behind the red-brick façade and barred windows was my nemesis, Hatter Fox. I had been summoned, so apparently my help was needed. Still I tried to imagine being sentenced to such a place; I shook my head to clear it, went into Room 214, and found myself facing another empty desk with a neat nameplate identifying the nonperson as Mary Hopper.

Mary Hopper was no place in sight. But beyond the desk, I saw an open door leading to an inner office, and I heard a man's voice speaking on the telephone. There was a protest of "No," a long pause, a statement of "He's on his way up," and another pause. He raised his voice. "I said it had been long enough. Is that clear?" There was another pause; then he hung up.

I cleared my throat.

"Dr. Summer, is that you?" he called.

"Yes."

"Come on in."

I went to the opened door, and before I noticed anything else in the office, I saw a window on the far wall with a view of other red-brick façades, the cold, sunless day, and, God forbid, snow. The sleet had turned to snow. Driving home would be difficult if not impossible.

Dr. Levering materialized from behind a large desk. He was a man in perhaps his late fifties, tall, very tall, and equally as gaunt. His cheeks were sunken and his eyes completely submerged in deep black shadows. I had the immediate impression of a terrible illness—one just over or yet to come, I couldn't tell. His handclasp was firm, though; he had a nervous habit of pushing his hair out of his eyes, and a full head of hair, only partially graying. Balding was not and never would be his problem. He wouldn't live long enough.

In rapid succession he thanked me for coming, asked me to sit down, and apologized for the absence of his secretary. "When it snows out here, life stops." He smiled, but seemed bewildered by something. "You're so young," he said. "For some reason I was expecting someone much older."

"Twenty-eight," I said. "But I try hard."

I took a chair opposite his desk and waited as he opened a large filing cabinet, all the while muttering to himself, "Hatter Fox, Hatter Fox, Hatter . . ." As he searched for the file on Hatter Fox, I looked about the office and found the standard framed diplomas and degrees. Very impressive. I also found the standard couch, the standard dying rubber plant in the corner by the window, the standard third-rate Southwestern landscape painting, and the standard family photograph depicting a smiling, rather timid-looking woman and three somber-faced, hollow-cheeked boys. Early teens, I guessed.

Dr. Levering found the file and cleared his throat, as though to summon me from my inspection. "Now, Dr. Summer," he began, in the deliberately fatherly fashion of a standard shrink, "we need any help you might be able to give us regarding this particular inmate." He smiled again—an artificial muscle spasm, no warmth. "She is proving to be quite a problem. She consistently resists all discipline as well as all rehabilitation." As he spoke he continued to flip through the pages of the file—a rather lengthy file, I noticed—interrupting himself now and then to read aloud to me the number of times that Hatter Fox had been sent to solitary confinement, the number of hours she'd spent in D.P., whatever that was, and other initialed forms of punishment which I could only guess at. In addition, he read in orderly fashion her offenses: the fire, the flooding of the dormitory, the number of escape attempts, the attempt to knife another inmate. The list was endless, and the weariness in Dr. Levering's voice and manner was suddenly accountable.

"So you see," he continued, apparently having trouble catching his breath, "she has given us no alternative but to keep her in constant restraint, and I haven't been here for so long that I've forgotten that nothing is accomplished in round-the-clock restraint. We need help," he concluded simply. "Tell me everything you know about her, please. Everything. Leave nothing out. Let me be the judge of whether or not it's important."

I was sincerely impressed by the man's earnestness as well as by his dilemma. He seemed to want very much to find the solution to the mystery of Hatter Fox. And I felt doubly bad when I thought of how pitifully little I knew about her. But I told him the few things that I knew, concluding with the last time I had seen her in the isolation cell in Santa Fe.

When I finished he looked very disappointed. He studied me for a moment, then the falling snow outside the window, then the opened file before him, then me again. "And that's all?" he asked.

"I'm afraid so."

"You had no contact with her before the drug arrest?"

"None. I'd heard of her, but I'd never seen her."

He'd placed his pencil between his lips and pushed it back against his mouth. It made a grotesque face, like a poorly done death mask. Again I felt sorry for him. The gauntness now seemed to be accountable, the frame of a man who had merely been worn down by dealing too long with the impossible human equation. Some genetic formulas simply don't work, and I was convinced that Hatter Fox was an unworkable genetic formula. She would be in one kind of institution or another for the rest of her life. Regrettable. I told Dr. Levering this, and he seemed to listen. He nodded now and then, and finally agreed that perhaps I was right, although he hated to admit it. He jammed the pencil back against his mouth again and stared blankly down at the opened file. Between and around the pencil I heard him say, "I was hoping you could tell us so much more," and he shook his head and stared some more, saying nothing.

Snow seemed to be blanketing the inside of the office. Disappointing people is a hard pastime. I'd done enough of it in my life: a lackluster childhood, unimpressive at best, no achievements to speak of, no awards, nothing outstanding; parental eyes hoping to see so much, and seeing nothing. Now again I was disappointing someone. I considered for a moment making up some elaborate case history for Hatter Fox, filling his ear with tales of sibling rivalry, incest, sadism—familiar words that I was certain would brighten his face as well as his day. But I couldn't. It wouldn't help matters. And he was a decent sort in spite of his standard office. I'm a pretty fair liar, but unfortunately I lie best to bastards, so I said nothing. Through the closed windows, I felt the cold of the day as I sat watching Dr. Levering wedge the pencil even tighter against his mouth; I remembered his backward-slanting signature, and kept quiet.

The phone rang, a sudden shrill sound which jarred both of us out of the tableau. As he answered it, I moved away from the desk and his disappointment to stare out the window at the snow and wonder how in hell I was going to drive home. At the window I discovered I was looking down on a courtyard of sorts. Three red-brick buildings joined the administration building to form a tightly enclosed square. On the ground below, in the middle of the courtyard, I saw what appeared to be four or five cages. For the dogs I'd seen at the front gate, I supposed. The cages were made of chain link and were about as tall as a German shepherd, at best three feet by five.

Dr. Levering was speaking in a low but insistent voice into the phone, telling someone again that it had been long enough. He said it twice more, and waited for what obviously was a dissenting voice on the other end.

I stayed at the window, trying not to listen, staring blankly at the dog pens in the courtyard below. Through the snow I thought I'd seen movement. I remember thinking, Poor dogs.

The conversation behind me grew more heated. The weather was mentioned again, and again a time limit of some sort. Someone was giving him a hard time.

The movement in the cage below continued to hold my attention. Through the snow flurries, it somehow didn't seem to resemble an animal. Whatever it was, I saw it try once to stand up on its haunches, but the height of the pen did not permit standing up. From where I stood, the angle downward was too severe to see clearly; there was also the screen of snow. But at one point I thought I saw a hand reach for the top of the chain link pen. I moved closer to the window in an attempt to see through the snow and around the downward angle. Unfortunately, I saw enough to know that whatever there might be in that cage, it was not a dog. Whatever it was had long black hair and appeared to be wearing a formless gray dress of some sort. And whatever it was had legs and arms and shoulders. It looked up then toward the falling snow, and I saw that it had a head and a face. And whatever it was had been locked in the pen in the snow. And whatever it was was trying very hard at that moment to get out, a frantic animal-like movement on all fours, hurling itself against the side of the chain link cage, stopping finally, apparently exhausted, and huddling in a shapeless heap in one corner.

I was no longer in contact with the standard office, or the standard shrink, or the fact of the snow, or the inconvenience of the trip itself. The caged thing had caused my pulse to beat unhealthily fast.

Suddenly I saw a door in the east building open; two white-coated aides stepped out, stopped for a moment to brace themselves against the wind, then walked, heads down, toward the cage. They unlocked the door of the cage, and one aide stooped down, apparently to say something to the thing inside. A minute passed. Then the other aide reached in and grabbed an arm and dragged the thing out, and together, one on each side, the aides half carried, half dragged it back toward the open door of the east building.

Snow had partially covered the black hair, and from the downward droop of the head, the thing looked to be half conscious. The aides were no more than four or five feet from the open door when suddenly there was a struggle. Energy from somewhere erupted in the thing being dragged. It tore loose from its captors and darted rapidly away toward a far corner of the courtyard. The aides started after it, neither in any great haste, for there was no way out of the courtyard. It ran toward a closed door in the west building, tried frantically to open the door, and failed. Arms extended, it started toward the solid red-brick wall of the south building, and clawed at the bricks; then it ran past the dog pens, the aides in slow and solemn pursuit; finally trapped, it cowered in the corner of the west building and sank into the snow. There were no blows, no violence of any sort. One aide stooped down and grabbed its ankles, and the other aide lifted it up by its wrists, and they carried it, hunter-fashion, toward the door of the east building.

The spectacle was over. The door closed behind them. Snow continued to fall in the courtyard.

At some point I was aware of movement behind me. Dr. Levering was standing at the window with me, looking down on the empty courtyard. Then he closed his eyes and shook his head. As he moved back to his desk, I heard him say, "I'm sorry."

It seemed such a useless thing to say.

He went on. "Dr. Summer, please don't misunderstand. I realize what we're doing here." He picked up the pencil, and I remember thinking that if he jammed it into his mouth, I was going to go a step further and jam it down his throat. But he merely watched the pencil as he talked, an interesting device in that it relieved him of the necessity of looking at me.

He went on. "She slashed twelve mattresses yesterday in the dormitory. We cannot tolerate that kind of destruction. We barely have the budget to feed and house them. The administrator is a stern man. He believes in the doghouse."

The doghouse! A quaint euphemism left over from childhood. "You'd better get that room cleaned up or you'll be in the doghouse when your father gets home." But it was a euphemism, nothing more.

Dr. Levering was still talking to the pencil. "I don't approve," he said. "I have never approved of it, although I must confess it seems to work with some girls. It's more effective during the warm-weather months than in winter. Then the other girls use the courtyard, and you have a very effective H.F."

"H.F.?" I asked, still stunned by what I had seen.

"Humiliation factor," he said, rather brightly. "The girls gather in the courtyard before each meal, and anyone in the doghouse comes in for considerable teasing. Generally one time is enough. But in her case it's been a weekly punishment since the day she arrived."

I asked him to identify "her," although it was an unnecessary question.

"Hatter Fox, of course," he said.

I turned back to the window and looked down at the snow and the dog pens, and the closed east door. I remembered the delicate Navajo features of the girl in the battered policeman's helmet, the way she had directed traffic in the bloody cell, the undisguised terror in her eyes as she had looked at me. And I remembered the regal outline beneath the blanket, and the stench and filth of the isolation unit.

"Would it be possible for me to see her?" I asked.

"Not today. She has to spend time in solitary after the doghouse."

"Tomorrow?"

"I don't know. What purpose would it serve? She talks to no one, has never been heard to speak a word."

"I'd like to see her."

"Look, Dr. Summer, believe me, I don't approve of what you just saw. I'm very sorry you saw it. But I don't run this place. Even if I had the authority to do anything I pleased, I don't know what I'd do with a case like Hatter Fox."

"Still, I'd like to see her. It's more or less what I came for."

"You don't believe me, do you? You think that I condone what you just saw."

"No, but surely there's another way."

He shook his head wearily. "If there is, we haven't been able to find it. We have to feed her intravenously because she refuses to eat. If we release her to the freedom of a dormitory, it's only a matter of hours before catastrophe occurs. She has been barred from all classes because she either attacks the other girls or makes an attempt at self-destruction. The other girls are terrified of her. The entire institution seems to breathe easier when she is either in the doghouse or solitary. It seems the safest place for her. And us. I've asked for permission to try various drugs on her, but the state has turned me down. Frankly, I don't know what to do, which is why I wrote to you in the first place." He smiled as he shifted the responsibility to my shoulders, and stood up behind his desk, indicating that the meeting was over. "Come after twelve tomorrow. I'll see if I can get permission for you to see her. You can't drive back to Santa Fe in this storm anyway. Can I get you a room in town?"

"No, I'll manage. I'll be here tomorrow. Thank you." It was a curt exit. I bore no real ill will toward him. It was just a matter of having seen and heard enough for one day. I wanted only to leave. Everything. The smell, the red-brick walls, the worn, tired face of Dr. Levering, and the image of the caged, trapped, desperate girl.

I have an absolute and childlike faith in the goodness of man. When I was with the Peace Corps in Bolivia, I saw a group of natives slit open the belly of a dead baby and eat its intestines. The Bolivian cannibals ate the dead baby only because they were hungry, and hunger is not yet a sin. It was more a need to preserve that concept of goodness that I had asked to see Hatter Fox. There was a reason for her. There had to be.

There were no cars on the highway; most people had better sense. I remember I looked back at the reformatory. Under a mantle of falling snow, it had a quaint New England look about it, a warm place for troubled females who needed only a gentle hand to guide them back to the straight and narrow. Probably there were fireplaces somewhere inside the complex, and girls were stringing cranberries and popcorn in preparation for Christmas, and there were gigglings and female secrets, all taking place under the kind but watchful eye of a plump matron who was everyone's mother. I knew better, but the fantasy made it possible for me to blot out the image of dog pens. Occasionally self-deception is necessary, even healthy.

The Ramada Inn provided me with a room and a fairly decent steak. The dining room was filled with stranded travelers on their way to California in one direction, Chicago and points east in the other. There was an air of excitement in the room, of schedules delayed, plans changed. At best, a snowstorm is Nature's way of relieving the tedium of living. Everyone smiled at everyone else, and shared stories, and became more human. Not one of them even suspected the existence of dog pens less than ten miles away.

In my room I watched the late news, listening half-heartedly to the commentator's flat reporting of various calamities. He too seemed not to know about the dog pens. And ultimately I was left with a test pattern, a hard mattress, an overheated room, a window which refused to open, no change of clothes, and the suspicion that I was the only person in the entire world who knew about the dog pens and had seen the caged thing trying to escape.

I am not a deeply religious person. In the past it has been the poetry of the church more than anything else that has sustained me—rote recitation, but comforting somehow all the same. "I believe in God, the Father Almighty, Maker of Heaven and Earth, and in Jesus Christ, His only Son, our Lord, born of the Virgin Mary . . ."

I believed in all of it.

But still I could not sleep.

At dawn I went out to watch the snowplows. The snow itself had stopped. Not a bad storm by Massachusetts standards. Traffic was moving again, mainly trucks at that hour. I walked up and down in front of the motel, oblivious to wet shoes and cold feet. A sleepless night had taken its toll. My thought processes seemed to be moving in circles.

I helped a couple of men separate a car from a snowbank. I watched a woman in a cleaning shop hang a plastic *Merry Christmas* sign in the window. I saw three kids run out of a grocery store and fall down in the snow on their knees, and look upward and laugh, as though they were giving thanks. And occasionally I forgot to remember that I had an appointment at twelve noon.

No need to go into detail. Everyone has been there, when you've committed yourself to something and then had bleak afterthoughts consisting mainly of what in the hell have I done? I knew all too well what I'd done, knew that nothing could possibly come from an interview with Hatter Fox. If ever the Creator had wittingly or unwittingly created a victim, she was it.

About midmorning I found a pancake house and a cup of coffee. Revived, I made my way back to the room and took a hot shower. I checked out of the motel and guided the jeep through a snowbank and out onto a reasonably clear highway, narrowly avoiding a collision with a large Coca-Cola truck. There was a stop at a Texaco station for gas and an earnest discussion with a cowboy hauling an empty horse trailer on what a "heller" the storm had been.

Then there were no more stops, no more excuses. Every clock I saw said eleven thirty. Apparently twelve o'clock would come that day. Unlike most people I function fairly well on a little sleep. Like most people I don't function at all on no sleep. Between the Texaco station and the turnoff to the reformatory, I developed an irrational sense of urgency, as though I were looking forward to the appointment.

About twenty minutes later I saw the red-brick complex sitting innocently on a field of fresh snow. There was a different guard on duty at the gate. He either sensed my irrationality or had been warned of my coming, for the gate was opened immediately and a gloved hand waved me through. On the other side, the sense of urgency was replaced by a god-awful depression. The mere sight of the buildings reawakened every memory of the day before. The depression and the remembrance conspired against me, and I sped too fast around the circular driveway, lost control of the jeep, and slipped out of the ruts and off the road into a snowbank. I closed my eyes for a moment and saw a thousands suns and cursed everything—the snow, the day, Hatter Fox—and stepped out into a knee-deep snowdrift.

The front hall of the administration building was

deserted, the desk and chair empty. I took the stairs to
the second floor running; this time I knew where I was
going.

On the second floor, I found the office and saw
light coming from the open door. I heard a voice call,
"Dr. Summer, is that you?"

I said it was, and Dr. Levering appeared in the
doorway, clutching a sheaf of papers in his hand, looking even more exhausted and ill than the day before.
He smiled and said the exact same thing he had said
the day before. "When it snows out here, life stops." I
assumed it was his standard winter comment. He
added, "I'm not surprised to see you, though—an old
New England man. I'm from Rhode Island myself."

I tried to think of a suitable comment but couldn't.
I appreciated his attempts at small talk, but I hadn't
come for small talk. When he invited me into his office
and told me to take a seat, I asked bluntly, "Why? I
thought I had come to see Hatter Fox."

"Oh, you will," he said. "Shortly. I feel we should
talk for a moment."

I took a seat and began to notice small, barely
perceptible changes in Dr. Levering. As he sat behind
his desk, I saw him reach for a pencil, then drop it,
as if he knew that his gestures with the pencil the day
before had been revealing. He kept his hands in his
lap for a moment, lifting the right hand only to open
the folder before him. Then the hand disappeared
again safely out of sight. He seemed totally unwilling to
look at me, even though at that moment he was
asking inane personal questions such as had I found
a room, and had I slept well?

I said yes and no, said yes, I thought the storm
was over, and it really hadn't been too bad, and yes,
I'd had breakfast, and yes, I planned to drive back to
Santa Fe today, and all the time I was fascinated by
his new rigidity.

Finally I had had enough small talk. "When can I
see her? I'd like to start back soon."

Once again the hand made a quick movement toward the pencil, and once again the mind interceded and said no. It was my guess that he'd recently given up smoking, and now he was making a concerted effort to give up the habit of jamming pencils into his mouth.

"Yes," he said, to nothing in particular. He sat back in his chair and made a visible effort to draw a long, lung-filling breath. "I think you should know, Dr. Summer," he began, with immense deliberation, "that as of yesterday afternoon I filed a recommendation with the administrator of the institution suggesting that Hatter Fox be transferred to the State Hospital."

The vocabulary and manner of bureaucrats who mindlessly control the lives of others! I'd heard it before.

"The mental hospital?" I asked, without having to.

He nodded.

The bastard. File the recommendation and thereby be relieved of all responsibility, no matter what happened. I filtered my actual words into a plea for reason. "Dr. Levering, she may not be receiving the proper treatment here, but surely you know that she will receive no treatment at all there."

"Oh no," he protested, "not true. They have the authority to try certain techniques and methods that are not permitted here."

Shock. And drugs. He was needle-happy. Find an insoluble problem and stick a needle into it, daily, and keep it in a safe, manageable twilight sleep.

"Drugs?" I asked.

"Yes."

I stared at the window, began to walk toward it, and remembered what I'd found the day before. "Why are you telling me this?" I asked, turning back, suddenly feeling my fatigue, and wondering what in hell I was supposed to do with this new information.

Dr. Levering continued to concentrate on the open folder, still talking to the sheets of paper. "The administrator here is a . . ."—he paused—"a dedicated man." It was the adjective that had caused him trouble. "He takes great pride in believing that he, ah, we can make a difference in these troubled lives. He is of the old school. He believes that discipline solves all. I just felt that if I could get you to agree with me and my recommendation, it might help to persuade him that nothing can be done for her here, except perhaps to make matters worse. Do you understand?"

I understood—too well. He did not need me to see and talk with Hatter Fox. He needed me to plead his case with his superior and thereby keep face and professional reputation in good order. Of all the roles human beings ask other human beings to play, the role of pawn is the most despicable. There was an edge to my voice that I did nothing to alter. "I can't make any recommendation in good conscience until I see and speak with her personally. You understand, I'm sure."

"Of course, of course," he agreed. His manner now was very solicitous. "And we'll get on with that right away." Then he said a foolish thing. "Remember what you saw here yesterday, and realize that whatever is in store for her at the State Hospital couldn't be worse than that."

But it could. I've seen state hospitals. But the important thing to remember here is that all this time we were talking about a human life: flesh, brains, bones, blood—and feelings. Admittedly a difficult human being, but a life all the same. In perfect leisure we were plotting her future hells. And, more alarming than that, I didn't doubt for a moment our authority or ability to carry it all out. I have seen the drugged insane. The worst I can say about them is that they live forever.

As I stood to leave, Dr. Levering shoved a piece of paper across the desk. "One more thing," he said. "I must ask that you sign this."

"What is it?"

"It's self-explanatory." And it was, a simple pledge stating that I, the undersigned, would keep confidential anything that I witnessed there that day.

"You have to be kidding," I said.

He didn't smile and obviously he wasn't kidding. "It's a standard form."

"Standard for whom?"

"For most state institutions of this nature. We do the best we can under difficult conditions. The outside world doesn't always understand. You understand."

No, I didn't, but I signed the paper and shoved it back at him. I wanted only to get it over with, what I had come for, and then leave.

He took the paper, inspected my signature, smiled his thanks, and filed the pledge away in the top right-hand drawer. Perhaps more than anything else it was his slightly smug smile which prompted me to say, "I have a condition of my own. When I see her I want to talk with her alone."

He looked doubtful for a moment. Finally he said, "If that's what you want."

It wasn't what I wanted at all. But when an institution forces you to sign an oath of secrecy, you naturally figure that secrecy on the part of someone else is going to bug hell out of them. My request didn't particularly seem to bug him. He seemed rather amused by it.

"I'll have to limit the time, of course," he said. "She's still in solitary, and generally no visitors are permitted there. The administrator granted us permission rather reluctantly. I'm sure that neither of us want to take advantage of his generosity."

I'm not a very good instant judge of character, but Dr. Levering never ceased to amaze me. I had to revise an initial impression. The deep-seated fatigue on his face was not the result of dealing with the complex problems of a complex world. I was convinced now that his fatigue was the result of a life of ass-kissing and politics.

"Lead the way," I said, wanting only to end the meeting.

He made a half-hearted attempt to straighten his desk. From the top drawer he withdrew a ring of keys: then he locked all the drawers, including the one which contained my recently signed pledge of secrecy, and joined me at the door. "Sun looks good after the storm, doesn't it?" he observed.

I agreed and wondered vaguely what combination of personal hang-ups had led him into psychiatry.

"This way," he said, politely enough, and I followed him into the hall, down the steps, and past the desk and the woman with the cropped gray hair, tight skirt, and hope of rape in her eyes. Apparently she had just arrived and was busy shaking snow off her boots. She gave Dr. Levering a pinched, disagreeable look. "What a terrible morning," she said. And the man who had just commented on the beauty of the sun agreed.

We walked past more offices filled with filing cabinets and secretaries talking about the horrors of the storm the night before. As we passed by, several called out cheerily. "Good morning, Dr. Levering." Beyond the secretaries we walked past a closed, silent door labeled "Administrator," and Dr. Levering watched it closely, as though he was afraid it might burst open at any second.

Then there was a small, chilly arcade, obviously the joint where the administration building joined the east building. Here we encountered our first locked door. Without a word he produced a ring of keys, selected the right one, and after a moment's fumbling, opened the door. I heard a different noise then, the sound of girls talking and laughing, and I saw before us another long corridor with what appeared to be classrooms on either side.

After relocking the door behind us, Dr. Levering confirmed my guess. "They attend classes in this building," he said. "We are rather proud of our curriculum. A girl can finish high school if she wishes, or take a variety of classes just for the fun of it. You'd be surprised how well they do."

I nodded in response to this information and glanced in the open doors. The classes appeared to be lively, and the rooms were sunny and attractive, a few decorated with student artwork. It might have been a small rural teachers college. Admittedly I looked very hard for something to criticize, but the students all seemed to be having a good time. As we passed one of the doors, a young female voice called out, "Hi, Dr. Levering," and she was joined by several others. In a good-natured, fatherly fashion, Dr. Levering called back, "Get to work, or Santa Claus won't come." They giggled at this, and Dr. Levering smiled and shook his head in the manner of a man who has too many children and loves them all very much.

Between the apparent warmth coming from the classrooms and the loving response of Dr. Levering, I caught myself foundering on feelings of ambiguity. There was nothing suspect here. There was nothing to loathe or resent or regret or report. Only giggling girls in sunny, pleasant surroundings. Obviously what Dr. Levering had said earlier was true. They were doing the best they could under difficult and limited circumstances.

At the end of the corridor there was a large, simple, but adequate room which he identified as the dining hall. There were rows of sturdy tables, and in the center of each table there was a large red Christmas candle surrounded by a wreath of holly. To the right was the cafeteria line; beyond that were girls working in the kitchen—the picture of industry. Some were washing and drying, others were stacking and putting the dishes in the cupboards. Perfect cooperation. Again we were treated to smiles and waves, and someone whistled. Dr. Levering said the whistle was for my benefit. "They're healthy females," he said, smiling. "They know an eligible male when they see one."

At the other end of the room, there was a small stage with an upright piano, and at the center of the stage about a dozen girls were busily decorating a handsome Christmas tree. Seated around on the floor about a half-dozen more girls were stringing, I swear it, popcorn and cranberries. My fantasy of the day before had not been too far off. I noticed something else. As we stopped in front of the stage, I saw before me one of the most beautiful ethnic smorgasbords I've ever seen in my life. Blacks, Mexicans, Indians, Anglo-Saxons—all were working together in blissful ignorance of their differences. A peculiar equation: Confinement produces tolerance?

A tall girl on a stepladder called down, "How does it look, Dr. Levering?" She was adjusting a string of lights. Of Mexican descent, she was very attractive, with a long, graceful neck and an erect head, the picture of self-confidence. I wondered how she had managed to end up in a place like the reformatory. She might have been president of a student council or editor of a school paper.

"It looks fine, Ramona," Dr. Levering said. "By far the best Christmas tree I've ever seen."

She smiled, and the other girls smiled at her and seemed somehow to bask in her reflected glory.

Dr. Levering said for my benefit, but loud enough for all the girls to hear, "The tree was Ramona's idea. She organized all the committees, took charge of the collections, and purchased the tree herself." He looked so proud—the father again.

And I was impressed with everything, particularly Ramona. "It's great," I said.

Then Dr. Levering made an introduction I could have done without. "Girls, this is Dr. Summer."

They smiled and nodded politely, and I felt the inquisitive weight of female eyes. Ramona asked the questions they were all dying to ask.

"Is he going to work here?"

"No."

"Then what's he doing here?" The question was blunt but honest.

Dr. Levering was evasive. "He's come to visit someone."

"Who?" It was Ramona again. The girl would go far if she could ever get out of this place.

"Just someone."

"Oh, come on, tell us who, Dr. Levering." At that point she was joined by a full chorus of cajoling, pleading females. Apparently visitors were rare treasures. They wanted to know who had been singled out for the honor this time.

But Dr. Levering seemed loath to reveal the information. Finally he did. "Hatter Fox," he said.

Their faces changed. The giggling stopped. Their smiles were replaced by cold, simple condemnation. Without another word they turned back to their various jobs. Only Ramona continued to stare down at me, as if I had offended her in some way. Finally, she too shrugged, as though to say there was no accounting for some people; she then turned on the ladder until her backside was facing me, and silently proceeded to attach the string of lights to the upper branches.

I was puzzled by the reaction and searched Dr. Levering's face for an explanation. He took my arm and said quietly, "Let's go." From the door he called back, "Keep up the good work." But there was no response from the girls.

In the next corridor I saw a row of offices labeled "Dietitian," "Purchasing Agent," and "Infirmary" —all institutional titles in a gray institutional hall. I wanted to know what had happened in the dining hall, why the mere mention of Hatter Fox had produced such a reaction.

Instead, Dr. Levering commenced telling me about Ramona. "She's quite a girl," he said. "A real leader. She's the father of one of the strongest families in the school."

"Father?"

"They organize themselves into families," he continued. "Very strong social units complete with fathers and mothers, aunts and uncles—their way of creating the security of a structure they didn't have in the outside world. There's a little sexuality involved, though not much. Mostly it's just the harmless role play and the natural affection that exists between young girls. Ramona's the strongest. She leads them in the right direction. You wouldn't believe her IQ. I'm trying to get her a scholarship for next year."

Good for Ramona, but I was still puzzled. "Why the reaction back there when you mentioned Hatter Fox?"

He seemed to think on the question. "They are all bright girls," he said. "In a way they sense the destructiveness of Hatter's nature. They are afraid of her." Then in a complete change of subject, he said, "Here's our infirmary. We have a registered nurse in residence at all times, but we need a doctor."

The guided tour continued and I was left with the task of digesting all my unasked questions. The sleepless night had caused a ringing in my ears, and Dr. Levering seemed to be talking very loudly as he explained the layout of the complex. "It's a workable structure," he said. "The administration offices and reception rooms are in the front or north building. The classrooms, dining room, and storage areas are in the east building, and the dormitories and recreation rooms are in the south and west buildings. Such an arrangement permits us to maintain tight security without the prisonlike appearance of maximum security."

I was mildly impressed and very tired, and was about to comment on both when we came to the second locked door. He produced the ring of keys again, there was more fumbling, and then we were in the second arcade, the second joint connecting the east building to the south.

"One of the dormitories!" he announced with pride, indicating a large room with perhaps fifty beds, all neatly made and arranged in two rows, one on either side. Behind each bed, I noticed small bulletin boards. They were decorated with the personal treasures of young girls: a boy's photograph, a faded corsage, pieces of ribbons, old letters. A few of the beds had stuffed animals on them, painful reminders of how close these young offenders were to childhood. Again I found nothing to quarrel with. Curtains at the windows hid the bars; in front of a few beds, I saw small, brightly colored throw rugs, and here and there a potted plant. It was not an unpleasant room by any standards. So far

I had seen nothing questionable, nothing to relate to the memory of the brutal scene I had witnessed in the courtyard the day before.

For once, Dr. Levering proved to be perceptive and seemed to read my thoughts. He said, "We have four other dormitories identical to this one. The girls take great pride in them. For some, it's the only home they've ever known. If they cooperate, we provide them with a good, productive, constructive atmosphere, a second chance."

And if they didn't cooperate? There was no need to ask the question.

We passed through two more dormitories on the ground floor of the south building. At the end of the corridor we came to the third locked door. More keys, more fumbling, then a right turn and a walk of about twenty feet to steps leading down. At the top of the steps, against a far wall, I saw a stack of what appeared to be new mattresses, mute testimony to the last outrage of Hatter Fox.

All Dr. Levering said was, "Those things cost a bundle, you know?"

I nodded sympathetically and said nothing, fascinated by the sudden changes that were taking place around me. Even Dr. Levering seemed to have undergone a major change. He walked more rapidly now, no longer conducting a leisurely guided tour. We started down a windowless staircase. The cozy smells of popcorn and Christmas trees faded and were replaced by the all-too-familiar smells of jail cells: old urine and older sickness. The steps were very narrow, lit only by bare bulbs hung from single cords and spaced about every ten feet. We walked single file then, Dr. Levering in the lead. We turned one landing and started down again, heading toward what could only be a subbasement. The air became clammy and chilly. He muttered, "It's damn hard to heat this place," and in the dim light, he looked almost angry. And still we walked down steps, another landing, another turn, more steps, even less light, and a sharper chill.

Finally we struck bottom. About five feet beyond the last step, we encountered the fourth locked door. The routine was boringly familiar now—the key ring, the fumbling. Then we were through the door and standing in a short, very narrow corridor. There was a turn to the right directly ahead of us, from which spilled a brighter light, brighter than the dim bulbs overhead which had dotted our passage down.

A man's voice called from around the corner, "Who is it?"

Dr. Levering identified himself immediately. His voice had a slightly melodramatic tone to it, as if behind the bright light was a fixed bayonet ready to attack.

"Come ahead, Doc," the voice replied. The suspicion was gone, replaced by the warm cordiality with which all the girls had greeted Dr. Levering. Obviously he was liked and respected by everyone in the institution.

We turned the corner in to a small, brightly lit room that resembled a provincial sheriff's office. Looking around, I saw a large desk against the wall, several filing cabinets, a long tube of fluorescent light overhead, calendar pictures of seminude females on the wall, a hot plate with a coffee pot bubbling on it, no windows, and a heavy-looking, closed door directly ahead of us.

"Claude, this is Dr. Summer," Dr. Levering said. I nodded and extended a hand across the desk, and Claude stood and took it, while with the other hand he quickly shoved a girlie magazine beneath the large blotter on the desk.

"Pleased to meet you, sir," he said, and the "sir" momentarily won me over. He was probably about my age, very large, perhaps an ex-football player, definitely an athlete of some sort. He was wearing white—soiled white, but white all the same. I remembered the white-coated aides I'd watched from the window the day before. I felt reasonably sure that Claude had been one of them. He looked ill-at-ease now, embarrassed, his eyes moving constantly from my face to Dr. Levering's.

I listened half-heartedly while my credentials were trotted out, and wondered what the hell did Claude care where I came from. Finally the amenities were over and Dr. Levering got to the point. "Dr. Summer wants to see Hatter Fox," he said, and there was again that weariness in his voice, almost an apology for the fact that there was even a person named Hatter Fox.

Claude's reaction was honest if nothing else. "You're nuts," he said, shaking his head at me and grinning. "Sylvia's still in there. Why don't you see Sylvia?"

Dr. Levering didn't seem to appreciate the humor. "Unlock the door," he said.

"Can't," Claude replied, bright enough to know a put-down when he heard it. "Clito's feeding her. He'll be out in a minute." He opened his desk drawer and withdrew a ring of keys almost as impressive as Dr. Levering's. Keys seemed to be the primary status symbol at the institution; the more keys you had, the more respect was due you. Claude fondled his and asked Dr. Levering, "How long does this go on? The tube, I mean. There's only two of us down here, you know, and one of us seems to be busy with the Indian all the time."

Dr. Levering was annoyed by the delay, or the question, or both. He now paced up and down in front of the desk. "I've made a recommendation," he snapped. "That's why Dr. Summer is here."

The hell it was. It wasn't at all why I was there. I felt a small annoyance of my own. Dr. Levering's professional reputation and position in the reformatory meant less than nothing to me. I had come to see Hatter Fox—against my better judgment, it was true, but I had come all the same, and as long as I was there, I was determined to stick to my original purpose. At that moment, the heavy door at the opposite end of the room swung open, and another white-coated aide appeared. Clito, I assumed.

"Visitors!" Claude called out quickly as though to

warn him against doing or saying anything out of the ordinary. Clito looked up from relocking the door, a strong, rather blank-looking Mexican face. So this was what ex-football players did for a living. His shoulders and arms were at least as beefy as Claude's. He was juggling intravenous paraphernalia, shoving tubes and bottles into both pockets. In spite of Claude's warning, he too seemed embarrassed, as though we had caught him at something.

"Doc," he smiled, bobbing his head in greeting. He wiped both hands down the front of his jacket and finished the process on the seat of his pants.

"How is she today?" Dr. Levering asked, apparently impervious to the breach of sterilization which had just taken place before his eyes.

"Mad. As hell," Clito said, with very little accent. "We got her fixed real good in there, but she still manages to spit now and then." He wiped the side of his face, although there was nothing there. He walked self-consciously toward the desk where Claude sat, an alignment of sides, Claude and Clito in one corner, Levering and I in the other.

Clito said, "There's no way you're going to get her ready to leave here, Doc. Ever." And he made a flat, rather stiff gesture with his hands. "Even when we got her strapped down, it still makes me nervous just to be in the same room with her. She's strong; goddamn but she's strong."

Claude nodded in agreement while Dr. Levering contined to pace back and forth in front of the desk, his neck growing red. At that moment he made it clear that he had many things to do and we were all wasting time, and if Clito would be so good as to unlock the door, we would get on with what we had come for.

"I'd stay a good distance away from her, both of you," was Claude's parting advice. Dr. Levering ignored him, and his annoyance grew as Clito fumbled with the keys.

"I have it here," he said, producing his own key

ring. But at that moment Clito found the right key and the door swung open.

On the other side I found total darkness, or what seemed like total darkness after the bright light of the outer room. After my eyes had adjusted, I saw that we were in a room with two small barred cells on either side of us, four in all. Three of the cells were empty. In the second cell on the left I saw a small light bulb—no more than twenty-five watts—screwed into a ceiling socket, throwing inadequate light down onto the cell below. In the cell I saw a cot, a slop jar, a tray of half-eaten food, and in a corner the squatting figure of a girl.

"Good morning, Sylvia," Dr. Levering said, his tone as pleasant and warm as it had been upstairs with the girls decorating the Christmas tree.

The girl named Sylvia did not respond in any way. She continued to squat in the corner, head down, playing with her fingers. Levering moved close to the bars. "It won't be long now. You'll come to my office on Monday afternoon and we'll talk again. All right?"

He was undeniably kind and seemed genuinely concerned with the girl. He waited a moment longer for a response, but Sylvia continued to squat, her face hidden behind a muss of hair. She interrupted her finger play only long enough to give him the finger.

"None of that, Sylvia," he said. "It solves nothing. You're smart enough to know better." He was stern, but still kind. As we walked on beyond the cell, he said quietly, "She's been used by her father and five older brothers since she was nine. We have quite a ways to go with her."

A quaint way of putting it, I thought, like telling a terminal cancer patient he has a "ways to go." There are such things as terminal mental illnesses, permanent damage done to the psyche as virulent and deadly as that done to the body by a cancer virus. The thumbnail sketch of Sylvia's past led me to agree that they did indeed have a ways to go.

But where was Hatter Fox? I had no investment

of blood and discomfort in Sylvia. I had come to see
Hatter Fox, and yet we had run out of cells, and were
now standing before yet another locked door.

"She's in here," Dr. Levering said.

Why was it that I always found Hatter Fox behind
the last locked door? As again the damnable ritual of
key-fumbling commenced, I tried to straighten myself
mentally and physically for the impending encounter.
The foolish question of why I had come no longer
seemed important. I was here, locked behind numerous
doors, as much a prisoner as Hatter herself. There was
no way out until the key-keepers said, "Let's go."

I have never suffered from claustrophobia, but in
the moment before the door opened, I found it very
hard to catch my breath. In the semidarkness of the
passageway I felt again the high toll of a sleepless
night, and stole a backward glance at Sylvia, squatting,
still playing with her fingers. Watching her, I felt the
unpleasant weight of total hopelessness. What could
one do? What could ten thousand Dr. Leverings do to
heal the Sylvias of the world? As fast as he healed
them, the world would simply create more to take their
place.

Clito dropped the keys. Dr. Levering said, "Light
might help."

Clito said, "No. Orders from upstairs. Cut down
on electricity."

Then the door was opened. On the other side
there was a single cell, again dimly lit, but I could see
that it was larger than the ones we had just passed.
There was a space of about three feet before the bars
started, and these bars seemed heavier, thicker.

"Well, there she is," Clito said. He pointed toward
the center of the cell and what appeared to be a hospital bed. No simple cot this time as in the other cells.
She was covered with a blanket, and thick canvas
straps had been laced over her entire body. There were
straps binding her ankles, her knees, and her waist;
two heavy straps came around and under each shoulder
and looped back over her forearms. There was even

a narrow strap across her forehead. She was totally restrained. I had come back to see and talk with this? All human qualities seemed absent from the cell, erased in the profusion of straps. Apparently someone had already passed judgment; she was being treated as though she were incurably insane.

"I need light," I said to anyone. "And unlock the door."

Clito looked to Dr. Levering for confirmation of the order.

"Go ahead," Levering said.

"He don't know what he's doing," Clito protested.

"I'll take responsibility," Levering said. "He wants to talk to her."

"But she don't talk to anyone, and you know it."

Levering lost patience. "Do as I say, Clito." Then softer, "It'll be all right."

Clito was still unconvinced, but he had been outranked. Begrudgingly, and still muttering, he found a switch and flipped it. For a moment, nothing; then a blue-white sputtering illuminated the room, and I saw the dreary place clearly and was almost sorry I'd asked for more light. However, my plan—if it could be called that—was based on recognition. I wanted to see if she recognized me.

"I'm telling you, this is—" Clito was still shaking his head. But Levering was firm.

"Now open the door, Clito," he said patiently, as though directing a child.

I kept my eyes on the thin figure beneath the countless straps. As far as I could tell, she had not reacted in any way to the change in the environment. She had not averted her eyes when the strong light overhead had come on; she had not struggled against the head strap to see the excitement of visitors. Again she appeared to be focusing on a spot on the ceiling, and that spot was of greater interest to her than anything going on around her.

I started into the cell with Levering right behind

me. I stopped abruptly, reminding him of our bargain. "I said alone. Remember?"

Clito said, "Goddamn!"

But Levering retreated. "All right. We'll be outside."

I thanked him, and waited while Clito, still shaking his head, started to lock me in the cell with her. But Levering protested. "No. Leave that door open. We'll wait outside."

They retreated back through the door into the other cellblock. I saw the door close behind them. Then I turned back toward the high bed and Hatter Fox.

For the specifics of what I found, I can only repeat that I have never seen such total and brutal restraint. Also, she had lost weight. If she had been merely thin that first time I'd seen her in the jail cell in Santa Fe, now she looked skeletal, not unlike the concentration-camp photographs from the last war. Her cheekbones seemed to be pressing against a thin layer of skin; the way the light struck her face, the bone itself appeared to be showing through. Her eyes were lost in deep hollows, although again the light caught on dark diamonds of pupils staring. Her body beneath the straps made only small rises and falls, and I noticed that new notches had been taken in in the straps to properly restrain her. Her hair was still long and dark, but hopelessly matted now, and I saw the top of what appeared to be the same gray, shapeless dress she had been wearing the day before in the dog pen. These, then, were the physical specifics of what I saw: a skeletal female form in consummate restraint, a skull-like head tilted up under the forehead strap, no movement of any kind, and dark, dark eyes staring at an invisible spot on the ceiling.

My emotional reaction to what I found was more difficult to describe. I stood a few feet from the bed, and my first perfectly lucid thought was, What a foolish predicament for a human organism to get itself into. Also, I let my mind wander over the grim possibilities of what she might have been subjected to down here in this cold sub-subbasement behind countless locked doors, hopelessly restrained, at the mercy of Claude and Clito. But such speculation was foolish. I had enough facts to keep me busy, and the most important fact of the moment was that I had come back to talk with her, and could not, again, form words of any kind.

If she was insane, words would make no difference. But I had the strong feeling that she wasn't insane, that the same intelligence that had organized twenty kids stoned out of their heads into effective platoons of marchers, and the same intelligence that had eluded cops and slashed mattresses and flooded dormitories and wielded knives—that that same intelligence was very much alive and functioning behind those glazed, fixed eyes.

Of course I had no way of knowing this for certain, and since she clearly wasn't going to start the conversation, it was my move. The straps were ugly and pulled tight. I tried not to look at them, and moved closer and tried to concentrate on her face.

I spoke her name. "Hatter?"

Suddenly her eyes widened and darted to my face. There it was again—ungovernable fear, terror beyond description. I saw her rate of breathing increase as, struggling, she arched her body beneath the straps as though she were trying to push deeper into the bed for safety, for protection. The forehead strap cut into her flesh as she tried to inch back away from my presence. She groaned, her breathing now a panting, her eyes flinching at the appearance of a nightmare too horrible to endure.

Quickly I tried to reassure her. I reached out and touched her shoulder. At the touch, she screamed; her eyes fluttered closed. Her breathing appeared to stop altogether. A stillness settled over her. A moment later her eyes opened, pupils distended, fixed on the spot on the ceiling, unblinking. Her breathing was slow and even, her body relaxed. She appeared to be in some sort of a trance, as though in my presence she had felt the need to send the most vulnerable part of herself away. Only a shell remained.

I called her name twice, but there was no response. Mystified, I stared down at her. What had I ever done to her to provoke such terror, the same insane fear I'd seen in her eyes in the cell in Santa Fe? I tried to think of something to say to call her back, but my head was empty.

Then it was that a very painful and impalatable truth dawned on me. And the outline of that truth was that after countless years of education, I was totally unequipped to deal with this situation. I'd suspected for some time that education was at best a grossly overrated thing. But in that frustrated and uneasy moment, I came to know it in a way I've never known it before. I could think of no man, living or dead, whose thought processes, philosophies, or discoveries could help me. Not Guthrie and his blood test, not Klinefelter and his syndrome, not Salk and his vaccine, not Jung and his symbols, not Turner and his mongolism, not Lévi-Strauss and his hot-cool societies, not Rousseau and his happy savage, not Sartre and his no exits—no one, not one man whose brilliant intellectual efforts I had committed to memory and made my own could come to my aid in that desolate place. Twenty-eight years after the day of my birth, armed with one of the finest educations this country could give me, licensed to dispense health and well-being, I stood in a cold subbasement in a solitary-confinement cell, confronting a thin, abused, terrified, totally restrained Navajo girl. And could think of nothing to say. It was a sizable defeat.

But I rallied, and with no thanks to my education or the ghosts that had filled it. I rallied largely because intuitively, instinctively, I knew that it takes two human beings to have a good talk, and if one of those human beings is restrained to the point that she can't move, then the talk isn't going to go so well.

In the fever that accompanies delayed action, I moved toward the ankle straps. It took me a moment to figure out the complicated strap-and-buckle system, then the process went more rapidly; moving up to her knees, then her waist, I threw off the straps, hoping, praying to see her move, stretch, enjoy the agony of exercising dormant muscles. The strap on the forehead was the last to go. And she was freed. I remember I said another stupid thing. Pleased with my accomplishment, I said, "There! That's better, isn't it?"

Nothing was better. There still were a half-dozen locked doors between her and sunlight, still the possibility of dog pens and of a drugged future in the State Hospital, still not enough food or the right kind of food, still the remembered terror in her eyes, still not even the remote possibility that she would be permitted to function as a human being within the safety and comfort of her own dignity.

I knew all this even as I viewed my accomplishment of relieving her at least of the burden of straps. Still I felt she should have made some gesture of gratitude.

But apparently she didn't agree. She lay upon the high bed as rigid and unmoving as if the straps still bound her. Her eyes had not shifted from the ceiling. Her face was unlined and the skin was tight and shining across her cheekbones. Her intense black eyes had found sustenance and safety elsewhere.

Generally, frustration makes itself known at a time when one is weary from honest effort, and therefore more vulnerable. I found myself growing impatient with her. I spoke to her again, this time more bluntly than before. "This is pretty stupid, Hatter, you know? There are girls upstairs above you having a good time. Did you know that? You don't have to stay down here. The only one who put you down here is yourself. And that's what I call foolish, don't you think?" It sounded pious, and I knew it sounded pious, but it was better than standing and staring at her.

Pious or not, it provoked nothing. I turned my back on her and walked a few feet away and tried again. "The first time I saw you back in Santa Fe, they told me you were pretty intelligent." I looked back at her. "They could have been wrong."

Make *her* angry, I thought. Make her spring to her own defense—anything to provoke movement, a hint of life. But no, apparently there was nothing I could do or say to provoke anything. She remained where she had been bound, unable or unwilling to cope with any reality save that spot on the ceiling.

I remember thinking, Maybe she's dead. But even from a few feet away I could see the slight rising and falling of her chest, sufficient testimony that the heart was still beating, that life was persisting. I thought of a few other possibilities: a catatonic state, the chance that drugs had already been used. But I couldn't bring myself to believe any of them.

Then I could think of nothing else to say to her, so I decided to speak my mind and heart briefly, and leave. I spoke her name again, and waited. Nothing. I said, "I'd like very much to help you," and I meant it. I said further, "There are others outside that door who would like to help you. But we can't do anything until you decide to let us help you. Do you understand what I'm saying? I know somehow that you can hear me, and I also know that you remember me. What I don't know is why you are doing this." Nothing. She hadn't moved. It was useless. I stood up from bending over her. "I'll leave my phone number with Dr. Levering. If you ever want to see me or talk with me for any reason, have him call me. I'll come. I promise you, I'll come. Please believe me."

Somehow you can tell when a person is listening to you. You can tell by the eyes and the position of the head that your words are being received. And, I swear, at that moment Hatter Fox was listening to me. But obviously there was nothing of substance going on in that grim cell but my own useless monologue.

I have known more than a few defeats in my life: the rapid and somewhat dishonorable exit from Bolivia and the Peace Corps, a low rank in my class at med school, the always slightly disappointed expression in parental eyes.

You'd think that if you lost enough times, you'd eventually grow accustomed to the habit of defeat. But you don't. And without going into a description of self-pity, I must confess that I think I felt sorrier for myself than I did for Hatter Fox. I suspect that behind my somewhat shapeless motivation for going to see her in the first place was the still, small hope that I would gain in stature, that I would sleep better at night knowing I had made a difference in a human life, that I, a small god, had picked someone up and put them back together again. Tricky business, Christian charity.

Of course, none of this had happened. I had made no more difference in the life of Hatter Fox than had Claude and Clito—perhaps less. I still suspected that she had good reason to fear them, but then she feared me too, a fear which went beyond fear into dark, paralyzing terror. I waited a moment longer beside her bed. When nothing was forthcoming, I turned to leave.

I'm not certain I can reconstruct what happened in the next few minutes. First of all, it happened with incredible speed, and there was not only the element of surprise, but of shock as well. I remember clearly turning away from the bed, feeling rather sorry for myself, and thinking once that I heard movement, a slight rustling.

A step further, and I heard it again, or thought I heard it—more rustling, more distinct this time. As I lifted my head to look back, I caught an image in that split second of slightly distorted and peripheral vision. I thought I saw something crouching on the bed in the position of a person about to start a race. I saw a blur of black hair tumbling awry, obscuring features. My second thought was that someone had been under the blanket with her all the time, and had only now emerged.

These were the only thoughts I had time for because in the next moment, the thing crouching on the bed was airborne with a leap worthy of a leopard, and the thing was heading directly toward me. No time to duck or move to one side. In the next instant she was on my back, her heels digging into my groin, her teeth making themselves felt through the thickness of a corduroy jacket, and her hands gripping the sides of my head, the fingernails trying to move around toward my eyes.

There was no sound, either from her or me. I knew enough to keep my head down and my eyes closed, but beyond that I didn't know what to do. I could hear her breathing, and could feel the incredible strength of her legs; I was constantly aware of the probing, jabbing fingers and sharp fingernails, which at that point had given up the search for my eyes, and had contented themselves with merely scraping down the sides of my face.

I could not dislodge her. The struggle took us around the cell in a crazy-quilt, piggyback ride, both of us fighting with all the strength we had, she to stay on and inflict as much damage as she could, and I to throw her off before she inflicted that damage.

I must have yelled at some point, although I don't remember yelling. But after what seemed an interminable length of time, the outer cell door flew open, and Claude and Clito appeared followed by Dr. Levering. Again, no words were spoken, either by them or us. Claude and Clito ran behind me, and I was aware of the pressure of her legs leaving my body, her hands and arms being wrenched backwards. I thought I heard her cry out at the wrenching of her arms, but that was the only noise save for the sound of labored breathing—hers, theirs, mine.

Freed completely of her, I looked back to see Claude and Clito forcibly return her to the bed. I watched the straps being jerked into place, and watched her smoldering rage subside under the insistence of restraint. She struggled a moment or two longer, and arched her body as they drew the shoulder straps tight, securing her arms and feet before they attended to the middle section.

Then it was over. I could feel the condemnation coming from Claude and Clito, a distinct "We told you so." And outside the cell Levering seemed to be suffering from acute agitation. But my main interest at the moment was the cool fluid running down the sides of my face, which I assumed was my own blood. That, and the fear-contorted profile of Hatter Fox, who was still breathing heavily beneath the straps, her eyes focused once again on that spot on the ceiling.

Levering was calling out a series of questions to me. I ignored them all. Claude and Clito were busy putting the cell in order, straightening the overturned slop jar and water bucket, and glancing up at me now and then, as if curious to see what I was going to do next.

I didn't know what I was going to do. I felt a surge of release, as if Hatter Fox had just absolved me from all responsibility to her. I felt absolutely certain that she was beyond help. The sight of her totally restrained body now had a curiously pleasing effect on me. I dabbed at the cuts on my face and saw the red confirmation of blood. I moved very close to her, leaned over her face, took the place of that spot on the ceiling and forced her to look at me. The black eyes jerked and made contact with my eyes, and her eyes were so clear that I could see myself in them. It was probably one of the purest moments of absolute fear and hate I have ever experienced.

She had an added bonus for me. As she looked up, her lips moved. She whispered two words.

That was all. I'd had more than enough. I raised up from bending over her and backed away from the high altar of her bed, and wanted in a peculiar way to see Claude and Clito come and pull the straps even tighter.

Outside the cell, I found a very exicted and apologetic Dr. Levering. My head was pounding, and he added to the discomfort with a repetitious barrage of questions.

"Are you all right, Dr. Summer? Did she speak to you? What did she say? You'd better stop in the infirmary and—"

I led the way back through the other cells where I saw Sylvia, stirred by the excitement of violence, standing at the bars, giggling. The door on the other side of Claude's office was locked. I tried to open it, and in anger kicked at it.

Dr. Levering was there with his key ring. "Just a moment. I'll do it," he offered. "She said something to you, didn't she? What did she—"

Then the door was opened and I took the narrow steps two at a time, trying hard to outrun Levering and his questions and his whole sick world. All I wanted was freedom and a clear exit from that place. But Dr. Levering couldn't see this. He jogged from one side to the other, trying to keep up, still asking the same questions over and over again. Was I all right? Had she spoken to me? What had she said?

I found my way back through the labyrinth of dormitories and classrooms, through the connecting arcades, back to the familiar territory of the administration building. Light was coming through the front doors, and I saw the old one-eyed janitor wisely move to one side as he saw us coming. I doubled my speed, and still Levering pursued me, asking those same questions over and over again. The first sharp blast of cold air was like a healing balm. I went down the partially shoveled steps and would have continued on to the privacy of my jeep.

But at that moment Levering stopped at the top of the steps, and ceased asking questions. In a different tone of voice, he merely said, somewhat sharply, on what might have been his last breath, "Dr. Summer! Please!"

At the bottom of the steps I stopped. I knew it would only be a matter of seconds before the questions started again. Clearly pleading now, he asked, "Please tell me what she said to you." I looked back and saw him draw his jacket about him, meager protection against a cold I had yet to feel.

"All right," I began. "What she said, Dr. Levering, was 'fuck off.' Her very words. And that's just what I intend to do. You can't help her. No one can. She doesn't want help. The daily punishment is probably the very thing that is keeping her alive. Send her anywhere you like. She's your problem, not mine. I'm not equipped in any way to deal with her. For some reason, I terrify her. So do with her what you will. But don't involve me any more. I have had it. Do you understand?"

He seemed puzzled by something. He squinted down at me. "She said . . . what?"

" 'Fuck off,' " I repeated, enunciating very clearly and vowing to myself that within the next ten seconds I would be in my jeep and on the way back to Santa Fe.

In the rear-view mirror I examined the condition of my face: superficial scratches for the most part, except for one long laceration which slid down the cheekbone and connected with the bottom of the jaw. I made a mental note to give myself a shot when I got home. She was undoubtedly infected with something.

The growl of the motor was a pleasing sound; the tires fought the snow, then held, and I was backing out and around, bidding a silent and heartfelt goodbye to the still-gaping scarecrow figure of Dr. Levering standing at the top of the steps. His problem was he didn't know when to give up.

The guard at the gate was cooperative, even friendly. He waved me through and shouted something about driving carefully, and I gunned the motor and sped through the gate, wrestling the tires across hard-frozen ruts, determined only to put as much distance as possible between me and Hatter Fox and the State Reformatory.

At the intersection which led to the highway and

Santa Fe, I found chaos. Cars were sliding about, and a large semitrailer truck had overturned and was now blocking traffic going north. The flashing red party hats of a half-dozen police cars were trying to make order out of it all and, as far as I could see, fighting a losing battle.

I shouted my destination to a nearby policeman. He merely shook a red and frozen face and yelled back, "No way, buddy, not tonight. Roads are closed."

Damn it. I knew how to drive on ice, and the jeep could take any road. I started to protest again, but it was a simple matter of no energy. I rolled up the window and followed the direction of his glove back toward town.

At four in the afternoon the motels were doing a land-office business. I went back to the Ramada Inn, only to learn they were full. Five motels later, I got the last single room in a little third-rate place called the Dream House Motel. It was not a dream house, but the room was fairly clean and it was better than spending the night in the lobby.

I bought some tasteless hamburgers at a drive-in next door, and went to my room and ran a tub of hot water and sat in it until my skin puckered, and cleaned my face and wondered how in hell I was going to account for the scratches to curious and morbid friends.

In bed, I stared at the television set—faulty picture, no sound. The horizontal hold was on the blink. The distorted image had a hypnotic effect. That, in addition to thirty-six hours without sleep, produced a state not unlike an instant coma. One minute I was awake, and the next minute I was gone. Healing sleep, no dreams, no remembrances of Hatter Fox and her leap from the bed, no recall of fingernails or dim, smelly, solitary-confinement cells, or slack-jawed, white-coated aides, or restraining beds. Just sleep—black, smooth, peaceful.

About eleven o'clock that night, the phone rang in my room. My brain opened right away, but my eyes stayed closed. Groping for the receiver, I thought, It's a mistake. The switchboard operator has plugged in the wrong room. Then I heard the now familiarly weary voice, and saw in my mind's eye the cadaverous face that went with the voice, the whole, persistent image of Dr. Thomas Levering.

"Dr. Summer? Is this Teague Summer?"

"Yes."

"Thank God. I knew you wouldn't be able to drive home because of the roads, and I've been calling every motel in town."

"What is it, Dr. Levering? It's late."

"I know, and I'm very sorry to be bothering you." He seemed to be using some sort of assuaging technique on me, and I resented it.

"Then why did you call?"

He cleared his throat and became very business-like. "The reason I called, Dr. Summer, is because Dr. Winton asked me to get in touch with you."

His tone of voice implied that now everything had been explained. "Dr. Winton?"

"He's our administrator. You've never met him. Of course he heard about what happened today, and he found it very encouraging."

Admittedly my brain was still foggy and sleep-bound. I sat up and tried to clear the cobwebs. "He found it what?"

"Encouraging. He wants to talk with you if it wouldn't be too much trouble. Could you stop by to-morrow?"

I was wide-awake then, but I still wasn't able to make any sense out of what he was saying. "You say he found it what, Dr. Levering?"

"Encouraging."

"That's what I thought you said."

Levering went on. "Well, she *did* speak to you, responded to your presence, and that's encouraging."

"Is that what you call it?" I was losing patience. "Look, I told you this afternoon exactly how I felt. It will serve no purpose for me to stop by tomorrow or the next day or the day after. She doesn't want my help. For some reason which baffles me completely, I seem to provoke absolute terror in her. And I'm sure you'll agree that terror is not the best basis for a sound therapeutic relationship. I don't know what I've done to her. I haven't the faintest idea what threat she sees in me, or thinks she sees in me. But it's there all the same. For the life of me I can't see how you or anyone else could call what happened today encouraging. I have work waiting for me in Santa Fe, and I plan to leave first thing in the morning. I'm sorry I couldn't be of service to you, or Hatter Fox. But I've done all I can do, and I'd appreciate it if you'd convey that message to Dr. . . ."

"Winton."

"Yes, Dr. Winton."

There was a pause. I heard another voice in the background. Someone was saying something to him.

"Dr. Levering, did you hear what I said? As far as I'm concerned, the matter's closed. I approve of your recommendation to transfer her to the State Hospital. Transfer her any place you like. Tell Dr. Winton I won't be able to stop by tomorrow. And again, good luck."

"No, wait! Don't hang up."

"There's no need to talk any further."

"I . . . how are the cuts on your face?"

He was stalling. "My face is fine. Now please, it's late."

"Dr. Summer?" My God, he was relentless. "Are you there?"

"Yes."

"What would you say if I told you that Hatter had asked me to phone you?"

"I'd say you were lying." I waited for confirmation that he was lying. But he said nothing. It was a ploy to drag me back into his hopeless world. "It *is* a lie, isn't it?"

"She *did* respond to you."

"The hell she did."

"Dr. Winton asks you to reconsider for your own sake."

My God, they were a clever bunch. "For my own sake?" I exploded. "Is that Dr. Winton there with you? Let me talk to him. Put him on the phone."

"I don't think that's necessary."

"And I don't think this conversation is necessary. Now listen carefully. I am not a psychologist or a psychiatrist. I'm not an anthropologist or a sociologist. I'm not even an Indian freak. I'm just a plain, second-rate M.D. There is nothing I can do for Hatter Fox, and there is absolutely nothing further that I want her to do for me."

"Dr. Winton says he'll be in his office all day tomorrow. Whenever it's convenient for you to—"

"Good night, Dr. Levering."

I don't as a general rule hang up on people. But I hung up on Levering. I could imagine him on the other end of the line, looking more skeletal and lost and defeated than ever.

It didn't hit me until the following morning and my third cup of coffee, the possibility that Hatter Fox had actually requested that Dr. Levering phone me. True, I had told her to have him call if she wanted to talk to me at any time. But only she knew that. Surely it was a coincidence, what he had said on the phone. Perhaps he had been listening. Through a closed and locked door? No, it was only coincidence.

The morning was clear and sunny; the snow was melting rapidly. Christmas sights and sounds filled the air. Even the waitress wore a holly corsage and a big smile, and was concerned enough to ask, "Been in a cat fight, honey? Looks like you lost."

But the eggs were cooked well and the toast was crisp, and the coffee hot and strong. It was only coincidence that Levering had said Hatter Fox had asked me to come. Mere coincidence.

I needed a shave, but wasn't quite up to the wisecracks of a barber. I would shave that night in the privacy of my trailer. It was only coincidence, what he had said.

The skiing would be good on the weekend. I had that to look forward to. It was coincidence, nothing more.

Incredible, what doubt can do to you. What if she *had* asked for me? And why me? Even that, the classic cry of the victim. How could Levering have known that I told her to have him call if she needed anything? And what would happen if she *had* asked for me and I didn't go back? Probably nothing. What was left to happen to her? Obviously she had taken a good look at the white world and had rejected it. Society does not look kindly upon people who reject the world. So her future was pretty well mapped out: more bars, more restraining beds, and the new, added excitement of drugs—a vegetable future, silenced so that her cries of protest and criticism wouldn't cause too much embarrassment, safely out of sight and sound. No, it wasn't right. But what, in this best of all possible worlds, did she have to object to?

No one would miss Hatter Fox, would even lose a night's sleep over the fact that she had ever existed. Who said, "If there can be no history of goodness, there must be no history at all, for ignorance is better than a history of evil"?

But the fate of the American Indian wasn't my fault. The melting pot or poverty were not my alternatives for them. Others had learned to adjust. "Adapt or perish"—that applied to all of us. Since I'd been in Santa Fe, I'd been rather impressed with our attempts to apologize to them. We fed them when they couldn't or wouldn't feed themselves. We provided them with free medical services and made concerted attempts to enlighten them, to destroy their myths and taboos. We made pets out of them, mascots for our football teams. We studied them, made graphs and statistics out of them, wrote anthropological tracts on them—a technological society's way of saying "I'm sorry." Who said, "When a Democracy that advertises trust in God practices genocide, whom can you point a finger at and call villain?"

Still—what if she *had* asked for me? What if, after Claude and Clito had worked their special charms on her, she had remembered only a portion of what I had said to her, and had opened her eyes and said, "Call Dr. Summer."

About fifteen miles out of Albuquerque on the road to Santa Fe, there is a roadside establishment called Chief Sitting Bull's Trading Post. It is a combination snack shop, souvenir stand, gas station, and picnic area. The proprietor has nothing to do with the original Sitting Bull except for the fact that he is of Indian blood, as was the great chief.

The Indian with the bogus name who owns the trading post is a pudgy little man with an enormous beer belly and liver spots on his hands and sell-out on his face. In a headdress made of artificial feathers he poses for parents with cameras and kids. He shuns the native crafts and specializes in plastic tomahawks and assembly-line beadwork made in Japan. He is not liked or trusted by his own people but he drives a Cadillac, so who cares? Looking into his face is like looking into the darkest side of the American soul.

I had seen his place before, so I knew precisely what I was doing when I stopped again that morning for a lukewarm cup of coffee that I didn't want, and looked into his face, alive with profit, and looked deeper for even a single vestige of his heritage, and found nothing, not even the dead look of a survivor. The genes existed somewhere, I was certain, the characteristics of what he had orginally been. But they were out of sight now, buried, obliterated by Christian genocide.

Near the bottom of that bad cup of coffee, I overheard a conversation between the false chief and a gray-haired couple strapped in by their cameras. The white man said, "You don't close up here in the winter, huh?"

"No, sir," replied Chief Sitting Bull. "Who'd be here to serve the likes of you?"

The white woman adorned with diamonds smiled coyly. It was nice to be served. She asked, "What tribe do you belong to?"

"No tribe," Chief Sitting Bull said. "Just the American tribe," and he pointed behind him to a large soiled American flag splattered with dead flies and a faded photograph of Richard Nixon, hazy under a patina of insect repellent.

Everyone was happy there. Obviously one could not change the course of God's will. But at the end of that lousy cup of coffee, I changed my own course. Suddenly the "troublemaker" back in the reformatory seemed to be the most honest organism within a radius of fifty miles. I had seen many things on her face, but sell-out was not one of them. As I pointed the jeep back toward town, I felt that relief that comes when at last the mind and heart work in perfect conjunction.

The genuinely pleased expression on Dr. Levering's face when he came down to the reception desk to meet me was reward enough—at least for the time being.

"I didn't know know if you'd come or not," he said, shaking my hand with both of his. "How's your face? Not bad. Be gone in a week. I can't thank you enough for coming."

"*Did* she ask for me?"

"We'll talk in a minute. Dr. Winton will see you now. This way."

He was being evasive again. But I didn't force the question because I wasn't absolutely certain that I wanted to hear the answer.

Dr. George Winton. About five feet seven—shorter than I might have imagined—probably close to a hundred and ninety pounds, sixty to sixty-five years of age, could have played Santa Claus, and undoubtedly had at some time in his life. Ruddy cheeks; perhaps suffering from hypertension, but otherwise in good

health; everybody's young-at-heart grandfather. His office was more plush than Levering's: carpeted, fresh
flowers on the desk, the desk itself large, mahogany,
arranged with a Dictaphone, a couple of telephones,
and a neat stack of papers. He had the comfortable,
assured, and slightly glazed look of a man who has
not seen fit to change his philosophy since it was first
formed, over forty years ago.

Dr. Levering made the introductions, a slight flush
on his face. "Dr. Winton, Dr. Summer," he said.

A handshake, not a bad one, slightly clammy, re-
inforcing the suspected hypertension. But he smiled and
said, "Sit down," and it wasn't an invitation, and everyone sat.

Levering arranged the chairs. I was provided with
the seat of honor, a large, comfortable, overstuffed
chair. He took a straight-backed, cane-bottom one.

"So!" Winton said, seating himself behind the
desk and holding his hands before him as if he were
about to lead us in prayer. "I suppose you know why
we have asked you to come back," he began.

I thought I knew, but wasn't certain, and said no
to be safe. Winton and Levering exchanged a glance.
Winton took the floor with the confidence of a man who
knows whose floor it is. The following speech is his,
not mine, the opening thought so predictable that I almost smiled—but didn't.

"We run a tight ship here, Dr. Summer, under
very difficult conditions," he began. "These girls are
sent to us by the state because there is no place else
to send them. Now we don't run a prison, but neither
do we run a resort hotel. Some are more difficult than
others, but not once in seventeen years of serving as
administrator of this institution have I had to say uncle
to one of them. Sooner or later I've been able to give
them all back to society, reformed. That is my job. You
know what they say: there's no such thing as a bad
girl, just an unhappy one."

Yes, I'd heard that. I noticed Levering was studying his fingernails as though he had heard the speech too many times to count. It's a peculiar feeling to find yourself bored with Santa Claus.

I tried very hard to look impressed and said nothing because I had the feeling that there was more to come. And there was.

"Now, I've been known to search the four corners of the earth for the one person who holds the psychological key to a difficult inmate. And there is always a key, I can assure you of that. Sometimes it's a brother, an uncle, an old teacher, a family friend." He smiled. "I'm not above asking for help, Dr. Summer. I'm just above giving up."

I smiled back, and tried to look impressed. And in a way I was. A questioning, searching man wouldn't last five minutes in such a job.

He went on. "Regarding the inmate, Hatter Fox —and by the way, I'm very sorry for what happened yesterday, but you should have known better. We don't place inmates in restraining beds without good reason. There is no brutality here. Our goal is to create supervisable individuals."

Somehow I felt that the last two words fought with one another, but I nodded, and accepted the information as well as the reprimand. Still he went on, his hands folded neatly before him, no nervous ticks like Levering, no eating pencils or fidgeting or looking uncertain and weary and worn. He just looked supremely confident.

"Now, regarding the inmate, Hatter Fox, her case has proved most difficult because we can find no past for her. No relatives, no one who ever knew her as a child. Oh, we've turned up a few kids, drug addicts for the most part, but they are of absolutely no help. And so now we come to you." His smile broadened. "The words she spoke to you yesterday, Dr. Summer were remarkable."

"I have a way of bringing out the best in people."

"Do you realize they are the first words she has spoken to anyone in all the months she has been here?"

"Maybe she has nothing to say."

"In order to live in society, Dr. Summer, you know we must make an effort to communicate."

Did I know that? I thought about it for a moment, and while I was thinking, Dr. Winton went right on.

"What we're saying to you, Dr. Summer, is that we need you on our team for a while. To work with her, talk with her, see if you can reach her in any way. Levering here is ready to pack her off to the insane asylum, but I'm not. My job is to reform her, and by God, I will. Those things go down on records, you know. Wins, losses, draws. I've had a clean record here for seventeen years and I intend to keep it that way. Dr. Summer, help me keep it that way."

I had no suitable response for him. He was asking me to help him keep his record clean. The girl downstairs in the restraining bed was a blotch on his record. I found it difficult to look at him. He was asking for my help, and I was considering giving it because I had been told that I was needed, that my presence in the world did make a difference. And what about the girl? Nothing about the girl.

Then came the proposition, and like a good whore, I listened. "I've already spoken to the Bureau of Indian Affairs," he said. "They aren't happy about it, but they are willing to release you for a short period of time from your duties in Santa Fe. Without pay, of course. I'm afraid the state can only put you on three-quarters pay, but we'll throw in room and board. What do you say to that?" The image of Santa Claus was gone.

"Nothing, Dr. Winton, not yet. I'll see her again today because I'm here and because I was told she'd asked for me. But I have no faith in my abilities as a therapist. So I say no to your offer. Let's just keep it on the basis of an interested by-stander."

"Whatever you say." At least he knew enough not to push. And why should he have to push? I was there, wasn't I, ready to do what I could to keep his record clean? But I was appalled by the way we kept losing

Hatter Fox. It's a national pastime, a societal bad habit. Winton's interest in her extended only in so far as she affected his clean record. Levering, while slightly more subtle, still viewed her as an insoluble problem, a professional embarrassment. And what exactly had been my motivation for making that U-turn at Chief Sitting Bull's Trading Post? Because it made me feel good to do so.

Apparently the monologue was over. Winton stood up, looking for all the world as though he was about to pronounce a benediction. His closing words were too choice to omit. With his hands still clasped together, he said, "All right. I think we have a pretty good team here. Now, let's go get the problem." He smiled again and sat back down, and made it pretty clear that the "we" who were going to go get the problem did not include him.

Through the amenities of parting, and his last-minute invitation to call on him personally if I needed anything, I caught myself wondering if Dr. Winton had ever seen all of his reformatory. His office on the outside of the ground floor did not look out over the dog pens as did Levering's second-floor office, and I wondered if he even knew the way through the turns and twists of halls that led to his cold solitary-confinement cells and restraining beds.

No answers, not even time to voice the questions. I overheard him giving instructions to Levering to prepare one of the guest cottages for me. It implied a stay of long duration, and I objected.

"That won't be necessary," I said. "I told you I would see her today because I'm here. I have to go back to Santa Fe tonight."

He nodded as if grateful I had refreshed his memory. "Well, we'll see," he said. "We'll talk later."

The hell we would. Bureaucrats! They seem to go conveniently deaf to anyone's wishes but their own. True, the man was no villain. As there are few genuine heros left, there are also few genuine villains. I'd found nothing blatantly evil in him, just a professional man, adequately trained, self-serving, objective, political. Nothing exactly wrong with him. But a world filled with his kind would never have very much right with it.

Then Dr. Levering and I went on our way down to the subbasement, moving through the arcades and locked doors, back through the corridors filled with giggling girls, through the dining room filled with lunch smells and the decorated tree, poignant with human effort and homemade decorations.

No word had been spoken during our long walk Levering looked like a man who was afraid to open his mouth for fear he'd say the wrong thing. As we entered the south building, I had a question, and I asked it.

"*Did* she ask for me?"

Conveniently he was fumbling with keys again, and appeared distracted. I waited until the locked door of the moment had swung open, and asked again. "Did she—"

"Yes, in a way," he replied.

"What's that suppose to mean?" He wasn't going to answer my question. He had no answer. I knew that now.

He went on, safely changing the subject. "Look, I want to thank you for coming back. It's very important to Dr. Winton."

"Yes, I gathered that."

"I've told you. He's not a man who gives up easily. Now, do you have a plan?"

"Plan?"

"How are you going to approach her?"

"Face front," I said, making a poor attempt at humor.

"Doctor Winton suggested that later on you use a tape recorder."

"Why?"

"We might be able to tell more from what she says to you. No offense, of course."

"All this is assuming that she says anything."

"Yes."

We turned the last corner and passed the stack of mattresses and started down. Plan? What sort of plan should I have? What could anyone do or say that would make the slightest difference to Hatter Fox? Somehow I had trouble conjuring up an image of her sitting obediently before a microphone, happily spilling out her life story. Foremost in her catalogue of things to hate were white faces. Once, on my rounds of the reservation, a young Indian came up and said to me, "Get your white ass off this reservation." We'd pushed a few of them too far. A tape recorder? With Hatter Fox?

Claude and Clito were playing poker. They looked up as we entered the room. Clito groaned. "We just got her settled in."

Levering said, "Dr. Winton's orders," and that was all he said.

"How long does she have to stay down here?" I asked.

"A week," Claude answered. "We got her on Tuesday, she goes up on Tuesday. But she'll be back. She always is."

It was then Thursday. Four more days. At last I'd found an excuse. "I doubt if we can accomplish much as long as she's restrained," I said.

"Oh, she's out of bed," Claude replied. "We moved Sylvia upstairs this morning, and she's in Sylvia's cell. She's behaving herself, even ate a little this morning." He grinned. "She don't like that big bed."

Again Levering asked, "How do you want to work it? Do you want me to go in with you?"

I said no, and looked around the room for a peace offering. I smelled fresh coffee. "Give me two cups of that," I said, pointing toward the hot plate.

Still shaking his head, Clito went for the coffee while Claude went for the keys. They both accompanied me to her cell door. Clito called out cheerily, "He's back again, Hatter. Take it easy on him this time, you hear? You'll know what you get if you don't."

Claude's parting advice was brilliant. He leaned close to me and whispered, "Just don't say nothing to rile her." He left her cell door opened, but I heard the outer door close and lock. I was alone with her again, standing stupidly in the doorway, burning my fingers on two cups of coffee that I had the feeling neither of us wanted. There was always the possibility she was using her intelligence to make fools out of all of us.

She had shunned the chair and the cot and was sitting on the floor in the far corner, her legs tucked demurely to one side, hands folded in her lap, head down. The gray dress seemed fresh, though coarse and unironed. Her hair was still hopelessly tangled and matted. She looked up and saw me. There it was again, that darting fear in her eyes.

To reassure her, I said quickly, "I brought you coffee," and took a step toward her, then changed my mind. I placed her cup on a small table beside the cot. She was now scrambling backwards into the corner, as though trying to find an exit where the walls intersected.

"Hatter, please, I'm not going to hurt you. I mean you no harm."

I was not more than five or six feet from her, and noticed raw places on her wrists and upper arms. The straps, I supposed. Pity stirred, possibly the worst emotion imaginable. I considered taking the chair, then changed my mind again, and sat on the floor opposite her, my back resting against the bars of the cell. I decided to try to wait out her fear, let her see that I was not going to hurt her.

The coffee tasted good, and I urged her to drink hers. She pressed farther into the corner, her face toward the wall, shivering slightly. The stone floor was cold. I crossed my legs, uncrossed them, finished my coffee, and waited. She had appeared relaxed when I came into the cell. Now here she was again, terrified, refusing even to look at me.

I tried to imagine what she was thinking about in her long silence. Certainly she had accumulated enough memories just within the last two days to keep her mind busy: the sensation of being placed in the dog pen, the beginning of snow, the painful and futile attempts to stand erect, the one brief bid for freedom from Claude and Clito, and being trapped finally and carried off in the position of a dead animal. But I hadn't done those things to her. I wasn't responsible. Why was she so afraid of me?

In the re-creation of events, I studied my fingers, recalled Sylvia playing with her fingers, and began to understand the tales of finger play and masturbation that supposedly take place in solitary cells. What else was there to do?

But Hatter was not playing with her fingers. Now her hands were limp in her lap as though she had used up the last measure of some very important energy source, as if she had sent away everything that was vital and left only the husk for the white asses. In that continuing silence, I thought about touching her, in line with the sensitivity theorists I'd read about who believed that any human doubt, fear, or insecurity could be soothed away with an all-encompassing embrace of nonpossessive human warmth. But did the theorists know anything about a hate and fear the size and depth of Hatter Fox's? Could those be soothed away by the touch of a hand? I had my doubts and kept to my place on the floor, shifting slightly as the bars against my back caused undue pressure on the old knife wound, trying to figure out a way to convince her that I did not want to hurt her, that I wanted only to help her. At some point, I decided that words—any words —were better than the continuing silence.

"Do you know who I am, Hatter?" I asked, whispering for some reason, as though someone was listening. "Do you remember?"

Nothing. She sat facing the wall, head erect, stoical, trance-like unresponding.

Then it occurred to me that maybe she didn't know how to play the white man's game of talk therapy. Maybe she didn't know that she was supposed to tell me everything about herself, that I was to listen and pass professional judgment. Then I would start the game. Name, birthplace, losses, fears, liabilities.

And I did. I began in the loud, clear, objective manner of a boy reciting his lessons. "My name is Teague Summer," I said, always watching closely for the slightest movement on her part, the faintest indication that she was hearing, was even listening.

The statistics were dull: early childhood, parental influence. But at some point, I began to enjoy the sound of my own voice, the accounting of a morbidly normal, slightly indulged childhood, safe in an all-white world. At some point I became less interested in watching Hatter Fox, and commenced reliving the highs and lows of my twenty-eight years. I skipped rapidly over the vacuum of junior and senior high school, and informed the walls, the bars, and the floor of my decision to enter med school because it was a paternal wish, even though it was against my better judgment, knowing even then that I would never be more than a second-rate doctor. I shifted throughout the long monologue, hearing things from my own lips for the first time, literally enjoying and needing the clean slate that was Hatter Fox. I was glad she was not responding. I did not want response. I merely wanted the blank of her presence.

Bolivia was recounted in full, the incredible hopes with which I'd entered the Peace Corps and the equally incredible disillusionment with which I'd left it. In the telling of it, I relived it and almost forgot about her presence, less than five feet away. And all the time I was talking—telling her about my experiences with the Indians and the communes, and even bringing her up to date on the first time I had seen her in the crowded jail cell—I had the peculiar feeling that I had split, that part of me was standing to one side, leaning against the bars, shaking his head, and saying, "You jackass," and the other part of me was still on the floor, spilling out my life story to a dim cell and a motionless fear-ridden Indian girl.

But near the end of my speech, she suddenly was no longer motionless. Caught midsentence, I watched, fascinated, as her hands stirred, watched as though I were watching a miracle as she lifted her arms without turning her head; then, in a gesture as slow and deliberate as anything I've ever seen in my life, she raised her hands to her head, one hand on either side, and gracefully but firmly stuck the index finger of each hand into her ears. With no words spoken, she had communicated brilliantly.

I had bored hell out of her. For a split second I was angry, but the anger was soon replaced by the more neurotic emotion of hurt feelings. The fact that she had listened and perceived, at least enough to be bored, mattered not at all to me.

I muttered a sarcastic apology and waited for her to remove her fingers from her ears. When she continued to sit in that ridiculous position, I shouted at her, "You can come out now. I'll shut up." But still she sat with her fingers in her ears, head erect, still facing the wall.

Another shout, but it didn't make a bit of difference to her. A third shout brought Claude and Clito to the outer door. Claude inquired, "Anything?"

Seeing us seated on the floor a distance apart reassured him. Seeing Hatter with her fingers stuck in her ears aroused his curiosity. "You playing a game?" he inquired.

I stood up and straightened the kinks out of my back. "No game," I muttered. "I'm through here."

Clito came in with a tray of nondescript food. "Well, it's time to feed her and bed her down anyway. You two can play some more tomorrow."

I stood in the cell door and watched her, the fingers still in her ears. Useless. She was not even aware that I had stood up and was now leaving and would not come back.

"Least you didn't rouse her today, Doc," Claude said, as he brushed past me. "That's something. You looked beat, though. She takes it out of you, don't she?"

I made it as far as the outer door, and then curiosity prompted me to stop and watch the feeding and bedding-down process. Both Claude and Clito saw me stop, and neither of them seemed to like it. A look passed between them which from that distance I couldn't read. Then they went about their tasks, Clito placing the tray of food on the table, and Claude going to where Hatter was sitting. Not unkindly he put an arm around her shoulders and lifted her to her feet. She permitted him to lift her up, even seemed to help a little. Her hands fell back down to her sides as she permitted herself to be guided to the table and placed, robot-fashion, in the chair. She still never looked directly at anyone, but followed obediently all of Claude's suggestions, lifted the spoon, and started earting.

Beside her on the table was my peace offering, the cup of coffee, now cold. Claude and Clito were busy behind her, straightening the cot. So I was the only one who saw her put down the spoon, and for the first time during that long afternoon, I saw her lift her head and look directly at me through the bars, her eyes black and fearful. And still looking at me, as though she was trying hard to conquer her terror, she lifted the cup of cold coffee to her lips and drank it—more than drank it, drained it in all its cold bitterness. Her hand trembled as she returned the cup to the table, but not once did she take her eyes off me, nor did I dare stir for fear that she would take her eyes away. Again, with no words spoken, she had communicated.

It is difficult to describe my feelings at that moment. Her gift to me, the simple act of drinking the coffee, I still consider one of the most treasured I have ever received.

Claude looked over his shoulder and saw I was still there, saw too that she wasn't eating, and became doubly annoyed. "You still here?" he said. "Levering wants to see you in his office, and he don't like to be kept waiting."

But I couldn't move. She was still watching me, still speaking. Volumes were being communicated through those eyes—indecipherable volumes, to be sure, but she was speaking. I had the feeling that she was still terrified, still saw me as some kind of a threat, but was at least making an effort.

Claude was losing patience. He leaned over her shoulder, clearly threatening. "The stuff's hot, so eat. That big bed of yours is right in there, if that's what you want. You hear?"

She heard. Her eyes wavered, broke contact with mine. She lowered her head over the plate of food and used one hand to put the spoon into the stew mixture.

"That's better," Claude said. "See you later, Doc," he called out. "The doors are unlocked, so help yourself. Levering's in the front building." It was clearly a dismissal, although I couldn't understand the need for haste. My presence seemed to make both men uncomfortable, and I couldn't understand that either. But there was nothing more to stay for. I watched her a moment longer, the mechanical movement of her hand guiding the spoon from the plate to her mouth, then back again; she appeared not to even chew the food, but to swallow it whole, the sooner to get it over with.

What I think I felt most strongly in that moment was a sense of possession, a feeling that she had at last made an effort to reach out, an SOS sent from her to me. For the first time, I was loathe to leave her. Possession and protection. Perhaps neither were the right feelings.

Hatter Fox. After hundreds of years and the plague of Christianity, after incredible apathy, active conquest, and passive resistance, in a death-ditch stand, and with no words spoken, she had finally made contact. With me.

I remember little of the long walk from the solitary-confinement cell to the administration building. When I reached Levering's office, I went in without knocking and went straight to the window that looked out over the courtyard. The sun was setting, the afternoon was over. Staring down at the dog pens, I vowed to myself that that would never happen again. Not to Hatter Fox.

Levering was surprised by my sudden and unannounced entrance, and totally misread my mood. "Nothing, uh?" he questioned. "I was afraid of that. Well, we have no right to ask you to stay, but I want you to know that we all are grateful for your efforts."

"Winton mentioned something about a deal," I said, still looking down at the dog pens. "Three-quarter pay, and room and board? Where's the room?"

"Room?"

"A room, a place to stay. Didn't he say that room and board were part of the deal?"

"You're staying, then?"

"Yes."

"Why? What happened?"

I looked at him and wondered how I was going to explain to him what had happened. "Nothing," I said.

"Did she say anything?"

"No."

"Then why?"

"She drank a cup of coffee," I said. "I'd like to try and work with her again. Is there a place for me to stay?"

"Yes, of course, the guest cottages at the—"

"That'll be fine. How do I get there?"

"I'll have to call a girl to take you. But I still don't understand."

Neither did I, and I felt a peculiar inability to talk about it. Certainly the man was entitled to an explanation. It would have taken little effort on my part to catalogue the events of the afternoon. But I couldn't bring myself to do it. Fresh from Hatter's presence, where no words had been necessary and so much had been accomplished, I found myself under the spell of her silence. I wanted only to isolate myself as she was isolated, to know silence as she knew it.

Levering gave up temporarily. He made a phone

call to someone, said he wanted a guide, said no twice, then said yes, said to send her right up to his office, and hung up. He sat back in his chair and watched me pacing at the window.

Interesting, the differences in silences. The one with Levering was awkward, almost embarrassing, as if the very act of being quiet was wrong somehow. Two professional men had to fill the blank places with words, or something was at odds. But the silence with Hatter had been different. With her, words had been the abnormality.

"Weather's cleared up," I said finally, pretending to study the dark-blue but clear dusk sky.

Levering grunted. He wasn't interested in skies or a weather report. He launched his own topic of interest in a roundabout way. "So you were encouraged this afternoon?" he asked, moving carefully around the words.

I said I was. I rubbed the growth of beard on my face and realized that something had to be done about it. "Do you have anything for this?" I asked, pleased to change the subject.

He looked at me, made the mental transition, reached into a bottom drawer and produced a cord and an electric razor. "Keep it," he said. "There's a plug in the cottage. I'll get it later."

"Thanks."

He nodded. More silence. Where was that guide?

"Look," I began, "Couldn't you tell me how to get there and—"

"She'll be here in a minute. You need keys."

Of course. It was impossible to go anywhere in the institution without keys.

Then he tried a new approach. "You know that Dr. Winton will be interested in hearing about what happened. What shall I—"

"Tell him?" I broke in, then hesitated and tried to figure out what Levering was to tell him. "Tell him that I changed my mind, that she . . ." What had she done?

Levering sat up and tried to help. "And you say she didn't say anything?"

"No."

"Then what did she do?"

"She did nothing, Dr. Levering. Something about her mood. She seemed to be in a more cooperative, receptive frame of mind. She's still afraid of me, but you know she's eating now."

"I know. For the wrong reasons. Because she's afraid of—"

"It's a start."

He continued to look at me as though something were puzzling him. "You've had quite a change of heart, haven't you?"

"Not really. I've wanted to help her since the first time I saw her. Now I think there's a chance that she might let me. I could be wrong."

I couldn't be absolutely certain, but he seemed almost disappointed that I had decided to stay. Was he so devoted to his recommendation that he couldn't stand the thought he just might have made the wrong one? I had the unpleasant feeling that I had been caught in the cross fire of a petty political battle between Winton and Levering. I had encountered the same sort of battle before, in med school, in my internship, in the Peace Corps, in the Bureau of Indian Affairs—minor men jockeying for positions of power, and the least qualified always winning. It shouldn't have surprised me to find it firmly entrenched in a state reformatory, but it did. Somehow the stakes were too high, the victims too helpless. Damn Levering's recommendation. He would just have to learn to live with the embarrassment that was Hatter Fox.

Fortunately, at that moment there was a knock on the outer door. Levering called, "Come in," and a strapping, broad-shouldered Mexican girl appeared, a stack of fresh linens in her arms, and a businesslike expression on her face.

"Mango, thank you for coming," Levering said, cordially enough.

Introductions were made, and I was told that Mango was a trustee, that she'd been in the reformatory a year and a half, and she was going home after Christmas. "Unless," Levering added, "we can persuade her to stay here. She knows how to run this place better than most of the aides."

Mango blushed becomingly under the weight of his compliment. She was close to six feet tall—I looked her in the eye—and she probably carried a hundred and eighty pounds on her large frame. She wasn't pretty in the conventional sense, but had the strong, almost masculine, sultry beauty of certain Mexican women.

She smiled when Levering said she'd take good care of me, and waited patiently at the door while he gave her further instructions regarding which cottage was to be opened; he also told her to prepare my dinner in the kitchen and serve it in the cottage.

"There are four cottages behind the institution," he said to me, "for relatives who wish to spend weekends with the girls. They were Dr. Winton's idea, the cottages; he raised the funds and saw to their construction. I think you'll be quite comfortable."

Interesting, that the same man who had conceived of the dog pens had also conceived of visitor's cottages. I thanked him and assured him that I would be quite comfortable. "How early can I see her in the morning?" I asked.

"Mango will come for you after nine. The cottages are outside the fence. She'll have to show you how to get in."

They *did* trust Mango. I thanked him again, and followed Mango's broad shoulders out into the hall. Midway down the steps, I offered to take the stack of linens for her. She shook her head and shifted them to the other arm, as if I had intruded into her realm of responsibility.

In the front hall she asked. "Do you have a car?" I nodded.

"Then let's take it. It'll be quicker, and they don't

like to leave parked cars in front of the building overnight."

I didn't ask why. I had the feeling she could have
told me. She couldn't have been more than sixteen,
but she acted much older—all business, very efficient,
and obviously pleased with her importance.

The outline of my jeep was a friendly sight, reminding me of the outside world. In institutions you
have a tendency to forget that there is another world
minus locked doors and keys and rules. I experienced
a brief longing for my trailer, for the familiar sights and
haunts of Santa Fe.

Mango crawled eagerly into the jeep and hugged
the linens and gave me curt instructions. "Through the
gate and to the left."

The road to the left was gravel and made a broad
arch around the institution and cut back on itself near
the rear of the south building. There it headed toward
four small houses which resembled summer cottages.
Obviously the road had not been used since the snow,
but the jeep had no trouble cutting a path.

Mango said, "Jeeps are good."

I agreed.

"My brother-in-law had a jeep once, but he
wrecked it. Over there," she said, pointing to the first
cottage.

The units appeared to be very small. They reminded
me of the overnight tourist camps, the predecessors to
the luxury motels which now covered the highways.
No frills, no extras, just a place to wash your face and
go to sleep. Inside, there was a couch which made into
a bed, a desk, two chairs, a picture on the wall of
Christ in Gethsemane, bright red curtains with nondescript yellow flowers, a well-worn brown rug on the
floor, a clattering radiator, and behind a partition at
the rear, a toilet and a shower.

"This is it," Mango said, pleased, as if she'd had
something to do with it.

"It'll be fine. Thank you."

I stood to one side and watched her make the bed.

I thought a couple of times about offering my help, but decided against it. She was doing very well and needed no help from me. As she smoothed out the sheets, she said, "You're here to see her, aren't you?"

"Who?"

"You know who I mean. The bad one." She looked up briefly from her labors and smiled, signifying that she knew we were playing a game. "Hatter Fox, the Indian," she said, folding the sheets under the corner of the mattress.

"Why do you call her the bad one?" I asked.

She stopped abruptly, looked at me as though she were wrestling with a decision. Then suddenly she pushed up the sleeve of her shirt and extended her arm for my inspection.

There was a very raw-looking, ugly scar on her forearm, about five inches long, and still pink and perforated with the holes of stitches. She seemed proud of it. "She did that to me," she said. "She's a bad one, all right. No one with good sense will go near her."

"How did it happen, Mango?"

She threw the blanket up into the air, sailed it down over the bed, and commenced tucking in the corners. "I had bathroom duty with her one day," she began. "She was cleaning the inside of the stool, and just like that she raised up from scrubbing and reached down and took a knife out of the cuff of her jeans, and shoved it toward me and asked me to kill her. I said she was crazy in the head, that I couldn't do that, I'd get into trouble. And she got all mad and started crying and started begging me to kill her. I guess she knew what I was in for and figured I knew how to do it better than anyone else." She smiled almost coyly and gave the blanket a final smoothing-down.

"What *are* you in for?" I asked.

"I tried to kill my old man. He's a bum. Anyway I told her I wouldn't do it, and couldn't do it, and that she'd better get rid of the knife and get back to scrubbing that john or we'd both get in trouble. And then she got real mad and came at me with the knife. And this is what I got out of it."

Again she thrust her arm out for my inspection, then turned immediately to fluffing the pillows.

"I thought she'd never spoken to anyone," I said.

"Oh, she never talks to the big boys up front. But she talked to me all right, that day. Wish she hadn't. She's crazy in the head, like all Indians. You'd better be careful."

I took a chair beside the desk and watched her put the finishing touches to the bed. The image of a sobbing Hatter Fox begging someone to kill her did not surprise me.

Mango arranged the towels behind the partition said she'd be back shortly with my dinner, and for some reason told me to lock the door after she'd gone. I thanked her and said I would. But I didn't. I stayed in the chair by the desk and thought about Hatter Fox. *The bad one, she's crazy in the head like all Indians. . . . She talked to me all right that day, crying, begging me to kill her—*

Sometime later, Mango returned with a covered tray and a scolding. "You didn't lock the door," she said.

"Sorry."

"It's a rule," she said, "and rules are made for your own good."

I had the uncomfortable feeling that I was talking to a "supervisable individual." She placed the tray on the table. "It was the best I could do," she apologized. "The cooks don't like meals after hours."

"It'll be fine," I said. As I started to eat, she seemed not to want to leave. I invited her to sit down, and she looked pleased.

"Mango," I asked, "when you leave here after Christmas, where will you go?"

She shrugged. "Back to El Paso, I guess."

"Is that your home?"

She shrugged again and nodded.

"What about your father?"

She looked directly at me. "He's still a bum. But I won't try to kill him this time. I'll just stay out of his way, and he'd better stay out of mine."

Her bulk became suddenly ominous. I looked at her and wondered what had been solved. And what if the bum didn't stay out of her way?

Finally she said good night, and said she'd be back first thing in the morning. I thanked her again, and again heard her parting admonition to lock the door.

I knew she was waiting on the other side of the closed door. She probably would have stood there all night if I hadn't left the chair and slid the night latch. "Okay, Mango, you can go to bed now."

No answer, just the sound of footsteps crunching snow. *Rules are rules.* A true convert.

There was fried canned meat on the plate, cold corn, watery mashed potatoes, and two prepared cupcakes in little cellophane coffins. I did my best, not wanting to offend the cooks further by returning a plate of uneaten food.

I showered and shaved, moving the razor carefully around the lacerations. I discovered that they looked worse on a clean-shaven face, as raw as Mango's fresh scar. We were both victims of Hatter Fox, the victim.

I wrapped up in an extra blanket that Mango had left on the bed, drew a chair close to the radiator, and turned off the light. I closed my eyes, and still I saw her lifting the cup of cold coffee that no one wanted—that no one in his right mind would drink—saw her drinking it all, then lifting her face and finding my eyes and staying with them long past a chance encounter. What a remarkable thing it would be if I could somehow help her. But if it worked at all, it would have to be on her terms, not mine. I would have to discover the cause of her terror; I would have to become skillful at interpreting silences, reading blanks, understanding her nonactions as well as her actions. On *her* terms. What a remarkable thing that would be.

Strong in my new determination, I went to bed.

And I slept. On a mattress which felt as though it had been made of tin cans. And I felt for the first time anticipation for my meeting with Hatter Fox the following day.

The next morning I awakened in the dingy little tourist-camp room. It was Friday, about a week and a half before Christmas. The sun was shining through the red curtains, casting a blood color on the floor. My feet were frozen, and Mango was knocking at the door. My watch said nine o'clock. She had not only learned all of our rules, she'd also learned that most peculiar axiom of the white, civilized world: the good are punctual.

Still wrapped in my blanket, I went to the door, slid the latch, and opened it.

She grinned. "Getting in the mood for the Indian?" A would-be father killer with a sense of humor! She stomped snow off her boots and came in carrying another tray. "All right," she said. "What am I supposed to do this morning?" she asked.

Still half asleep, I sat on the edge of the bed and pulled the blanket tighter. "What do you mean?"

"I was told to take you any place you want to go," she said, holding up a monumental key ring loaded with keys. "You must be pretty important. Orders from old man Winton himself."

I didn't feel very important, sitting naked under the blanket. "Is that coffee?" I asked, nodding toward the covered tray.

It was, and she served it to me, still amused by something. "Your face looks terrible," she said bluntly. She moved the table close to the bed and revealed a plate of indescribable scrambled eggs, and two pieces of burnt toast. "They're no good cold," she said. She grinned. "They're not much good hot." Then she took the chair I had abandoned by the radiator, and sat down and watched me.

The coffee was fine and occupied all my attention for the moment. But I was aware of her staring at me. She said, "Got any cigarettes?"

I shook my head.

"Don't you smoke?"

"Used to. Gave it up."

"I wish I could. That's the worse thing about being in this place—no butts unless someone brings them to you, and then they are gone like that."

I made a mental note to pick up a carton of cigarettes for Mango. Lung cancer was the least of her worries. I made a stab at the eggs, but couldn't quite do it. She giggled, "Rotten, aren't they?"

I agreed, and we sat in silence, she watching me, and I watching the black coffee.

"Can I see your back?" she asked suddenly.

"My back?"

She nodded. "I heard all about you last night. You must be some sort of dumb-ass to want to see her again. After what she's done to you."

I sensed a grapevine, a very efficient one. No, she couldn't see my back, and if she'd kindly leave the room, I'd dress and we'd be on our way.

She shrugged. "Didn't mean to make you mad."

"I'm not mad, Mango. Why don't you take the trays back and I'll meet you out front in about ten minutes."

She shrugged again. It was her favorite gesture. "So where do you want me to take you?" she asked, stacking the dishes on the trays.

"Down to solitary."

"To see her?"

"Yes."

Now her expression clearly said, You *are* a dumb-ass.

Without another word she lifted the trays and left the room. I had a strong suspicion that she was mildly jealous. Her reward for learning the rules and for being good was the right to show visitors around. Hatter Fox's reward for ignoring the rules and causing havoc was the gift of the visitor himself. It didn't seem right. But then few things did.

I dressed quickly and went out onto the porch to

find a clear, but very cold, day. The ground was still covered with snow, and the red-brick complex had a picture-postcard quality, if one didn't look too closely at the bars on the windows.

Mango appeared a distance away on the other side of a closed gate. I waved at her in a friendly attempt to assuage her jealousy and called out, "Shall we walk or drive?"

"Walk unless you're lazy."

She was displeased by something. By the time I had reached the gate, she had it unlocked, and we walked up a curved path which led to the rear of the south building. Along the way I thanked her for bringing breakfast, and for taking such good care of me.

Again she shrugged, a self-effacing sort of movement which seemed to say, At least I'm good for something. I was sorry I had not come to see her, and sorry that she was hurt or jealous or mad, whatever. I wondered if I could make her understand.

"Have you ever been in solitary confinement, Mango?" I asked.

She heard my question, but didn't answer right away. Finally she said, "No, but I had a friend who was there once. For a day."

"And what about the dog pens?"

"What about them?"

"Have you ever been in them?"

It was obvious that the questions were embarrassing her. She shook her head in the negative and said nothing.

"How many times has Hatter Fox been put in the dog pens?"

She gave a short laugh, an empty sound which had nothing to do with amusement. "Good God, who counts?"

"And solitary? How many days has she spent in solitary?"

Suddenly she was angry. She stopped walking and confronted me on the sidewalk. "Well, she asked for it, didn't she? They ain't done nothing to her that she didn't ask for. Rules is rules, and you can't have a place like this without them."

I readily agreed, impressed again with her knowledge and fear of rules. I reconsidered my assessment of Mango's future. Maybe she wouldn't be back after all. I had the feeling that she would fit nicely now into a rule-bound society. The poison was still in her system, but she had digested it—successfully, I hoped—and was now ready to conform to anything that bore the name "rule."

She walked on ahead of me then, clearly angry. I had accomplished nothing, had made her understand nothing. It was an inauspicious beginning to a day that had dawned in anticipation of success.

At the rear of the south building, we came to a steel door with no doorknob, and, wonder of wonders, no outside lock. She rang a bell and waited, keeping her face turned away from me, more interested in studying her footprints in the snow. A few minutes later, the door opened and a white-coated aide I'd never seen before stood on the other side.

No one said a word; we passed through the door and I found myself on familiar territory, the dormitory corridor that led to the narrow passageway and the steps down.

"Ned will take you the rest of the way," Mango said, and stomped off down the hall. I called thanks after her, but there was no response, just her massive hulk moving angrily away.

Ned too looked mad for some reason. With a jerk of his burr-shaved head, he indicated that I was to follow, and I had the curious suspicion that Hatter Fox's unpopularity was rubbing off onto me. I had come to see the untouchable. She and I had been granted special privileges, and in this enclosed world of offense and punishment, goodness and reward, we had somehow broken a major rule.

So be it. I couldn't solve all the problems at once. There ahead was the familiar passage down, the dim bulbs hanging from the ceiling, the narrow stairway, and a chill in the air as sharp as if we were still outside. I tried again to imagine the feelings of a young girl being escorted down those steps for the first time, the ritual stripping and donning of prison garb, the hard, harsh hands and expressionless faces of her guards, the cells, the humiliation of a slop jar, the closed and locked door, and then only the dim light and the silence.

Reform? How could such an experience reform anyone? Still "rules is rules!" Yes, Mango, you're right. And you can't run a place like this without them. But there had to be a better way.

Ned, who had not spoken a word all the way down turned me over to Claude, who likewise looked less than happy to see me. "When you gonna give up, Doc?" he asked.

"Not right away," I said, trying to be pleasant.

"Come on in," he said, "but I'd better warn you, she's acting up again today. Frankly I'll be glad to see her get the hell out of here." He unlocked the inner door and led the way to her cell. "Look at that, will you?" he said.

She was on her back on the cot. Her arms had been drawn over her head; her wrists had been twisted back and down and handcuffed to the crossbars beneath the cot. She was struggling against the restraint and the awkward position, her body arched, legs thrashing, her head tossing from side to side, her arms pulling against the handcuffs, against the position of her wrists twisted backward into an inhuman position, her breath coming in short spasms. If she knew I was in the room, she gave no indication of it. Even her fear of me was diminished in the face of this new torture.

The sight was intolerable. "Why?" I demanded.

Claude was chewing gum. His tongue moved around the obstacle of gum with an explanation. "She wouldn't stay on the cot last night," he said. "Kept getting down on the floor. It's a rule here. They gotta stay on the cot at night 'cause the floor's cold, and they get sick, and it's all a big mess. I told her, I warned her over and over again, but every time I'd go in, she'd be there on the floor. I got no sleep at all on account of her. It's a rule here, they gotta sleep on the cot. But she wouldn't listen. So I got her onto the cot all right, and there she is, and there she's gonna stay."

All the time he was talking I was looking into his face, and I had the sinking feeling that behind that smooth forehead was the mentality of a dull-witted twelve-year-old. I could still hear the struggle coming from the cot, moans now and then as she inflicted pain on herself by twisting her wrists against the steel handcuffs. And between the moans behind me, and the slack-jawed, gum-chewing, rule-abiding countenance before me, I considered quite seriously wrestling him for the key to the handcuffs, killing him if necessary —anything to release her from this new and stupid agony.

But reason stepped in. To have fought with Claude would have solved nothing. Besides, I had the feeling he could have beat the hell out of me. There were other ways to deal with twelve-year-old mentalities. I took his arm and led him to the locked cell door, shaking my head sympathetically at his lost sleep, at his impressive responsibility.

"You do quite a job down here, Claude," I said. "Why don't you unlock the door?"

"It ain't easy, Doc," he said, obediently unlocking the cell door. "Some of these gals are like wild animals, and wouldn't you know it, I get the wildest ones down here."

"I know, I know."

The door was unlocked, and we were in the cell, standing only a few feet from the continuing struggle on the cot.

"Ain't she something?" Claude asked. "She's been at that most of the night. But at least she's on the cot, and that's the rule."

I nodded broadly, not trusting myself to speak. I

squatted down and pretended to examine the handcuffs. Her left wrist was bleeding.

"Look here, Claude." I invited him to squat down beside me. "Looks like there might be a mess after all."

"Uh?"

"She's cut herself. If she keeps that up, there will be an infection, and she'll get sick, and there'll be a big mess after all."

He bent close for his own examination. "Dumb broad," he muttered. "I didn't do that to her. She done that to herself."

"I know, but all the same, maybe you'd better take them off now before it gets worse. What do you think?"

The agony of indecision was on his face. "I dunno."

"Some infections can be terrible, Claude. Cost money. Medicine and all. You'd have to account for it."

Suddenly, as though cooperating with me in my efforts, Hatter gave one enormous struggle; her wrists bent backward until they were doubled against her arms. The steel cut deeper, fresh blood flowed.

"Goddamn, you'd think that'd hurt," observed Claude.

"Why don't you let her go now? Night's over." I noticed a thin edge to my voice. If he didn't make a move soon, I'd have to try to take the keys from him.

But finally he stood up, fishing through his pockets, still grumbling, "I didn't do nothing to her that she didn't ask for—"

"I know."

"You're my witness, Doc. I didn't do nothing to her."

He moved carefully around the blood on her wrists, as though he didn't want to soil his hands. The tiny locks clicked, the handcuffs fell to the floor, and the struggling ceased, although her arms continued to hang limply over her head.

"That's good," I soothed. "Now, look, Claude, if you could get me some warm water, and maybe a first-aid kit somewhere, I'd see what I could do about those cuts. We don't want her to get that infection, do we? It would just be between us."

"Would you do that, Doc? I'd appreciate it." The child had been won over. He was on my side now. "You're okay," he grinned from the door. "I'll be right back."

I smiled my gratitude for his stamp of approval and let him know that I was pleased with our alliance. I waited until I heard the outer door close and lock. Carefully I lifted her arms and placed them beside her on the cot. The cuts were not deep, but her hands and arms were cold from lack of circulation. She was still breathing heavily, and her face was all but obscured with thrown, tousled hair. I brushed the hair to one side and looked down on her forehead wet with perspiration. Her mouth was open, lips dry, her eyes were closed. Her struggle had been so futile.

I pulled the blanket up around her and asked quietly, "Was it worth it, Hatter? Was all this worth wanting to sleep on the floor?"

Her eyes fluttered opened. She saw me, groaned, tried to move away from my touch. She turned her head away from me. Somehow I couldn't quite bring myself to lecture her. It was the old fear again, groundless, mystifying. But I remembered my pledge of the night before, to meet her on her own terms, and these apparently were her terms of the morning: lacerated wrists, chills, strained muscles, and total exhaustion.

There was so little flesh on her, such meager protection for the constant war that she apparently had chosen for her existence. Her collarbone and the bones of her neck were clearly visible. And in lifting her arms, I had observed that the upper arms were very little larger than her wrists.

I knew so little that morning of what to do or say. But I did know that if something wasn't done

soon, her wish would come true. She would die. Her
breathing subsided. Her head rolled back and forth a
few times. Again she opened her eyes and looked up
at me, but some new pain or fear caused her to turn
away again. I placed a chair beside the cot and sat
down. Finally she became quiet. She wasn't asleep exactly, just still and vaguely triumphant in the face of
this new and painful defeat. I wondered if she even
knew the meaning of the words "triumph" and "defeat"? And more important, did she know the difference?

Beyond the brief opening of her eyes, she did not
acknowledge my presence in any way. She kept her
face turned to one side, eyes closed. It occurred to me
again that every encounter I had had with her had been
in one kind of cell or another, behind bars and a
locked door. Beneath the blanket, she looked harmless
now, scarcely a major threat to society. In fact, there
was a strange, almost primal, mystical beauty to her,
lying there, her features glistening with perspiration,
her lips opened. She looked as if she had just undergone
some strenuous rite of initiation, tribal royalty put to an
agonizing test to prove her worthiness. But this was
mere fancy. She had meager credentials for royalty. Apparently no one had even been able to find out where
she came from, who her parents were, where she had
been born. She was Indian, Navajo, about seventeen, perhaps younger, and went by the name of Hatter Fox. That was all. Scarcely the qualifications for
royalty.

Still she dominated that grim cell, just as she had
dominated the cell back in Santa Fe, occupied it and
conquered the ugliness somehow, made it seem paltry
and unimportant when compared with her spirit, her
stubbornness, her will.

But how to approach her? How to reassure her
that I meant her no harm? How to salvage what was
good and heal what was ill? How to save her from
her own massive powers of destruction?

It was very quiet in the solitary cell. No clocks ticking, no friendly hum of a refrigerator, or distant voices in an upstairs room. No sounds at all.

Claude returned with a basin of water, a small tube of something, and a roll of bandage. Clito was right behind him carrying a tray, listening intently to Claude's account of the night. They stopped talking as they came into the cell, and started telling me about the excitement of the moment.

"I had to steal this crap," Claude said, placing the objects on the table. "We got a nurse upstairs that you wouldn't believe, Doc. Big as a house and horny as a toad. Old lover boy here warmed up to her, and I lifted them clean as a whistle."

"Good," I said, trying to imagine what sort of female would be distracted by Clito.

"Is the Indian bad off, Doc?" asked Clito, hands on hips, staring down at Hatter on the cot.

"I don't think so. Just minor cuts, but we don't want a mess, do we?"

"No siree. Daddy Winton believes in bringing them into line, but leaving no marks. He don't like marks."

An interesting theory of reform. I wanted them out of the cell. "Look, why don't you two go out there and keep watch?" I suggested.

"No need," Claude replied. "No one ever comes down here, and besides we got all the doors locked. Nobody but us has a key to that door. We got it all to ourselves."

How convenient! Having encountered mindless brutality so early in the morning, I found that my mind went easily in that direction. "All the same, I'd like to talk with her. In private. You understand."

Unfortunately, they thought they did understand. All too well. Clito grinned and poked at Claude. "You yo-yo," he giggled. "The doc said he wants to be alone with her."

A slow dawning light crossed Claude's face. "You betcha," he said. "There's more than one way to bring 'em into line, ain't that what you say, Doc? And it don't leave no marks either."

Somehow I felt that I had moved up a notch or two in their estimation. I was one of them, and this recognition pleased them. I found I could not look at them. I figured that at the outside they had about five seconds to get the hell out of there, or I would give them reason to use the handcuffs on me.

Claude said, "That's her breakfast, but you may want to give it to her later."

"Just knock when you're through, Doc. We don't want to rush you. Take your time. She ain't bad, if you like 'em bony."

Two, three, four . . . and they were gone, still grinning at the door, sharing their judgment of me, that I was one hell of a guy. With my worst suspicions now confirmed, I vowed to see Levering before the day was over and get her moved out of there. I had no proof, true, and even if Hatter were to make an accusation, I doubted seriously if anyone in that institution would believe her. But Levering would not refuse to believe me. I would see to it.

The bowl on the breakfast tray held a liquid mixture which looked as if someone had been sick. I pushed it to one side and turned back to Hatter. Looking down on her, I have never, at any given point in my life, felt such compassion for any human being. It occurred to me that perhaps the kindest thing I could do for her would be to place my hands around her throat—and press.

But I was a civilized man, had been taught to believe that it was kinder to prolong agony than cause death. The water in the basin was ice-cold. The salve was an old sulpha-base, a World War II relic, and the bandages were unwrapped and yellowed around the edges.

Better than nothing? It was all I had. She appeared to be sleeping, but I knew better. I sat down beside her and asked if I could see her wrists.

No response.

"The medicine will make the cuts heal faster. Please."

Still no response, except an attempt on her part to push deeper beneath the blanket, as though I were the one who had handcuffed her to the bed.

Moving very slowly, I lifted the blanket and drew it back. I had my hand on her forearm when suddenly she pulled away, shivering with fear.

"It won't hurt, Hatter, I promise. Please don't be afraid of me."

No response.

On her terms. Remember? I sat back in the chair and waited. About twenty minutes later, she turned toward me, and slowly placed her arm on the edge of the cot. It was a generous gesture. For her. I wasn't certain if it was a cessation of fear, or merely a lack of energy to resist. Without speaking, I lifted her right arm and examined the cuts. They were not deep; the flesh had been rubbed raw, chewed by the handcuffs. I cleaned off the blood and carefully applied the ointment and wrapped the wrists in a loose bandage; all the time she watched me as a very young child watches a doctor, with that incredible fear in her eyes.

Her breathing had become more labored. She was terrified, and I could think of no words to match the size of her fear. So I worked in silence, treated both wrists, each movement on my part as deliberate as a slow-motion camera. Not once throughout the ordeal did she take her eyes off me, as though she were waiting, on the alert, for the first excuse to withdraw.

Apparently I gave her none. She endured the treatment, watched closely as I returned the equipment to the table, and was still watching as I sat back down beside her. Her terms were hard ones. No words, no sounds of intelligence, just the indecipherable language of the eyes. More than once, I felt words forming inside my head, but made a conscious effort to send them away. Still, there was so much I wanted to ask her. But I knew better.

I could not outstare her. When I began to see two

of her, I leaned forward and rested my head in my hands and tried to rub away the double image. It was while I was sitting with my head down that I heard her stir. Without looking up, I listened carefully and tried to determine what she was doing. Within the range of my downward vision, I saw her bare feet touch the floor. She stood up, seemed to struggle for a moment for balance, and then, using the table for support, she made her way slowly across the cell to her corner. She placed her hands on the wall and laboriously lowered herself to the floor. There she curled herself into a fetal position, placed the bandaged wrists beneath her head, closed her eyes, and went to sleep.

Within only a few moments, her breathing was steady and rhythmical. Twice I placed the blanket over her, and twice she threw it off. The third time I gave up. It seemed the wisest course of action where her will was concerned.

I watched her for a long time sleeping on the floor in the corner. Again she had won. Whereas only a few days before I had wondered repeatedly what in hell I was doing there, now it seemed the only sensible place to be. In much the same way as she had conquered bare walls and bars, she had invaded and conquered me. I wondered if she had planned it that way. No matter. The commitment acknowledged, I moved the repulsive mixture of her breakfast to one side, laid my head down on the table, and joined her in a nap.

Sometime later, certainly no more than twenty minutes, I awakened suddenly. I looked up to see her sitting in the corner, unwinding the bandage on her left wrist. She knew I was watching her. I caught only a glimpse of those diamond-bright eyes. Her gestures, no matter how small, were beginning to say so much. And this one clearly said, "To hell with you. Don't think for a moment you've touched me."

"Suit yourself," I said. "I only wanted the cuts to heal faster," and with a conscious effort, I forced my head back down onto the table, seemingly impervious to who she was and what she was doing.

The movement stopped. I tried to count the seconds to five minutes. When I looked up again, I saw that she had gone back to sleep. The bandage on the left wrist was partially unwound. The bandage on the right wrist was intact.

Score one!

I did not go back to sleep. But she did, the deep, uninterrupted sleep of complete exhaustion. She turned a couple of times and hugged her arms to her, as though she were cold. But the rejected blanket was only a few feet from her. If she wanted it, she knew where she could find it. I spent the better part of the day watching her sleep, and learning firsthand about the special horrors of solitary confinement. I paced off the cell until I knew every square inch of it. I counted the bars: sixteen across, eight down the sides. I observed the cracks in the ceiling where moisture had seeped through and weakened the construction, and I found the outline of a mountain troll. I studied the short frayed cord and the dim bulb in the ceiling. I stared at the splattered dark-brown stains on the concrete floor and decided they were from food, or excrement. I recited the Gettysburg Address, the Twenty-third Psalm, the Lord's Prayer, and the Preamble to the Constitution. I said the multiplication tables and the Hippocratic oath, and recalled the opening lines of five novels. I tried to imagine spending a week's sentence in that place, and found the thought so terrifying that I started back at the beginning with the Gettysburg Address, the Twenty-third Psalm, the Lord's Prayer.

Incredible things happen to a person in solitary confinement. A kind of mental numbness sets in. You begin to think that your words and thoughts have no reality, that they don't exist at all except as figments of your imagination. With no one to receive or acknowledge them, you cease thinking in coherent terms. A vacuum occurs, and you don't rush to fill it with anything. After a few hours, I was convinced that no one could survive intact under such conditions. What in the name of God were we doing in our reform systems? And who was the jackass who conceived and created the first solitary-confinement cell?

The minutes refused to pass. I studied my watch. The second hand seemed to be stuck. Eleven forty-five. An hour later it was eleven forty-seven. Two hours later it was eleven fifty. In the beginning, God created . . . And they wrapped Him in swaddling clothes and laid him . . . Call me Ishmael . . . It was the best of times, it was the worst . . . The watch was broken . . . Time? . . . No time . . . Space? . . . Nothing but space . . . And silence . . . What was I doing there? . . . Why didn't someone come? . . . There wasn't enough air . . . The weakened structure of the building was going to collapse, and I was going to be buried alive . . . They had forgotten about me . . . They had led me down here, locked all the doors, and gone off and forgotten about me . . . Five fingers on one hand, five fingers on the other . . . I fell out of the apple tree when I was a kid, and broke my arm . . . I'm your first-grade teacher, Miss Caldwell, and you have muddy shoes. That's not acceptable . . . Why didn't someone come? . . . A ticket to New York, please—one way . . . On Wednesday morning there will be an orientation meeting . . . Be there . . . The natives are human beings, never forget that . . . The secondary vein is connected to . . . Massive bleeding occurs . . . Something is wrong with my heart . . . Your patient died last night . . . I'm so sorry . . . There's pain when I breathe . . . Throat cancer is the worst kind . . . Sixteen bars across, eight bars down . . . Fourscore and seven years ago . . . God help me . . .

I am a fairly reasonable, well-adjusted male, twenty-eight years old. The above is an honest recollection of the disintegration that was taking place within me that morning. Rehabilitate? Don't make me laugh.

In fact, one of the most glorious sights I've ever seen in my life was Claude's flat face when he came bursting through the outer door about two o'clock that afternoon, calling out "Ready or not, Doc, coming through."

He seemed disappointed at our seating arrangement, Hatter curled up in the corner, and me sitting at the table, holding my head in my hands as though I were trying to hold it together.

"Chow time," he said, appearing with another tray. Suddenly Hatter's position dawned on him. "Hey, I said no sleeping on the floor."

My mind was working, but my mouth could not form words. The act of verbalization. How was it done?

Claude was still upset. "Did you hear me, Doc? I said no sleeping on the——"

"Leave her alone."

Some private and very sick vision occurred to him then. He grinned. "You really put her through it, uh?"

The cell and everything in it had an unreal quality. Even Claude seemed to be made of some elastic substance. At times he seemed three feet wide, as tall as the cell, then he'd shrink to below my line of vision.

"You don't look so good, Doc."

"I'm fine."

"Message from Levering. He wants to see you in his office."

"Good. I want to see him." I stood up, pleasantly surprised to find that my legs still worked. So eager was I to leave that place that I almost forgot whom I was leaving behind. I stopped at the door. Claude was at the table, clearly annoyed with the uneaten breakfast.

"She knows what she'll get if she don't eat. You should at least have let her eat."

I walked back to the table. "Why don't you just let her sleep now?" I suggested. "You look beat yourself. I'll be back in a few minutes, and I'll see to it that she eats. I promise."

Something was troubling him; some new thought was slipping precariously across his smooth brain.

"How come she gets a private baby-sitter?" he asked. "I don't ever remember anyone else down here getting their own private baby-sitter. You know her, or something? What's she to you?"

"A job," I said, trying to sound casual. "Bills have to be paid, you have to eat."

He stared at me, uncertain, not quite believing. Then the new idea slid off the edge of his brain and out of sight. "You're right there," he agreed, "and it ain't easy these days to get a decent job."

I took him by the arm and led him out of the cell, commiserating with him all the way about the unemployment problem, the inflation problem, the cost of a six-pack of beer and ten gallons of gasoline. I looked back at the girl sleeping on the floor in the corner of the cell, and found myself hoping she wouldn't wake up until I'd returned. I had one burning goal then, to get her out of that place. If I had to tear the building down, I'd get her out of there. It was impossible to think of her opening her eyes to those sixteen bars across, eight down, the cracked ceiling with the outline of the mountain troll, the splattered floor. Maybe after several days, one grew accustomed to it. And that was an even worse thought.

Claude relocked the doors, still talking. All the way up the stairs, locking and unlocking doors, he considered and condemned: the Supreme Court, all Communists, Martin Luther King, and birth-control pills. About the same time that he told me he was a Wallace man, we reached the top, and I saw the sun.

"I can take it from here," I said. "I know the way."

"You got two more doors between here and the front office," he warned. "How do you plan to get through them?"

Good question. Maybe it was better to take him with me than to provide him with the leisure to return to her cell. He called out cheerily to a few of the girls we encountered in the hallway. It seemed to me that they did not respond as readily as they had to Dr.

Levering. A few bobbed polite heads, but I noticed others who turned away without speaking at all. Fear?

The girls' coolness seemed not to bother Claude at all. Between greetings, he talked breezily about the state of the world, the moon exploration, a planned hunting trip, half thoughts, faulty logic, massive prejudice—harmless by himself. But multiplied into the hundreds of thousands?

As we passed through the last arcade, he became more businesslike, as though he were entering a different sphere of influence that required a different kind of behavior. He walked the length of the corridor without saying a word.

But several secretaries in the main office caught his eye. He stopped and leaned into the door, and grinned a greeting. The girls scarcely looked up from their work.

"Look," I said. "I can take it from here. You deserve a break." I winked broadly and jerked my head toward the girls.

"You're all right, Doc," he said. "You just holler when you're ready to go back. You hear?"

I agreed to holler, and proceeded on my way alone, relieved. It would have been awkward to walk into Levering's office with the man I intended to accuse. In all honesty I didn't care what Claude did with his free time and excess energy. My only purpose was to get Hatter out of his suspect reach. There would be no accusations, just a simple plea on behalf of logic. Placing a patient like Hatter Fox in the care of a man like Claude was like handing a burn victim over to an arsonist. Levering had sense. Surely he could see this.

His office door was closed, the outer office empty. I was on the verge of knocking when suddenly the door opened and Levering appeared in the company of a delicate, fragile-looking little girl. She couldn't have been more than fourteen, maybe younger, and had long pale blond hair. She was weeping.

He saw me and sadly shook his head, then continued to comfort the distressed child. "We'll talk some more tomorrow, Anne," he promised. "But I think we've made real progress today, don't you?"

She smiled through her tears, and nodded, and permitted him to guide her to the door, leaning in toward his comfort and warmth.

"Do you know how to find your way out?" he asked. She nodded again, sniffling. "Then until tomorrow?"

He gave her a warm hug again, and she responded with a tear-stained smile. She looked so young, so innocent. What rule had she broken? What crime had she committed? She bore no resemblance to either a criminal or a rule-breaker.

These were my first questions to Levering when he returned from watching her on her way down the hall.

"A runaway," he said simply. "She ran away from home five times. The sixth time she was on her way to California with a sixty-year-old man. She'll be all right, though," he concluded. "She's very intelligent." He looked tired, but amused by something. "Why is it always the very intelligent ones?"

It was a rhetorical question. He wanted no answer, and I could have given him none. He motioned me into his office and into a chair, and I watched him struggling through the transition and felt a surge of compassion for him. He must be called upon to make dozens of similar transitions every day. It was required of him to march lock step from one private hell into another, nonstop, with only a moment to take a breath, chew a pencil or two, gaze out of the window at the dog pens, then proceed to the next agony. I hoped they paid him well, although I knew better.

"Well," he said, sinking finally into his chair, refocusing his eyes on me and his mind on the new problem at hand. He leaned so far back in the chair, I thought for a moment he'd fall over. "What can I do for you?" he asked.

"I thought you wanted to see me," I said, deciding to give him a break and not hit him immediately with the news that he might have a rapist on his staff.

He looked puzzled; then the light dawned. "Oh? Well, I just wanted to hear how things were going. Did Mango take good care of you last night?"

"She did, just fine."

"Was the room all right?"

"Perfect."

"And your meals?"

"Fine."

"Good." He leaned forward and reached for the nearest pencil. Into the mouth it went. He chewed it, and seemed to be waiting for me to take over. When I refused to do so, he asked, "And how was your session with Hatter?"

"No session. She slept all morning."

"She slept? Why?"

"Because she didn't sleep last night."

He was trying hard to understand, and failing. "Why didn't she sleep last night?"

"Because Claude had handcuffed her to the cot."

He lowered his head for a moment. I was sorry to add to his fatigue, but those were the facts. And that seemed to be the time to tell all. I began carefully, choosing my words, avoiding the dangerous accusatory ones. "Dr. Levering, would it be possible to move her out of there?"

He didn't answer right away, and when he did he avoided the question altogether. "The handcuffs are necessary if the inmate refuses to sleep on the bed," he stated flatly.

I repeated my question. "Would it be possible to get her out of that place?"

He did not even consider the possibility. He merely said, "Not until Tuesday."

"But nothing is being accomplished down there. If anything, it's making matters worse."

Then he made an unfortunate selection of words. He said, "It's a rule. They are required to serve their time in solitary, and it is also a rule that they sleep on the beds. There is no way that we can——"

Rule is a four-letter word, and by this point, it had become for me an obscenity. "Is it also a rule," I flared, leaving the chair and confronting him across the desk, "that they be chained like animals? And is it also a rule that they be subjected to complete humiliation? And is it also a rule that they be used and abused in whatever sick fashion the aides wish?"

He looked up. "What are you saying?"

"I'm saying that you have a girl down there on the verge of becoming a corpse. I'm also saying that you have locked her up and placed her in questionable hands so far away that you haven't the faintest idea what goes on down there."

He was struggling to understand. "Are you accusing——"

"I'm not accusing anyone of anything," I said, "I'm just trying to point out that you are accomplishing nothing with this girl in solitary. She *has* changed. I can assure you of that. When I first saw her in Santa Fe, she was strong, a leader, afraid of nothing. In a few short months, this institution has reduced her to a cowering, terrified animal. Is that what you have in mind when you say reform?"

He was visibly shaken, but intractable. "They must learn that rules are there to be obeyed."

"And how do you plan to teach them? By locking them up in a remote cell, and giving the only key to subhumans, then turning your back and closing your eyes and ears? She was handcuffed to the bed, Dr. Levering, completely defenseless."

It was as close as I had come to an accusation. He stood up, no longer weary. "You are making a serious charge," he warned.

"I am making no charge," I said. "I have no proof, nothing of substance. Just my suspicions. I was called here to see if I could help. I'm trying to help."

"Claude has been with us for over six years——"

"What in the hell is that supposed to mean? He is a simple, brutal man. You know that. No one else could perform that sort of a job. He told me this morning that no one ever goes down there. He also told me that he has the only key to the cells, and when I told him that I wanted to see her alone, he seemed to know exactly what I was talking about."

Levering sat back down in his chair. At least he was listening.

"I'm not accusing him, Dr. Levering. I can't, I have no proof. And even if I had Hatter in this office at this moment, would you believe her?"

No answer.

"All I'm saying is, let's not take any chances. Let's not cause more damage. Please help me get her out of there."

He covered his mouth with his hands and shook his head. Through the barrier of his fingers, he spoke, muffled. "We don't sentence a girl to solitary lightly. The infraction must be large enough and serious enough to warrant it. I counsel them before they go down to make sure they understand why. And I counsel them when they come up. Not one of them has ever said anything about—"

"Rape? Would they? Would that be the sort of thing a girl already in trouble would tell the authorities, particularly when she knew there was always the possibility that she would be sent back down, and placed in the same hands? How is she supposed to know where brutality stops and therapy starts?"

Still he sat there, shaking his head, half concealing his face from me, visibly disturbed by what I had suggested, but not quite able to believe it. "There are two ways," he said flatly, "for a girl to come up. She is ill and is sent to the infirmary, or she has completed her sentence. Those are the rules."

There was that word again. "Then you won't help me?" I asked, looking at the half-concealed face and already knowing the answer.

"How can I?"

"Then that's it," I said, and started for the door.

"What do you mean?"

"I mean she's all yours now. Yours and Winton's and Claude's. Only I wouldn't worry any more about whether or not to send her to the State Hospital. Give her about four more weeks, and you can bury her. How many deaths have you had here, Dr. Levering?"

He looked pale. "None."

"There's a first time for everything."

"Where are you going?"

"Back to Santa Fe."

"What shall I tell Winton?"

"Tell him anything you like. See you around."

"Dr. Summer?"

He called my name twice more before I reached the hall, but I was moving with greater determination than he. The corridors, the institutional odors of red wax and old coffee, the bars, the hopelessness—all this was beginning to take its toll. Somewhere in the world were fairly contented, fairly well-adjusted people. I wanted to find them and join their ranks.

In an unbelievably short time, I was seated in a dingy, second-rate bar in Albuquerque, trying like hell to get drunk. "One for the road" had been my explanation to myself when I'd reached the fork in the highway and had taken the road into town instead of the one to Santa Fe. I'd found nothing enjoyable or rewarding about beating my head against a brick wall. About three scotches later, I had embraced the adolescent philosophy that God arbitrarily points to a group of people and says, "You are the victims." I didn't care what He did or said, but I regretted like hell the fact that I was always running into them, the victims. So Hatter Fox was a victim. So let her play her role and get it over with.

Still, I had seen. I had witnessed. I had felt a personal disintegration after five hours in that cell, and I knew, as I have never known anything in my life, that what was going on back there was wrong. So wrong. And all the scotch and adolescent philosophies in the world wouldn't make it right.

At the back of the bar, there was a pay phone alongside a stinking men's room. I used the men's room and then the pay phone. For once the operator co-operated and found my number immediately, and sooner than I might have wished, I had Dr. Levering on the other end of the line.

"Teague Summer here," I said. "I have a proposition."

Again he sounded genuinely relieved to hear my voice. "I've been thinking," he began.

"So have I. Now listen. If we can't get her out of there, is there any rule which says I can't go down and stay with her? I'll take the cell next to hers."

Long pause. "There's no precedent."

"Then let's make one."

"I don't know. Special privileges have a way of upsetting the entire institution. Anyway, she has three days left. Are you sure you know what—"

"If she can take it, why can't I? At least I could keep an eye on her. And no one would even have to know. I'd come in late tonight. As far as the girls are concerned, I could have gone back to Santa Fe."

"Dr. Winton would have to—"

"Winton wants a clean record. You know as well as I that he doesn't give a damn what I do."

Another long pause. "Are you sure you know—"

"I know."

Apparently the man was making a noble attempt to find his backbone. Finally, reluctantly, he said, "All right, as long as you take responsibility."

I could have predicted that. "I'll be there in about an hour. I'll park behind the guest cottages. Have the south door opened."

I hung up, amazed. Unable to get drunk, I had just sentenced myself to three days of solitary confinement. That realization called for another scotch. Even then, I walked out into the night air stone-cold sober.

Santa Claus was standing on the street corner, ringing a bell. White fog exploded out of everyone's mouth. The street was crowded with shoppers carrying wrapped packages, and there were colorful blurs of Christmas lights, and coming from somewhere was canned music. "Silent Night."

Standing there, watching it all, I seemed to have my second clear realization of what I had done and where I was going. I stood on the curb and watched the passing crowds and tried very hard to relate everything I saw to my last image of Hatter Fox, wrists bandaged, sleeping on the floor. *Did* God perhaps sit up there and arbitrarily designate the victims? It seemed the only sensible conclusion.

Partly it was the season, and my negative reaction to it, but I caught myself with the impossible feeling, deep down, of looking forward to what was ahead. Why did I want to share her punishment? Because I was guilty. But of what? I suspected again that my interests differed little from Winton's and Levering's. They were of a different color, perhaps, but as vested as theirs. I did not return that night for Hatter Fox. I told myself that I did, but I was lying. If I was doing all this for Hatter Fox, then I ate a good steak dinner for Hatter Fox, walked the streets and breathed cold, fresh, free air for Hatter Fox, bought a couple of new shirts in my size for Hatter Fox, and a new toothbrush for Hatter Fox, listened for a while to street-corner carolers for Hatter Fox.

Finally the influence of the season had a mild impact on me. I stopped in a large Rexall Drugstore and purchased a carton of cigarettes for Mango, and two girlie magazines for Claude and Clito. As I was going through the check-out counter, I saw and purchased a small, inexpensive, pink-plastic mirror, comb and brush set. For, at last, Hatter Fox.

But in truth, these objects were not gifts at all. They were bribes. Even the comb and brush set was a bribe, a silent plea to her not to let me fail. Again.

It was all very clandestine and melodramatic—

the way I cut the lights of the jeep as I passed through the reformatory gate, and drove slowly around the complex to the cottages at the rear. I parked on the far side, well out of sight, and walked to the front of the cottages, trying to see through the dark to the south building.

Suddenly a voice jumped out at me from the steps of the cottage. "You said an hour. It's been close to two. I'm freezing to death."

Mango. Good old businesslike, father-killing Mango. Apparently Levering had decided it wasn't too important to keep the news of my return from the rest of the girls. If it was, we were all out of luck. I suspected that Mango was a one-woman communications center.

"Why didn't you wait inside the cottage?" I asked.

"We're not allowed in there except with authorized visitors. It's a rule."

Of course. I should have known. Her voice had all the warmth of the December evening. Adjusting my eyes to the night, I fished through my brown bag filled with bribes, and came up with the carton of cigarettes.

"Merry Christmas," I said, tossing the carton to her. "Could we go inside now?"

Never has a carton of cigarettes been so warmly received. "Goddamn," she exclaimed. "For me?"

"I don't smoke."

"But a whole carton, a whole goddamn carton."

"Mango, could you unlock the door?"

"Sure. Right away."

She was mine, at least for the time being. I had won her—heart and soul—with a carton of cigarettes. Inside the cottage she continued to examine her treasure, turning it over and over, murmuring, "A whole carton, a whole goddamn carton."

I told her to have a couple, that I was going to shower and change. "Then you can take me back to solitary."

"Anything you say, Dr. Summer."

While Mango chain-smoked, I took a steaming shower, brushed my teeth, put on one of the new shirts, and reappeared from behind the partition to find her counting the packages of cigarettes. With my bag of bribes in hand, I asked, "Ready?"

"Sure thing. I can't thank you enough, Dr. Summer."

"Yes, you can."

"How?"

"By keeping your mouth shut that I've come back here, and by answering, if asked, that as far as you know, I've left and gone back to Santa Fe."

She looked bewildered. "Why?"

"Because I brought you that carton of cigarettes," I said.

She shrugged. "Whatever you say."

She filled the pockets of her jacket and jeans with the cigarettes, and stuffed the rest down the front of her shirt. "If the others see them, they'll be gone like that," she explained. Then she locked the door behind us, and we started toward the steel door in the south building. I had the feeling that she wanted to ask a thousand questions. But she was a good girl, and asked nothing and rang the bell and waited, and thanked me again—several times.

We waited for what seemed to be an interminable length of time, slowly freezing. And finally the door opened and Clito appeared on the other side, disgruntled.

"Where in the hell is Claude?" he asked, as if we should know. "He said he'd wait here. I had to come all the way up from downstairs."

Mango said, "Sorry." Then she said, "He's all yours," and took off in a run toward the dormitories, undoubtedly to stash away her treasures before the other girls found out about them.

Clito kept looking around at the empty hall, muttering, "Where in the hell did he go? He said he'd wait here."

I shrugged, something I'd picked up from Mango, and tried to change the subject. "Clito, has anyone spoken to you about my plan?"

His face was a calm, reflecting pool. Nothing moved inside or out. He shook his head.

"Well, I'm going to be staying down there with Hatter for a few days."

Still nothing moved.

"Did you hear me?"

"Yeah, I can't get over Claude though. Where could he have got off to?"

"He'll turn up." I took his arm and headed him in the direction of the stairs, promising him along the way that Claude couldn't have gone far, reassuring him that he'd be back.

And he was. He was waiting for us at the top of the stairs, looking as sullen as I'd ever seen him. "What's you got up your sleeve, Doc?" was his greeting. "I never heard of such a thing. You staying down there with her. What's you got up your sleeve?"

Clito was asking him in mindless repetition where the hell he had been. But Claude was focusing the handful of his attention on me, waiting for an answer. Obviously Levering had just given him the word. And he didn't like it. "You don't think much of us, do you, Doc? You don't think we know how to handle things?"

He sounded more hurt than angry, like a child who has been betrayed. I tried to be at my reassuring best, and hoped that Levering hadn't told him everything. "It has nothing to do with that, Claude. Dr. Winton and Dr. Levering have a problem here they don't quite know how to solve. They called me to see if I could help. You understand, don't you? Besides, she's sick, and I'm a doctor."

Both men snapped to attention.

"What's she got?" Clito asked.

"I don't know yet, but she's not well."

"Hell, I'm not going near her any more," Clito said. "I don't want no goddamn Indian disease."

Claude was the smart one. He asked, "If she's sick, why don't they move her up to the infirm?"

With a perfectly straight face, I replied, "Well, she's not that sick yet. But I'm supposed to watch her."

He didn't buy it, not right away. He continued to slouch against the new mattresses. I still carried with me the bag of bribes, and decided this was the time. "Hey, I brought you guys something."

Stirred to interest, they leaned forward as I fished out the magazines, one for Clito, on the cover the photograph of a nude lying on her back, legs up in the air, balancing a Christmas gift on the bottom of her feet, a sprig of holly in her bellybutton. And for Claude, a nude on all fours, and riding on her back, a midget dressed in a Santa Claus suit.

They were both very impressed and grinned their thanks. "Didn't mean to get tough with you, Doc," Claude muttered. "It's just that we've never had anyone staying down there all the time who didn't belong there."

"I know," I said sympathetically. "And I won't get in your way, I promise. In fact, I'll help you. You said yourself, she was a handful, right?"

Clito was lost to the nude on the cover of his magazine, but Claude grinned and nodded, and restated his opinion of me. "I guess you're okay, Doc. Just if you got any beefs, bring 'em to me, not to Levering, you hear? Come on."

I took a deep breath and fell into step behind them. As we started down the stairs, Clito thumbed through his magazine, whistling appreciatively now and then, and let Claude do all the locking and unlocking, and offered to trade magazines with him when they got through. Claude agreed and led us down, down past the dim bulbs to the last door, and finally into the empty space of the office. There he stopped, still troubled. "Where in the hell you gonna sleep, Doc?" he asked.

"In the cell next to her."

"It ain't clean."

"It'll be all right." I didn't dare ponder too long the question of why the standards of cleanliness did not stretch to include Hatter. "And you can bring two trays from now on," I added. "And try to get something better than that slop you brought this morning."

"It's what they give us in the kitchen," he replied.

The key was in the lock, but again he stopped, still troubled. "I guess you can use our bathroom," he hesitated, trying hard to work his way through or around the insurmountable problems.

"Fine," I agreed.

Suddenly, in complete exasperation he shook his head and stepped back from the door. "What the hell, Doc? Am I supposed to lock you in too?"

I almost felt sorry for him, asking him to break out of the comfort and security of his rules. "You better keep this door locked," I said, indicating the outer door. "But we're not going any place in there, so why don't you leave the cell doors unlocked? Would that be all right?"

"Hers, too?"

"Yes."

Clito had taken the seat behind the desk, the better to devour the magazine. He looked up. "You know, you're some sort of dumb bastard," he said to Claude. "Do what the man says. Maybe he digs her."

Claude looked closely at me, as if searching for confirmation. Finally, worn out from his mental ordeal, he threw up his hands. "What the hell. I don't understand a goddamn thing. She's all yours, Doc. Levering said you'd take responsibility."

"And I will."

At last he unlocked the door, stepped back, and motioned me through. He unlocked Hatter's cell door and the one next to it. "She ain't eat a thing today," he scolded. "It's tube time tomorrow."

"I'll get her to eat," I promised.

From the door, he took a last look at me, still shaking his head. "You look like a smart guy. Can't figure you."

"Don't try."

I watched the door close, heard the lock slide. A moment later, the light in the next cell came on. It splashed a faint illumination in the dark corner of Hatter's cell. I saw her, still on the floor where I had left her. She was lying on her side, one knee drawn up to her chest, the other leg straight, one hand under her head, the other arm resting in a distorted position beside her. She wasn't asleep. Her eyes were opened. She was simply lying there, staring sideways at the legs of the table, as if some delicate balance had been broken, some conflict had reached unbearable proportions within her, some duality was on the verge of cutting her in two. And this was the result: limp form, glazed eyes, merely an organism with the heart still beating. She looked up and saw me. She moaned and turned away, as though to say that she had no more energy for facing new threats, let alone old ones.

I placed the package containing my last bribe on the table. It would do little good here. I squatted down close to her. Still no major movement, no alteration in the fixed and terrified eyes. Again I considered touching her. I had a strong impulse to do so—to gather her in my arms and hold her until the eyes moved, the mouth opened and formed words. But I didn't. I'm not certain why I didn't. Something to do with the old resolve to meet her on her own terms, I suppose. Holding her would have been my terms, not hers. Then, too, experience had taught me that she wasn't always what she appeared to be. Like some primal sorceress she apparently was capable of producing a knife out of thin air, and if the knife failed to materialize, my face still bore mute testimony to the effectiveness of her fingernails.

So I didn't touch her, I merely squatted close beside her and spoke her name once, twice, and a third time before giving up and returning to the table. Her dinner was before me on a tray: a pool of red beans, the ever-favorite fried canned meat, and a gelatinous ball of brown rice. It wasn't the sort of diet to produce a picture of robust good health, but it was better than nothing. From what I could see of the skeletal figure in the corner, it was no longer a matter of choice. She had to eat something. But how to convince her of this? How to go about getting the red beans from the tray down her throat. I remembered Claude's threat of "tube time tomorrow," and wondered if she had heard.

It's very difficult to speak sternly and with authority to someone you suspect is terrified of you and wants only to die. But there was no room for pity. She had survived this long solely on her strength of will. Then that would be my appeal.

"You know," I began, as stern as I could make my voice under the circumstances. "You know that you're letting them win, don't you? They have you just where they want you."

They. Good old faceless, nameless they. I wasn't absolutely certain whom I meant by "they," but I had a suspicion that she knew. Some people are born knowing who "they" are, every threatening face who takes all the food and all the land, makes all the rules, administers all the cockeyed justice, conceives all of the double standards.

I went on. "They're probably sitting up there right now thinking that all they have to do is wait a few days and they can come in here and stash you away in a pine box, and be rid of you once and for all. And why not? Obviously it's what you want, and obviously it's what they want."

It wasn't exactly movement that I saw—rather a new rigidity, a stiffening in her body as in a moment of acute terror. I remembered one of the no more than half a dozen facts I knew about the Navajos, a curious contradiction unresolved in the minds of those who make a profession out of studying such things. While the suicide rate was one of unbelievable proportions, they feared death more than anything.

"Lock you in a pine box," I repeated, playing on that fear, "and bury you under six feet of earth where the other ghosts live. Perfect. For everyone. It's what you want."

From where I sat I could see clearly the increase in her breathing. The left arm was no longer lying limp. It clutched and moved closed to her body. Both legs moved up to her chest, the fetal position.

Suddenly I had no appetite for the new fear I was instilling in her. Fear of me was the one thing that Hatter Fox had in abundance. Then reason, maybe. Quiet logic and reason. I had her attention now. It was worth a try. "It's so simple, Hatter. If you eat, you live. If you don't eat, you die. The food isn't the greatest, I know, but it'll keep you alive until you can get out of this place. *That* should be your goal. *That's* the most effective way to win. Are you listening to me?"

She was listening. There was simply no response beyond the fear, no indication of how she was reacting to what I was saying. It was like talking to the table. Curled in on herself in the corner, I had the feeling that a very simple battle was raging within her. To live? To die? At that point it was impossible to say who was winning.

"Hatter, there's food here. Come and eat. Please."

Nothing.

My temper is mild and not easily lost, but suddenly I had the impression that I was talking to nothing more than a spoiled child. Reason had failed. Even fear had failed. Only force remained. I said nothing. There was nothing to say. I reached down for her arm, and jerked her up. She lifted so easily, although once up, she began to fall again. Moving behind her, I grabbed both her arms and pointed her in the direction of the table. I had expected her to object, but there was no objection. The main problem was to keep her on her feet, while still moving her toward the table. Once I felt her try to pull away, but apparently there was no strength. I had taken her by surprise, and in her already weakened condition she had no choice but to follow the direction of my hands.

The tousled hair completely obscured her face so I had no idea how she was reacting. At that point I didn't care. The goal of the moment was the food on the tray, and I half carried, half dragged her toward the chair and finally sat her in it. There was a small stool in the corner of the cell. I pulled it up close beside her and said, "Now! Eat!"

She looked like something broken, her head down, that godawful mass of black hair covering everything, her arms with the bandaged wrists hanging down at her sides, the shapeless gray dress emitting an unappetizing odor.

"Did you hear me?" I said. "Eat!" The only utensil was a spoon. I reached for her right arm and placed the spoon in her hand. The fingers refused to close around it.

"Hatter, if you don't eat now, it's back to the bed tomorrow. You heard what Claude said. Now eat!"

But she didn't. And somehow I knew that she wouldn't. Suddenly I was tired of her stubbornness, her will. I picked up the spoon and went behind her chair; not so gently I pulled her head back and jerked the hair out of her eyes; holding her head with one hand, I used the other to scoop some beans onto the spoon and to aim it in the general direction of her mouth. To my surprise the mouth was opened. In went the spoon, the beans, and my finger. She bit down hard.

Then the broken thing came to life. With both arms she started flailing while I, still trying to hold her with one hand, examined the bean-blood mixture on my throbbing index finger. While I was trying to shake off the throb, she escaped to the far corner of the cell and stood defiantly, her eyes flashing, daring me to try it again. And I did. Suddenly she was the one who was thwarting my goal, and I went after her with no apologies to anyone, amazed at her strength, intent only on keeping her fingernails away from my face.

No holds barred. I reached and missed, came up from the side, and missed again, and finally caught her from behind and literally wrestled her to the floor. She was strong, but the strength did not last long. I maneuvered her to a position close to the table, and flattened her on her back; holding both her wrists in one hand, I sat on her and reached up for the plate of food. She saw it coming, and arched her neck backwards, and I moved farther up and pinned her arms and shoulders with my knees, and informed her with what breath I had left that now it was dinner time. With her arms pinned, I had both hands free. I could feel her legs thrashing behind me, but they were doing no real damage other than an occasional knee thump against my back. I placed the plate of food nearby, abandoned the spoon, grabbed a handful of beans, forced her mouth open, and shoved them in. She spewed them out, covering herself and me with the red-slime mixture. I remembered the technique of administering medication to animals. I went for a second handful of beans; this time I held her mouth opened, forced the food in, tightly closed her jaws, and gave a light thump on her throat. She swallowed in spite of herself, still struggling, still trying to pull free of my grip. Her face was slippery from food that had missed the target, but I held fast and gave her bite after bite in this fashion, becoming covered with the food myself, but enjoying a tremendous sense of accomplishment every time she swallowed.

Down it went, most of it, what wasn't on me, on her, or the floor. At some point her legs stopped thrashing, and I could feel her body go limp beneath me. And on the last few bites, there was no need to thump her throat. She swallowed by herself, between gasps for air. At the end we were both exhausted. But the plate was empty. We were covered with food, but enough had gone down to matter. The battle was over.

In a way I was sorry for what I had done, for what she had made me do. But there was comfort in the realization that it had been done on her terms, not mine. It took me a moment to determine if she was conscious or faking it, slumped in her rag-doll pose which, I was beginning to learn, was more a mental condition than a physical one. She was not unconscious. She knew perfectly well everything that was going on. It was a consummate example of tuning out. I had seen it first back in the isolation cell in Santa Fe, an incredible ability to subdue all the life forces, to send them away and leave a husk.

Weary, stinking and food-splattered, I stood up. My hands were covered with bits of rice and slobber. I held them at arms' length and yelled, "Claude!"

When he didn't appear within the moment, I began to kick at the door, and was still kicking when I heard the lock slide and saw his blank face appear through a crack. He took one look at me and opened the door all the way. "What the hell——" he began.

"She's just had dinner," I said. "Could you get her some clean clothes, and bring us both some towels and water?"

He repeated his exclamation. "What in the hell——"

"Goddamn it, Claude. Clothes and water. Now!"

At least he was smart enough to recognize the tone of voice. Quickly he closed the door and left me on the other side, still dripping beans.

I looked back into the cell to see if Hatter had decided to rejoin the living. Apparently she hadn't. She was still lying on the floor exactly where I had left her, the gray prison dress twisted about her legs, soiled now beyond recognition.

I called out to her full voice. "Hatter, we are going to do this three times a day. You've got a choice. You can take it there on the floor, or you can sit at that table with me. It's up to you. It'll be easier on both of us if you choose the table, but it doesn't make a goddamn bit of difference to me. You hear?"

But she was gone again, completely out of earshot. It wasn't a bad trick. I made a mental note to ask her someday how she did it.

Claude reappeared in a remarkably short time, balancing towels and a basin of water, and carrying a gray dress stuffed under his arm.

"They ain't supposed to get but one clean dress a week," he grumbled, handing the items in through the door.

"I'll remember. Now lock the door."

"You sure you don't need me?"

"Lock the goddamn door, Claude!"

He slammed the door shut. I carried the stuff to the table and tried to find a clean place to put them down. Bits of food were everywhere. I ordered Hatter to get up.

She didn't move. I lifted and carried her to a clean space near the front of the cell, and placed her on the floor. She groaned as I laid her down, and I had a moment of serious misgivings. With a conscious effort I sent away all pity, but tried to handle her more gently as I guided the filthy dress up over her head, pulling the injured wrists carefully out of the armholes.

What I found beneath the dress could only be called the beginnings of a skeleton. Every rib was visible; the shoulderbones were sharp, hard knobs; the pelvic area itself would have served nicely as a basin. I had seen bodies like that in Bolivia. I had not expected to find them in the richest country in the world. She seemed completely unaware that I had undressed her. She lay on the cold floor in a position of numb submission, shivering now and then, but otherwise unmoving.

I bathed her as quickly as possible, and noticed lacerations on her breasts and dark yellowish bruises on the upper area of her legs. Grimly I recalled Levering's plea for proof. I had his goddamn proof for him. Once she raised a hand up into the air as though she might protest something. But it fell back down, and a shudder passed over her; her eyes opened momentarily, saw nothing of interest, and closed again.

The clean dress was about ten sizes too large. She was completely lost in it. I carried her to the cot and covered her with the blanket, then tried to clean myself and the cell. Once I looked back to find her watching me, the black eyes opened now, curious, frightened, taking in every movement.

The cell still smelled of beans and fried meat, but I had picked up the stuff from the floor as best as I could. Before I headed toward the cot in the next cell, I tossed the bag containing the comb, brush, and mirror onto her bed. "Use it. You look like hell."

I stretched out on the cot in the cell next to her and tried to stretch the tight kinks out of my muscles, and examined briefly the teeth marks she'd left on my finger and wondered how in hell either one of us would survive such an ordeal three times a day. My head throbbed and the dim light bulb overhead burned like a noon sun. I covered my eyes with my arm and wondered where it was written that I spend three days in this pit with a half-mad, half-starved Navajo.

Failing to perceive an answer, I turned on my side, the better to watch her. She still resembled a broken toy, but something had been accomplished. She had been fed, bathed and put to bed. There would be no tubes or restraining beds tomorrow. And that was an accomplishment.

The bars between the cells divided her into eight sections, and all eight sections were completely motionless. Her eyes, however, were open and fixed on the ceiling. Suddenly she stirred, sat up, felt her forehead as though she were fighting for balance. She threw back the blanket and stood on her feet—wobbling for a moment, but on her feet all the same.

And I was on mine, aware that both my cell door and hers were unlocked. "Hey, where're you going?" I called, ready for another battle.

She turned very slowly, and seemed to be having trouble focusing her eyes. But she found me at last through the bars. Her mouth opened, her lips moved, and in a voice scarcely above a whisper, she said, "I have to pee."

Magnificent! It was a complete sentence. Not a very glorious one, but it had a beginning, a middle, and an end, and it had been addressed to another human being.

I sat back down on the edge of the cot and watched her make her way to the slop jar, saw her moving painfully, slowly, using everything within reach for support.

When she had finished, she caught her heel in the hem of the oversized dress and fell to one side, striking her head against the bars of the cell. I fought the impulse to go to her aid, and waited and watched as she lay there for a moment. Then the battle was on again, and she was raising herself to her feet, groaning as she pulled against the injured wrists, but making it finally back to the side of her cot. She lay down and pulled the cover up around her, exhausted from her effort.

And all the while I enjoyed one of the greatest feelings of accomplishment I have ever known. At the same time I felt stupid, the burning behind my eyes felt stupid, but I took care not to let her see the emotion on my face. I lay back down and again covered my eyes with my arms.

She was stubborn, frightened of me, willful, full of rage; she was bruised, abused, injured, and half starved. But perhaps she was redeemable, salvageable. Perhaps. That's all I could give her then, a "perhaps" for both her and me. But it was enough to go to sleep on.

I smiled. "I have to pee." Not very majestic words. I was beginning to learn that Hatter's gifts were small and generally slow in coming. But somehow they were worth the wait. I wasn't even particularly annoyed when a few moments later, I heard her stir again, watched her leave the cot and head for the rear corner of the cell and the cold floor.

So she didn't dig beds. I called out, "Good night."

But there was no answer.

You lose track of night and day in a solitary-confinement cell. The bulb overhead burns relentlessly irregardless of such natural luxuries as the sun and moon. I slept restlessly and checked my watch, groaning at the agonizing nonpassage of time, and still the light burned overhead. The thin canvas swing of the cot was meager protection against the braces beneath, and no matter how I turned, I felt them digging into my spine, my ribs, the side of my head. I was cold, and the light blanket helped not at all. And there was the silence again, the sense of time and the world having forgotten about you. I walked off the cell a couple of times and checked on her, apparently sleeping soundly in her corner on the floor. Maybe she had the right idea after all. But I was a product of civilization, and civilized man does not sleep on the floor. Even when he cannot sleep anyplace else, still he does not sleep on the floor.

About 2:00 A.M. I felt myself becoming irascible. Who did Winton and Levering think they were, asking me to do their dirty work? And it would at least have been considerate of Claude and Clito to stick their stupid faces in the door and find out if I needed anything. She could have killed me by now, but what the hell difference would it have made to them. It's the sameness more than anything else, the monotony of bars, gray walls, a single light. Nothing changes, and man as an organism demands variety.

How had she survived? Or perhaps a more valid question, *had* she survived? About 3:00 A.M. she went through an uncomfortable period, groaning and moaning, and several times crying out, "No." I went into her cell and stood beside her and watched the nightmare work its way across her face; I considered awakening her and decided against it. I sat with her and wondered about the specifics of the nightmare and why she was crying "no." Then she grew quiet again, and curled up, her face toward the wall. And with nothing left to watch and nothing left to speculate on, I returned to my cell, sat on the edge of the cot, held my head in my hands, and made my mind a complete blank.

I must have dozed, the sort of sleep that is worse than none. But at least I lost consciousness, because I awakened with a start. The only constants in that world were still there: the light burning overhead, the bars, the old smell of beans and meat, my watch. It said ten minutes before eight. Disorientation. 8:00 P.M.?

A.M.? Had I slept through the day to another night? Was it Friday or Saturday? I stood up too quickly; every cramped muscle in my body objected. There was still no sound, nothing. Everything was exactly as it had been the night before, or the day before. Whatever.

I looked through the bars into Hatter's cell, stared at the corner where I'd last seen her sleeping. Something had changed. She was gone. There are no hiding places in a solitary-confinement cell, but for one ludicrous moment, I actually launched a search for her. Under her cot, under the table, in all the corners. I returned to my cell and did the same thing, lifting the blanket as though she might be crouched underneath. At some point, reason caught up with me; I ran to the outer door and started pounding the hell out of it.

"Claude!" I called repeatedly and kicked and pounded simultaneously, but no one came. She was gone, and I could rouse no one in the world outside. Human limitations were nonexistent. I thought about blasting my way through the ceiling, or dismantling one of the bars set in concrete and breaking through the steel doors.

"Claude!" Where was he? And where was she? Had she alone been able to figure out an escape? "Claude!" No answer. And when the minutes passed and no one came, I resumed the pounding, kicking, and yelling. At least it was better than the silence. But in truth, nothing was better. All the accepted modes of escape were absent, or cut off. Telephones, the human voice, opened doors, cars. There was nothing. I was as trapped as . . . as if I were the prisoner. The realization was a sharp one, the insight into Hatter's behavior. Why talk? Why cooperate? Why not long for death? You're dead anyway when you're so trapped.

It was during this quiet that I heard noise behind me, heard the door of the isolation unit at the opposite end of the room opening, heard, without looking, a flat voice inquire, "What's all the ruckus about?"

I matched the flat voice to the flat face and turned

and saw Claude. With what breath I had left, I said, "She's gone."

"No, she ain't. She's getting ready for breakfast."

The mind moves so slowly under certain conditions. I had to repeat to myself everything he said in order to make the connections.

"She's what?"

"Getting ready for breakfast." He grinned.

"Where?"

"In here." He jerked his head backward toward the isolation room. The mind creaked over. Isolation room, restraining bed, intravenous feeding, tubes.

The connection made, I lunged at him the full length of the room. "I told you last night she had eaten—"

"The hell she did. I spent an hour cleaning up the food from the floor. It was a goddamn mess. Now if they don't eat for twenty-four hours, it's tube time, and that's a rule."

His slack-jawed face was before me then, and my hands had become fists, ready to do what instinct told them to do. But much as I hated to admit it, I needed this man, needed his cooperation at least for the next few days. I lowered my voice and shoved my hands safely into my pockets. I became his buddy again. "Look," I began, "she *did* eat last night. I swear she did. Not much, true, but enough. And I think if you'll leave me alone with her, I can get her to eat again today. You really shouldn't have come near her, you know. For your own sake. She's got something."

Doubt crossed his face. "What's she got? You're not talking to that dumb-ass Clito. I couldn't even get him in here to help me this morning." He still stood blocking the door. "Now look, Doc, I don't make the rules around here. I wish I did. I'd do things different. But for as long as I've been here, the rule is food or the tube." He grinned. "I'll say this for you. You sure taught her a lesson in how to mind. She didn't give me hardly no trouble at all this morning. I whisked her in 'fore she knew what was happening, and got her all fixed on the bed, and she ain't caused no trouble to speak of."

Hopeless. Then a new approach. Obviously the man's job meant a great deal to him. He even seemed to take pride in it. What if I were to threaten it?

I began slowly. "Claude, Winton and Levering called me down here because they had a problem, a big one. Now, I offered to try to help, but I said I'd have to do it my own way. They said fine, because they had this big problem. Now, if she dies, there's going to be all sorts of investigations and publicity, and the state might just say what the hell, we're giving the taxpayers' money to that reformatory when they don't reform at all. They kill them. And the state's going to cut back on funds, and some of you employees are going to get the axe."

He was listening. There was no way to tell if he was understanding. I went on. "I'm a doctor, Claude. Did you know that you can keep a person alive on intravenous feedings for just so long? It's a stopgap measure, not a solution. What we have to do is get her to eat food so she'll regain her streangth so we can get her out of here and solve Winton's and Levering's problem, and maybe try to save your job. Do you understand?"

"What the hell does my job have to do with it?" he mumbled. "It's my job I'm trying to do."

"The state pays you. Right? If she dies, the state will be embarrassed and unhappy and maybe the state will say we don't need Claude any more."

Something had penetrated. He was worried. "So what am I supposed to do?"

That was better. "Well, I think the safest thing to do would be to let me in there and I'll take her back to her cell, and then you go to the kitchen and bring us a couple of decent breakfasts, and a pot of hot coffee." I winked and nodded my head reassuringly. "She'll eat, I promise you."

He wasn't exactly convinced, but the threat of unemployment had been effective. Finally he stepped back from the door. "She ain't been no trouble this morning," he said, almost apologetically.

"I know, but she's been trouble enough for you. Let me deal with her for a while."

"You sure?"

I patted his arm. "I'm sure. Now go get those breakfasts. Okay?"

He shrugged. "She's in there." He started off toward the outer door. "I'll be back when you see me coming."

I waited until he was gone. Then I found her where I knew I would find her, in that god-awful bed, totally restrained. I felt helpless as she looked up. There was no struggle coming from the bed, as if the straps, the bed, the abuse, the broken promises—all this was now the only reality in her world. There *was* something different. Her face, held rigid, was upturned, the eyes were open, and there were tears, silent ones, just moisture in the corners of her eyes, falling down the sides of her face.

And why not? She had been promised only the night before that there would be no more restraints, and there she was, restrained. At least we were consistent. The lie was probably no different from the other lies she'd heard from every white face she'd ever known.

I went to her, and apologized and undid the straps as rapidly as possible, and lifted her into my arms, and for the first time I held her. There was no response, only the weightlessness of her body. But as I carried her back to her cell, I thought I felt her head pushing into the hollow beneath my chin—only a small pressure, as when a dog pushes against your leg after you've removed a thorn from its paw. I waited to see if she would push again, but no. Maybe it had only been my imagination the first time.

I placed her on the cot and told her again that I was sorry, and she seemed not to hear my apology. I drew up the chair, and sat down beside her, fresh out of apologies and excuses. I reached for her hand, but she withdrew it quickly, as though she had revealed enough of herself for one day. Emotion was not negotiable. It made one vulnerable and weak. She turned her face away and drew the blanket up over her head. And that was that, at least for a while.

One step forward, three steps backward. The rehabilitation of Hatter Fox. It was at best a joke. The kindness and dignity of death occurred to me again. Her struggle had become mine, and already I was weary of it.

Claude returned with two trays and an announcement. "Levering said everything would be okay. So I guess it is. You swing a lot of weight around here, Doc. I'm suppose to take my orders from you from now on."

I made a mental note to thank Levering. And I thanked Claude for the recognizable scrambled eggs, and the pot of coffee and told him that would be all for a while. I watched him leave, and wished like hell that I could go with him all the way up the stairs and out of the building.

But despair is conquered one step at a time. And the next step was to get her out from under the blanket and to the table where the food was. I was not up to another battle, and I didn't think that she was either. I touched her shoulder beneath the blanket and said, "There's food. Let's eat."

No response.

I begged. "Hatter, there is only one way out of this place, and you know what it is. Please."

Nothing.

I drew back the blanket, ready for battle. But she didn't object. She looked at me and spoke for a second time. She said, "I can't eat. Leave me alone."

"Why?"

"I'm sick."

"You'll be sicker if you don't eat," I reasoned. "Look, there's coffee."

She didn't look. But neither did she object when I helped her sit up and led her to the table. She felt warm, but food was the goal at that point. I sat her in the chair, indicated the spoon, and watched, grateful, as she lifted the first bite, then the second.

A few moments later she groaned and turned away. "No more," she said, and something about the way she said it convinced me—no more. She had eaten perhaps a quarter of the food and sipped the coffee. It was enough. I helped her back to the cot and as I drew the blanket up, I noticed that she was shivering.

Imaginary or real? With Hatter it was hard to tell. Experience had taught me that she was a skillful actress. I went back to the table and ate my portion, all the time doing what I was rapidly becoming an expert at, watching her. My mind had already raced ahead to the consequences of a genuine illness. True, it would get her out of this place, but then too, I ran the risk of losing my jurisdiction over her. I could well imagine the officious and inept medical staff of an institution of this nature. Sadism galloping around the edges of the Hippocratic oath. There is no punishment in the world quite as effective as repeated enemas, and it could all be accomplished in the name of good health. No, she was better off here. With me.

She never took eyes off me while I was eating. Nothing had really changed within her. She was still absolutely terrified of me. And there was nothing I could say or do to ease that terror.

Breakfast over, I poured the last of the coffee and offered it to her. She shook her head and then lay panting beneath the blanket, suddenly seeming to be far too warm. Her lips were dry, her voice hoarse as she asked, "Why are you following me?"

"I'm not following you. Don't you remember me? I came to help you."

Another question was forming on her lips. "Why?"

"Because I want to."

We were talking, exchanging questions and answers. But she was so afraid of me, and it was the fear that I couldn't understand. I'd done nothing to cause her to be afraid.

Again she asked, "Why?"

"Why what?"

But she didn't repeat the question or elaborate on it. Something was causing her discomfort. She pushed her head backwards, eyes closed. "Go away," she begged.

"I can't go away, Hatter. I don't want to go away." In an attempt to soothe her, I laid my hand on her forehead. She was not merely warm, she was on fire. No imaginary illness this time, unless she had devised a way to raise her body temperature. She continued to pant as though trying to dissipate the heat. The fever had suddenly activated the sweat glands; the metabolism was struggling for balance.

"Head hurts," she murmured and tried to toss back the blanket.

"No. Keep covered," I ordered, amazed by the rapidity of whatever was taking hold of her. I had no choice. I would have to take her to the infirmary. I couldn't care for her down here, and obviously she needed medical attention. No games this time. She was ill.

Again she cried out, "Go away, please."

She appeared to be delirious. The chills had returned, along with a whole new dimension of fear I'd never seen before. She clutched at the blanket, teeth chattering, muttering over and over again something about me being the one. She never completed the accusation, never made clear what offense I had committed.

The chills were as severe as the fever. I pulled the blanket up and tried to calm her. But it was hopeless. I couldn't leave her, and I couldn't go for help. So I yelled. For Claude, for Clito, for anyone.

Her eyes were closed then, a thin trickle of blood seeping out of the corner of her mouth. I hoped that she had only bitten her tongue. The breathing was still labored, but the chill seemed to have subsided.

Where was Claude or Clito? Suddenly she arched her body almost double on the cot. Her arms shot straight up into the air and her eyes opened wide; she looked at me and let out one bloodchilling scream. The chills had returned and were now convulsions.

I had seen enough. I went to the door, and as I had done earlier that morning, I started pounding. A few moments later, Claude appeared on the other side, mouth agape.

"What the hell—"

"Open the door, Claude. I'm taking her up to the infirmary."

"Huh?"

"I said unlock the doors."

"She sick?"

"Unlock the doors, Claude."

"If she's sick, I'm suppose to file a report."

"Forget the goddamn report. Move!"

I went back to the cot and found her unconscious. I lifted her, blanket and all, into my arms and carried her out the door and into the bright light of the office. Clito pressed back against the wall, muttering, "Some goddamn Indian disease, and I bet we all get it."

Claude walked ahead of me, still informing me of the rules. "This ain't right," he said. "I'm suppose to file a report, then call up to the infirm to let 'em know we're coming."

"They'll know we're coming when we get there. Hurry."

Never before had the ritual of locking and unlocking doors been so tedious. I could feel her fever through the blanket, and as I turned sideways to carry her up the narrow stairs, Claude kept looking back at me, half fearful, half suspicious.

"You know, she's a good faker," he warned.

"She's not faking this time."

"They always said I'm suppose to call ahead."

I tried to ignore his protestations and concentrate on the body in my arms. It was incredible, the speed with which something had overtaken her. I remember a case of a Navajo woman who had presented herself at the hospital and announced that in two days she would die. She was not ill or old, but her husband had left her, and embarrassed and alone, she had said she did not want to be alive. She could find no one who would bury her, so she had come to the white hospital. I examined her and found nothing wrong with her. She was in perfect health. In two days she was dead.

Didn't want to be alive. There are biological constants operative within the human body that do not recognize such whimsical demands as "I do not want to be alive." That's what I told myself then, and walked away.

These uneasy thoughts occupied my mind to the top of the stairs, blocking out Claude's persistent grumblings. The sun coming in through the corridor windows was too bright and momentarily blinded me. I found myself wishing that Hatter might have seen the sun. But she was seeing nothing. Her head drooped limply from my arm, and the bandaged wrists lay curled in the hollow of her body. No protestations, no groans. Just the fever causing a bright red flush on the smooth skin, and the dried blood in the corner of the mouth.

Claude ran a good interference, I'll say that much for him. Curious girls appeared out of the dormitories, some chattering, some hushed at the sight of the lifeless form in my arms. Claude scattered them like chickens and plowed straight ahead through the twists and turns of corridors, always producing the right key for the right lock. In the dining room, we encountered a grim-faced matron who demanded to know, "What's going on here?"

"He says the Indian is sick," Claude answered.

Disbelief spread across the hard female face. "She doesn't want to take her punishment, that's all," she snapped. "Nothing but trouble, that one. What can you expect?"

Behind her and framing her hate-filled face was the Christmas tree. I told Claude to go ahead. The woman called after us, "You'll just have to take her back down. Nothing wrong with her that a beating wouldn't cure."

Peace on Earth. Good will toward men.

Several girls peered out from the kitchen. I noticed Mango's broad flat face. She stepped out of a group of onlookers, and asked, "Dr. Summer, can I help?"

Good girl. "No thanks, Mango. She's sick. I'm taking her to the infirmary."

"What's she got?"

"I don't know."

Then someone yelled to Mango, warning her to get back, and she did. And I proceeded on alone. The infirmary was ahead, the walls had turned from gray to white, and I smelled the familiar odor of a hospital, alcohol, and disinfectant. Home ground. Good territory.

Claude stopped at the receiving desk and yelled a name. "Rhinehart, you got a customer."

In the pause, I studied the "customer" and tried to straighten my mind in preparation for a diagnosis. I considered the irony of a corpse. Had I come this far with Hatter Fox to lose her to a grave?

Claude yelled again. "Rhinehart? Double time. It ain't a splinter."

Suddenly a door down the hall burst open. I remember thinking, Good God. What appeared was female, at least two hundred pounds packed onto a five-feet-two-inch frame which from the beginning had been designed to carry no more than a hundred and twenty pounds. She looked like a woman wrestler. Every seam of her white uniform objected to the bulk. Her hair was a frizzy bleached blond color and covered her head in ringlets. She had no neck, just a couple of rolls of fat. And there was a grotesque purple birthmark which covered the entire left side of her face and vaguely resembled the outline of the state of Texas. She was carrying an enema bag, her hands were dripping water, and she was mad as hell.

"Damn it, Claude, how many times have I told you to call first," she exploded.

"He said there wasn't no time." Claude bobbed

his head in my direction, and Rhinehart's steel-blue eyes pinned me against the wall.

"And who is he?" she demanded, as though no answer would be good enough.

"A friend of Winton's and Levering's." Claude grinned. "You'd better treat him right."

"Winton be damned. I can't run a one-man show here and have people dropping in like it was a private club."

I stepped forward, tired of her officiousness, ready to call her bluff. "I'm Dr. Summer," I said, emphasizing the "doctor." "The girl is Hatter Fox. I don't think it's advisable to waste too much time. She's unconscious."

"Aren't we all?" she snapped. But she seemed to consider me and the still girl in my arms. Finally she jerked her head toward a door at the end of the hall. "Take her in there. I'll be with you in a minute."

The room at the end of the hall was an examining room—crude, but fairly complete for a superficial examination. I placed Hatter on the table, removed the blanket, and started at the top. Her pupils were glazed, fixed; the nostrils were clear, throat clear; the lungs had a faint rattle, but nothing to get excited about; the pulse was faint but steady, blood pressure slightly below normal. There were no open sores on her body except for the lacerated wrists, which were healing and showed no signs of infection. Down in the cell, I had made a haphazard first guess of pneumonia. But it was not pneumonia. Hepatitis? But there had been no vomiting and the stomach muscles were fairly relaxed. A virus of some sort? But what kind? Which one was virulent enough to cause this? I could think of nothing that would bring on a seizure such as the one I had just witnessed. I tried to rouse her, but couldn't. *I will die in two days.* It was nonsense. One could not will death.

Stymied, I stepped back from the examining table, as though distance might reveal an overlooked clue. At that moment, Rhinehart came in. She closed the door, leaned against it, and gave me only the slightest edge of her attention. She was carrying a clipboard and a pen and started writing.

"Hatter Fox," she said. "So! Well, I knew I'd get her sooner or later. Most of them go nonstop from Claude to me. What's she got?"

I felt inept and stupid. "I don't know."

"I thought you were some sort of doctor?"

"I am. Some sort."

Exasperated, she slapped the clipboard down onto a near chair, and strode to the examining table. "Do you always examine your patients fully clothed, Doctor?" In one of the most efficient gestures I've ever seen, she lifted Hatter's shoulders and torso and floated the gray dress up over her head. By the time I decided the least I could do was to help, the dress was on the chair covering the clipboard. Even Rhinehart's hard professional features flinched at the sight she found beneath the dress.

"Lord have mercy," she murmured. "Where'd you find her?"

"In solitary."

She seemed puzzled. "What were you doing down there?"

"Trying to keep her out of the State Hospital."

For the first time she looked at me and, I think, saw me. "Winton's idea?"

"No. Levering's"

"Aren't they clever?" Her voice bore just the faintest edge of sarcasm. In another efficient gesture, she reached beneath the table and whipped out a white sheet and covered Hatter. "We've never lost a one to the State Hospital," she said. "It's like a sport. Like rival basketball teams." Again there was that innuendo, faintly disguised, but perfectly clear to an ear ready to pick it up. I had the feeling that Rhinehart could tell a few stories.

She moved with extraordinary grace for a large woman. It was my opinion that she had been heavy all her life, and had learned how to cope with it. I noticed a scar at the base of her neck. Faulty thyroid? Perhaps. She was examining Hatter, going through the same motions that I'd just performed, covering old territory with the stethoscope. All small talk had ceased. She was a true professional. The sheet was lifted at the proper place to avoid undue humiliation to the patient. Her hands moved with confidence, yet a certain gentleness, over Hatter's body. The perplexed look grew on her face as it had on mine, but still she said nothing. Once her hands paused as she studied the old lacerations on Hatter's breasts. She moved immediately to the yellowish bruises on the upper area of the legs. Something, a tightness, seemed to pass over her forehead.

"Have you seen marks like that before?" I asked, indicating the bruises.

"Par for the course for girls in solitary," she snapped, as though she was angry that I had noticed.

"Why haven't you reported it?"

"What's to report?"

"How about rape for a start?"

She looked angry, but some stronger impulse won out and she said nothing. Instead she returned all her attention to Hatter, as though she were about to start the whole investigation over again. She felt Hatter's throat and skull carefully, looking out the window all the time, as though her fingers were skillful enough not to need the assistance of her eyes. Suddenly she stopped and turned Hatter's head to the right. She pushed the tangle of hair aside, and now focused in on something. "How did that happen?" she asked.

I moved closer and examined that area on the left side of her skull, but saw nothing.

"Feel," Rhinehart ordered.

There was a small knob there, a bump, but the skin had not been broken, so it was nothing to get excited about. "I have no idea," I said. "I've done worse getting in and out of my jeep."

"Fine, but you're still walking around, and she's not. Now, how did it happen?"

"I have no idea," I repeated. "She could have

done it any number of ways. I found her handcuffed to the bed yesterday. She could have done it then. But that wouldn't cause a fever, wouldn't cause her to lose consciousness."

"Not to us, it wouldn't," she said, and continued to examine the small bump.

I was beginning to lose patience. And there was always the possibility that we were losing valuable time. "I suggest that we transfer her into a city hospital for further tests," I said.

"Nonsense" was her reply. The bump continued to hold her attention. "You sure you don't remember how this happened?"

"No," and then I did. When Hatter had used the slop jar, she'd caught her foot in the hem of the dress and had fallen, striking her head against the bars of the cell. I related the incident to Rhinehart.

"Were you the only one in the cell with her?" she asked.

"Yes. What difference does it make?"

"I don't know that it makes any difference yet. What has been her general reaction to you?" she asked.

"To me?" I looked blank and tried to make the connection.

"Nothing personal," she reassured me. "I was just curious. How has she reacted to you, to your presence?"

I decided to be honest, although I failed to see the point of the question. "Fear," I said, bluntly. "She seems to be terrified of me, has from the first time I saw her, although for the life of me I don't know why. I only want to help."

She seemed to consider what I had said, and looked at me as though a theory were forming behind those sharp blue eyes. But ultimately she dismissed her questions and her theory, and said, "Let's try to bring her around." The "let's" was a mere courtesy. She did it all herself, moving around me for smelling salts and a cold compress. She slapped Hatter's face a couple of times and called her name, then leaned in to take advantage of the first raised eyelid. Slowly Hatter stirred, her hands lifted to push away the strong odor beneath her nostrils, and finally her eyes opened. She saw Rhinehart first, and the white uniform; Hatter's eyes fluttered open, then closed again as she fought to keep back unconsciousness, the brain trying hard to locate for the body any threats, visible or invisible.

I was standing near her feet, out of sight until she raised her head. She took one look at me and cried out, "Go away." And the struggle was on again, as sudden and violent as the one I'd witnessed downstairs in the cell, incredible energy and strength coming from some hidden source; Hatter was thrashing about on the examining table, trying to escape from Rhinehart's grasp and almost succeeding, and all the time screaming, pleading, "Go away. Make him go away."

I tried to reach for her ankles to help, but even Rhinehart yelled, "Don't touch her. Leave her alone." I did as I was told, and stood back against the far wall and watched them battle it out, Rhinehart using all of her ample bulk to hold the girl on the table, all the time uttering the most unbelievable nonsense I'd ever heard.

"He's not the one, Hatter," she soothed. "You have the wrong man. Claude's the one. Claude's the witch. Think back. Listen to me. Remember? Claude's the one who emptied your slop jar. He's the one. I know it. Think. He made the corpse poison and shot it through the door. There, feel that bump? That's where it entered. Hatter, listen. Claude's the one. Think of all the chances he had. It's not this man. He came to help."

Hatter was no longer struggling. She was listening to what Rhinehart was saying—not quite ready to believe, but no longer fighting to escape.

"It's Claude. He's the one," Rhinehart said again, repeating over and over the insane refrain, whispering low over the distracted face. "Claude's the witch. I've known it for a long time. This man brought you out of that place, took you away from the witch. You're going to be all right now. We're going to break the spell, I promise. He came to help me. If it hadn't been for him, you'd still be down there."

From where I stood, I could see Hatter, lying exhausted on the table, studying Rhinehart's face and struggling now only to digest her words. Rhinehart lifted Hatter's hand and guided it up to the small bump on her head. "There. See for yourself. Feel? That's where it entered. I know what to do. Don't worry. Just rest now. You're going to be all right. I promise."

Rhinehart was rubbing her forehead, smoothing back the hair from Hatter's eyes, still whispering something that I couldn't hear to her. Hatter's legs went limp; her body relaxed. Rhinehart pulled the sheet up around her shoulders, still murmuring, "You're going to be all right, I promise. Sleep now. Go to sleep, go to sleep, go to sleep . . ."

And she did, or appeared to. Rhinehart motioned for me. She took my hand and placed it on Hatter's forehead. The fever was down—not gone, but certainly lower than it had been. Hatter's face was relaxed. She was asleep.

Rhinehart looked at the disbelief on my face. "She thinks you're a witch. Are you? She thinks you want to kill her."

"I don't believe anything I saw here today."

"You'd better believe it. It's real enough to her."

"I don't understand—"

"It's simple. She thinks that a witch, some witch, has control of her. Corpse poison is a preparation made of powdered human bones, or feces. The witch penetrates the victim with the mixture and gains power over them. The bump on the head was the symptom."

She spoke matter-of-factly in a flat voice, all the time cleaning and straightening up, returning the smelling salts to the cabinet, apparently unaware that what she was saying was complete madness.

"Symptom of what?" I asked.

"That a witch is operative within her." She looked at me. "The trouble is, she thinks it's you. Since her present problems started with your appearance in the cell, she thinks you're the witch. Are you?"

I was beyond words. I slumped onto a stool, shook my head and stared at the tile floor. The year was 1973, and I was being interrogated on the possibility of being a witch. Again I shook my head and said nothing. What was there to say?

"Well, no matter." She dismissed the subject airily. "She'll sleep for a while. Then you have your work cut out for you."

"What do you mean?"

"Convincing her you're on her side." She looked at me closely. "And I believe you are."

It was a compliment of sorts, the best that Rhinehart could do. I glanced up, grateful, and asked, "How do I go about doing that?"

"Well, let's start with a cup of coffee. You look like hell. My apartment's back there. And don't worry. I'm not on the make. I gave that up twenty years ago."

I followed her down the hall and into small drab living quarters which bore a striking resemblance to the guest cottages outside. Colorless mid-thirties furnishings with a few—very few—personal touches here and there, a small synthetic Christmas tree near a window with a star-shaped sign on top which said "Joy to the World," a dressing table adorned in the manner of a woman of late middle age who has given up hope: no cosmetics in sight, only a box of Kleenex, a jar of Vicks, an ashtray, and a package of cigarettes. There was the standard sofa bed, an assortment of mismatched chairs and tables, a partition at one end which led, I supposed, to a bath and small kitchen. She told me to have a seat and disappeared behind the partition. I heard water running and cups clattering. I sat on the sofa and noticed a stack of unopened mail on the coffee table. She reappeared, drying her hands on a dish towel, and went to the telephone. She dialed one digit and waited, then said "Honey, this is Rhinehart. Get me Claude, please."

Pause.

"Down in his hole, I guess. Try to rouse him for me. And listen, honey, spread the word. The Indian's got hepatitis." She winked broadly at me. "Yeah, pretty bad. She's gonna be with me for a while. If Winton and Levering have any questions, tell them I'll be happy to see them."

Another pause. Again she looked at me. She said to the receiver, "He's here. With me. . . . Yeah, ain't I lucky? Now, get me Claude, will you, and how about bridge one night next week? . . . Fine. Thanks a lot, honey."

She held the receiver between her chin and shoulder, reached for the cigarettes on the dressing table, and lit one. She whispered to me, "I can count on you to back me up, can't I? The hepatitis, I mean. Everyone's scared to death of it around here. It'll give the kid a break for a few weeks. Keep her out of Claude's basement."

I nodded to everything. Why not?

Then she was speaking into the receiver again, her voice raised. "Claude? This is Rhinehart. Listen, I need you up here for a minute. Can you come right away?"

Pause.

"Well, let Clito watch your empty cells for you. Don't pout, baby. They'll send you another one real soon. I've got to keep this one for a while. . . . Yeah, real sick. You don't want what she's got. Just come on up for a minute. . . . I'll explain later. My apartment. I'll do you a favor sometime." She hung up and looked distractedly out of the window. She said, "Wouldn't it be funny . . ." but that's all she said. A teakettle was whistling in the kitchen, and she disappeared again. The floor vibrated as she passed. A moment later she was seated at the opposite end of the sofa, blowing on a cup of coffee, looking at me as though I were the prime witness in a star chamber.

"Okay, Dr. Summer, tell me who you are and why you're here."

I was busy blowing on my own coffee, and I dislike witness stands. I repeated my name and profession and decided to let it go at that.

But Rhinehart wasn't satisfied. "How did you end up in this place?" she persisted.

"Levering asked me to come."

"Why?"

"Because he didn't know what to do with her."

"And what's she to you?"

"Nothing." As I've said before, it was not my intention or desire to tell Rhinehart anything. But I did. She was a good listener. And in spite of myself I told her about the stabbing, and being drawn into the case against my better judgment. I cut a few corners here and there, but in essence I told her everything that had happened since the first time I'd encountered Hatter Fox.

When I had finished, she leaned back and drank her coffee. She smiled, almost sympathetically. "So, now you're hooked. All that remains to be done is for you to convince her that you're not a witch."

The skeptic in me became vocal. "Do you believe that? It's my guess that except for the genes, she's no more Indian than you or me; has never been near a reservation, any reservation."

"The hell she hasn't. She's a full blood. She may not remember who did the teaching, and she may not even like to remember the teaching itself. But she does. She did. Your proof's back there." She jerked her head in the direction of the examining room where we had left Hatter sleeping.

"It doesn't make sense."

"Not to you or me," she agreed.

"Then you don't believe it? You talked a good game back there."

She studied the coffee cup, evading the question. Finally she spoke to the cup. "What's to believe?" She shrugged. "I believe it if they do. Perhaps it's all in the mind, but the mind is not a toy to be taken lightly. Besides, I don't like dead girls lying about the place. They're bad for my reputation. It was a hunch, and it worked, and I've seen it work before with Indians. You said yourself I ought to report Claude. And you're right. We'll get him with witchcraft."

It wasn't what she said, but more the manner in which she said it—perfectly calm, reasonable; the efficient, skillful nurse. I almost agreed with her. Yes, witchcraft. Good idea.

Disoriented as I felt at that moment, I also felt a kind of ease that I had not felt before in that institution. Goodness becomes easily recognizable when you've seen so little of it. And Rhinehart was good. Overweight, lonely, and God alone knew what else, but good. It was my hunch that she was as shocked by the barbarism that went on around her as I was. That she hadn't by now done something about it was only a small but persistent question. Institutional wheels so easily grind up those who question. How could one confront the Santa Claus face of Dr. Winton with the news that he was assigning his incorrigibles to someone who was at best a sadist, at worst a rapist? I recalled Levering's reaction to my quasi-accusation. No, it was much easier not to see, not to hear. The wheels must turn smoothly or they don't turn at all. Rhinehart, I suspected, had learned to live with problems I couldn't even comprehend.

So I didn't dislike her, although I didn't dare listen too closely to her talk of witches and corpse poison. She was a colorful, brusque eccentric. Let it go at that.

Claude arrived, slightly out of breath from the run upstairs. Rhinehart greeted him as though he were a long-lost friend, calling warmly to him to "Come in, come on in." She offered him a cup of coffee, and from the bewildered look on his face, I had the feeling that Rhinehart had never offered him a cup of anything before.

"What's all this about?" he demanded, staying close to the door, as though he might have to make a run for it at any moment.

"It's not about anything," Rhinehart said, all sweetness and hospitality. "Good grief, you work hard

down there, Claude, and you do a good job, too.
You've done real well with the Indian, and I just
wanted to say thanks from all the folks upstairs."

But Claude was not buying. He looked at me sus-
piciously. "Whatta you been telling her?"

Rhinehart scolded him. "Oh, for God's sake,
Claude. He hasn't told me anything except what a
diligent and conscientious worker you are. Now sit
down and be human for a change."

I watched the little game from the sofa and decided I'd figure it all out later, along with a few other
things like witches and corpse poison. Rhinehart's sudden warm interest in Claude eluded me. She forced a
cup of coffee on him and literally pushed him into a
chair, all the time soothing, wheedling—two hundred
pounds of coquette.

When he found nothing to fight or run from, he
began to relax. "You got a nice place here, Rhinehart,"
he said, studying the drab furnishings. "A hell of a lot
better than that hole they put me in."

"You learn to make do," she smiled, circling
around him, studying him as intensely as he was studying the room. "What did you ask Santa Claus to bring
you for Christmas? It's about that time, you know."

As Claude described the joys of a new hunting
rifle, Rhinehart circled behind him again. I saw her
withdraw a pair of scissors from the pocket of her uniform. My first thought was, My God, she's going to kill
him. I sat up on the edge of the sofa, and she saw
the movement and gave me a stern look which said
freeze.

I did, and watched, fascinated, as she bent in over
his head and snipped off a piece of hair.

Claude's reaction was sudden and violent. He
stood up, spilling the hot coffee, ready for combat.
"What the hell—" he exploded.

"You had a cowlick back here," she soothed. "It
kind of marred the nice contour of your head. You
know what a stickler Winton is on our appearances."
She moved closer to him again, backed him up a few

steps until he collided with the dressing table. "And here," she said, reaching up for his collar. "A loose thread." Again she snipped, not just a loose thread, but a sizable hunk of his collar as well.

He craned his neck downward for a better look at the now-jagged edged of his shirt. For a moment I was afraid he was going to hit her. "Rhinehart, you goddamn bitch, look what you've done? What in the hell . . . "—he slammed the coffee down on the dresser, spilling more, and looked over at me as though I were part of the insane plot—"You both flipped? What's going on here? I'm getting the hell out of here, that's what I'm going to do. I'm just getting the hell out of here." And he did, without a backward look.

Rhinehart watched him go, her face and eyes revealing clearly how she felt about him. "Just trying to be hospitable, Claude," she called after him. "Come again. You hear?"

She examined the objects in her hand—the snipped hair and the piece of collar—and without so much as a word of explanation, she said, "Okay, let's go," all business again, a professional with an urgent matter on her mind.

I followed her down the hall back to the examining room, trying to think up a way in which I might ask Claude's basic question: "What the hell is going on here?" But every time I ran it through my head, I sounded like Claude. So I kept quiet and followed her into the room where we found Hatter, sleeping beneath the sheet as we had left her.

Rhinehart moved past the sleeping girl to a far table. I watched closely as she took a large roll of gauze out of a cabinet. She cut off a piece about the size of a handkerchief, spread it flat, and placed on it the hair and the collar fragment. Carefully she drew up all four corners and tied it, knapsack fashion, onto the end of a throat swab. It looked like traveling equipment for a miniature hobo. That job done, she looked around, spied a small basin, handed both the basin and the knapsack to me, and said, "Now, let's wake her up."

"Rhinehart?" I had a few questions which could not be postponed. "What am I supposed to do with this stuff?"

"Just follow directions," she snapped. "Stand back there and wait a minute." She indicated the farthest corner of the room, and then started toward Hatter. She stopped abruptly and asked, "Got any matches?"

"No."

Annoyed, she slapped the pockets of her uniform, then searched through the contents of a messy drawer. She tossed a book of matches in my direction, and the game was on again.

I did as I was told, and moved back into the corner, feeling worse than foolish, carrying the basin, the knapsack, and the matches.

Rhinehart stood for a moment over Hatter, felt her forehead again, and stared down for a long minute at the thin face, the tangle of black hair. I heard her whisper. "Okay, here goes."

Then she was slapping her, trying to rouse her from sleep, calling her name over and over again. "Hatter, wake up. Come on. It's time. Let's get it over with. We're going to make you well now. I promise. Wake up."

And Hatter did, begrudgingly. She turned her head away from the slaps, her eyelids struggling against the bright light of consciousness and the sting of Rhinehart's hand. But Rhinehart was persistent. "Come on now. You have to wake up. We're all ready, and we need you."

Finally Hatter wrenched her head backward; her injured hands moved up to her face to give protection against the slaps; her eyes opened and stayed open.

"Can you sit up?" Rhinehart didn't wait for an answer, but pulled the girl up into a sitting position, covered her with the sheet, supported the wobbly head against her shoulder, and directed her attention to me, still standing in the corner, holding the strange objects I had been given.

"There," Rhinehart whispered. "Do you see him there?"

Hatter's eyes focused on me. She gave a soft moan and tried to turn away. But Rhinehart held her fast. "No, now listen. He is not the witch. But look what he has in his hand." She indicated the knapsack, and I held it high for Hatter's inspection.

"There's the witch," Rhinehart murmured. "And he's the one who got it for you. He's holding in his hand the hair and sweat of the real witch. And he did it because he wants to help you."

Hatter's face, weak and drawn, was suddenly alive. Her black eyes were fixed, motionless, as she studied first me and then the small white knapsack that I held high over my head.

Rhinehart went on, leaning close to her ear. "Do you want to see it, Hatter? He'll show it to you if you want to see it."

No! Every muscle, every fiber in her body withdrew from the suggestion. Amazing transformations had taken place in both women. Hatter had an expression on her face that went beyond mere fear, that seemed to penetrate into the most primal mysteries of the universe. And Rhinehart the heavy, rosy eccentric had disappeared, had been replaced by a hissing, whispering sorceress of terrifying proportions. Even I felt caught up in the ritual, completely forgetting for the moment who I was and exactly what I was holding over my head. At some point I wanted only to get rid of it. Like Rhinehart and Hatter, the small white knapsack had itself undergone a transformation. Literally and quite honestly, I felt as though I were holding pure evil over my head. The end of the throat swab in my hand began to radiate heat, and the knapsack itself became incredibly heavy. Rhinehart whispered something to Hatter. I couldn't hear her words, and in the interim, my upraised hand and arm began to shake, the muscles in my shoulders cramped. The discomfort was real, and all out of proportion to the actual weight of the objects overhead.

Suddenly Rhinehart commanded at full voice. "Burn it!" Hatter was whimpering now, a dog sound. She drew the sheet closely about her, her breath coming in short, sharp spasms. Rhinehart, still at Hatter's side, instructed me to place the basin on the floor, place the knapsack in the basin, and set fire to it.

I did as I was told, although it seemed to me that the objects over my head fought the descent to the basin. Glad to be rid of the thing, I struck a match and threw it down into the basin. At the first sight of flame, Hatter gave a scream the size and dimension of which I had never heard before. She fell back onto the table, her body arched, a contortion of pain. Rhinehart held her on the table as best she could throughout the ordeal, reaching down Hatter's throat for her tongue and holding it fast between her fingers. For as long as the objects burned, Hatter seemed to be in the worst sort of human agony imaginable. As the small fire burned down, her agony subsided. I turned away at last, and closed my eyes and smelled, I swear it, burning flesh.

Then it was over. A small pile of black smoldering ashes filled the basin, and Rhinehart was left with nothing to restrain, for Hatter had passed out, her arms outflung, legs curled to one side, her body on the table resembling a distorted crucifixion.

Knees shaking, I made my way to the stool and sat down. Rhinehart went to the chair, pushed the clipboard off onto the floor with a clatter, and sat. For a long time we said nothing.

Reason was absent. I believed at that instant that a witch had been destroyed and a girl had been painfully liberated. So little difference in rituals. *This is the Body and Blood of our Lord Jesus Christ. Take and Eat. The hair and sweat of evil. Take and destroy.*

Rhinehart was the first to stir. She wiped perspiration off her forehead. "She's all yours now. I hope I've done you a favor."

I looked up. "Is she all right?"

"For a while anyway."

Rhinehart pulled herself up out of the chair,

straightened a strap inside her dress, and said, "Let's clean her up."

Together we carried her into a bathroom, ran a hot tub, and placed her in it. While Rhinehart scrubbed, I supported Hatter's neck and head, turning her this way and that at Rhinehart's command, my respect for the large woman growing as I watched her work, still talking to the unconscious girl, soothing, "You're all right now. No more Claude, no more dog pens. You're going to be all right, you hear?"

Hatter heard nothing. But I heard. And was moved. Rhinehart washed her hair, and brushed out the mats and snarls until it was smooth and black against Hatter's shoulders. Then we carried her back to the examining room, dressed her in a clean white hospital gown, and rebandaged her wrists.

The job done, Rhinehart stepped back, drenched from the bath. "We'll put her in the room next to my apartment. Come on."

I picked Hatter up in my arms, and followed Rhinehart back down the corridor. She led the way into a small room, no larger than a monk's cell. But the walls were white and clean, and there was a bed, a real bed with sheets and a blanket and a pillow. The window was barred, but there were curtains covering the bars. The door had a lock on it, but Rhinehart had opened it without a key. It was paradise compared to the solitary-confinement cell.

"When will she wake up?" I asked.

"When she gets ready to. Look, I've got to change clothes. You stay with her. I'll be back."

Rhinehart was clearly exhausted. When she reached the door, I said, "Thanks. For everything."

"Wait until you're finished with her before you thank me." She looked back and smiled, not a half-bad smile. "Then if you're still grateful," she added, "you can take me to dinner sometime. I dig foot-long hot dogs." And she was gone, closing the door behind her. I waited for the sound of a key turning in the lock, but heard nothing. We were not prisoners here. The thought of an open door was a comforting one.

There was a straight-backed chair against the wall. I drew it close to the bed and sat down, and stared at the sleeping face, so at peace now, and tried to imagine what she had gone through, the most recent ordeal of fire. There was no reasonable, logical explanation for it, as there had been no reasonable, logical explanation for the death in two days of that woman. A child, lost in the twentieth century, had slipped effortlessly back to the roots of her origin. There was no other explanation for it. Then. Or now.

She looked regal again, asleep on the bed, her hair smooth and clean against the pillow. I thought of how the whole thing had started, of the ragged, dirty female I had seen leading the marchers in the jail cell, the boy bleeding to death, the still-fresh sensation of the knife entering my back. I felt responsible somehow for everything that had happened to her. No more victim theory. She had gone through too much not to survive. I would see to it. The investment was too great.

I lost track of time sitting in the still white room. I remember thinking, She doesn't look Indian—as though it were wrong for an Indian to look Indian. The delicate Oriental features pleased me more than ever, the non-Indian look. It would be an interesting experiment to try to pull her back from oblivion, and head her toward . . . I wasn't at all sure what her direction would be, which one I would choose for her. But I felt it as surely as I have ever felt anything, a sense of possession, of owning, by right of investment. It was a simple but potent narcotic, the sure knowledge that I would succeed where everyone else had failed.

I glanced up then, and there she was, eyes open. I leaned forward on the chair. "How do you feel?"

She continued to look at me, saying nothing, revealing nothing.

"Hatter? It's all over now. Look. No more bars."

The fact pleased me. It seemed that it should please her as well.

But still there was no response. She continued to look at me as one might look at a vaguely familiar face on a crowded street.

I tried to refresh her memory. "The witch is gone, remember? Back in the other room, remember how we burned him? He no longer has control of you." I was making a conscious effort to sound like Rhinehart, pleading with Hatter to believe that I believed.

But she merely looked puzzled. Very softly she said. "You flipped? No such things as witches. Everybody knows that." She turned her head to one side and closed her eyes, as though she might escape from such lunacy back into the safe realm of sleep.

It was a device, clearly a device on her part to dislodge me from her private world of corpse poison and evil spirits. Private property. No one enters here unless they have the proper credentials. So be it.

She opened one eye, the other hidden in the pillow. "Will I have to go back down to the basement?" she asked.

"No," I said, with absolutely no authority to say no, but saying it anyway.

The news seemed to please her more than the news concerning the death of the witch. She looked up, both eyes open. "That's a rotten place," she whispered.

I agreed.

Then she began to look around at the walls and the ceiling, her hands smoothing the blanket, her fingers touching the white sheet. She studied her left wrist for a moment as if aware for the first time of the injury and the bandage. Her face clouded: suddenly, she looked toward the ceiling, as though she had remembered too much.

I told her again that it was all over. No more handcuffs, or solitary cells, or dog pens. Any of it. No more. Not for her. I promised.

But she looked disbelieving. "You don't know this place," she said.

"I know it well enough."

"They're doing all this for you. So you won't make a fuss. Soon as you leave, it'll be the same."

"Then I won't leave."

"They'll make you."

"No way. I promise."

But she would not be reassured. She wrapped her arms closely around her body, and turned away from my promises.

I sat on the edge of the bed, and forcibly raised her, making her look at me. I made my words as measured and firm as possible. "You will *not* go back down to the basement, I swear it. You must believe that."

She seemed to want to believe, and nodded; I laid her back down on the pillow, and watched the old memories battle with the new hope. The memories were powerful.

"Claude?" she asked, "Will he come back?"

"No." I started to remind her that we had done away with Claude and his control over her, burned him in a water basin. "You remember nothing of what happened?" I asked.

"When?"

"When I first brought you up here."

She looked directly at me. "No," she said. So it was gone, merely part of the delirium of high fever.

"I'm cold," she said.

I drew the blanket up around her. Promptly she pushed it back down and examined the hospital gown.

"How'd I get this?" she asked.

"Rhinehart and I gave you a bath. She's going to keep you here for a while."

"You . . . gave me a bath?"

I nodded.

She grinned, a flush of modesty. Now she pulled the blanket up to her chin and grinned again. "I was naked?"

"I'm a doctor, Hatter. Don't worry."

She was charming, grinning beneath the blanket,

once completely disappearing, only to emerge again more embarrassed than ever.

"Well, if you must know," I soothed, "Rhinehart did most of it. I just held your head."

She seemed to think on this for a minute. Her face clouded again, the embarrassment faded. Old threats returned. "They don't like Rhinehart here," she whispered, as though sharing a secret with me.

"Why? I think she's a very nice person."

"I guess she's okay. But—"

"But what?"

"All the girls try to get infirm duty because they like her, and that makes the others jealous."

It made sense. More important than what she said was the fact that she had observed, witnessed the relationships within the institution. She *was* bright.

Still the threats were present. She stared straight ahead at the closed door. Then matter-of-factly she asked, "What's going to happen now?"

I adopted her businesslike attitude and described a future which made perfect sense to me. "You're going to stay here and get well, eat properly and get your strength back, and we're going to have long talks, like now, and then you're going back to the dormitory and you're going to cooperate and obey the rules, and one day old man Winton's going to come to you and say, 'Hatter Fox, that's it. Goodbye.'"

She looked at me with the same expression she'd had on her face when I'd told her about the dead witch—complete disbelief.

"Bull," she said.

"No. It doesn't have to be. It's up to you."

She groaned, a loud fake sound, anger rising. "God, I'm so sick and tired of hearing that."

"It's true."

"The hell it is." She sat up in bed. "If it was up to me, I'd walk out of this place right now and in an hour, be so far away, you wouldn't be able to find me anyplace in the world."

"Where would you go?"

She grew defensive. "I have friends. Don't think for a minute that I don't. Good friends. And lots of them. They'd help me."

"Where were these good friends when you needed them back in Santa Fe? That crew I saw you with in the jail cell all got out and never showed their faces again. They left you there to rot."

She exploded. "They weren't my friends."

"Then who were they?"

"Just kids. Bums. Hicks They weren't my friends."

I was pushing her, perhaps too hard, but I persisted. "Then tell me, where are these friends? They haven't been to see you here. No one's come. Not a sign of them."

She was mad then, sitting in the middle of the bed, fists clenched, voice rising. "They don't know where I am. That's why they haven't come. They'd come if they knew; they'd help me get out of this place. But they don't know, you bastard. Don't tell me I don't have any friends."

Suddenly the door opened. Rhinehart stuck her head around the corner. "Brass coming," she hissed. "Keep it down, you hear?"

"You're all bastards," Hatter shouted. "Every one of you. Just let me out of here and I'll show you my friends."

Again I was made aware of her unpredictability. She had gone from a quiet and rather sleepy peace to full-blown rage in less than ten seconds. I tried to quiet her, but the minute I left my chair, her rage increased, and on her knees now in the middle of the bed, she delivered a most impressive string of oaths and curses, all hurled at scream pitch.

Hearing voices in the hall outside, I begged her to shut up, but she wouldn't do it. She merely called the roll of the administrative staff, classifying them all. "Winton's a bastard," she screamed, "Levering's a bastard, Rhinehart's a bastard. I have friends. Don't tell me that I—"

Quickly I left the room and closed the door behind me, hoping that my absence would quiet her down. But it didn't. The screams continued, more obscene and loud as ever. In the middle of the hall, I found a grim little group: Winton, Levering, Rhinehart, and the aide named Ned.

Winton looked stricken. "I thought you told us she was sick," he said, moving his words around and between the screams coming from behind the closed door.

"She is," Rhinehart said quickly.

"She doesn't sound sick," he replied.

Levering, I noticed, stayed back against the wall, clearly worrying about how much of this would be his responsibility.

The screams continued. Suddenly there was a new sound of pounding and kicking. Apparently she'd left the bed and headed for the door, no longer content merely to scream her fury. Obviously she was not accustomed to unlocked doors, for she never tried to open it, but contented herself with pounding and kicking, an ungodly noise that echoed and reverberated down the corridor, accompanied by her screams of "Bastards, you're all bastards."

Rhinehart gave me a withering look.

"It's my fault," I explained. "I pushed her too hard. She's upset." An understatement if there ever was one.

Winton's face grew more grim. "Upset or not, we can't have this." To the aide, Winton ordered, "Get a strait jacket."

"No!" Suddenly I was in the middle of the group, pleading. "Please don't, Dr. Winton."

"She's upsetting the rest of the girls," he said. "I could hear her in the corridor outside. We can't have it."

"She'll settle down in a minute, I promise. Please just leave her to me."

"And in the meantime the whole institution has to listen to that?" He turned to the aide again. "Ned, get her quiet. Now."

"Please don't," I begged again. "You're doing just what she wants you to do. Can't you see that? Don't restrain her. Let her wear herself out. It'll be over in a few minutes. She's in there waiting for you to do something like this. Dr. Levering, tell him, please. You understand."

But Levering said nothing, perhaps could say nothing over the screams. He looked at me, helpless, something in his eyes suggesting that I give up.

Ned disappeared down the hall on his mission. I turned to Rhinehart for help. "Tell him not to do it. Tell him that she's sick. It's all my fault anyway. I upset her. I moved too fast. Tell him."

But Rhinehart turned her ample bulk on me and said to Winton, "Frankly, if she wasn't sick, I'd send her back to Claude right now. Damn hepatitis. You know how contagious it is."

Winton nodded, seemed to appreciate her good sense. To me, he said, "You're new here, Dr. Summer. I realize that your primary interest is in the one girl. But I have over three hundred girls to consider. Besides, there are visitors in the building now. What do you suppose they're thinking about that racket? No, I can't permit it. I won't permit it."

So! That was the main objection. Visitors in the building. Keep the appearances neat and tidy, the wheels running smoothly. But I had to admit that it was an ungodly racket. Not once had the anger in the room subsided. Her curses were as foul and as loud as ever, the pounding as thunderous. Still I tried again. "I was talking to her, Dr. Winton, and she was responding. Now, that's more than she was doing a month ago, isn't it? I said the wrong thing to her. I moved too fast. It's my fault. Will you believe me?"

I never found out if he believed me or not. Ned reappeared carrying a heavy white canvas strait jacket and several straps. He stopped at Winton's side. Winton said nothing, merely nodded his head toward the door.

I tried a final time. "Please, don't, I beg you."

But it was no use. Ned shifted the jacket to one arm, then went into the room and closed the door behind him. I walked away to the far end of the hall. The curses coming from inside the room stopped for a moment, then started again, aimed now primarily at Ned. There was a tremendous struggle. Something, a chair, fell backwards. I could hear Hatter through the walls, battling, losing, then heard her begging, "No, please don't—"

And that was all I heard. The room was quiet then. I rested my arm against the wall and leaned my head over. What the hell? What was the use? Nothing accomplished. Everything undone. It *had* been my fault. There was that weight, too. My fault. The illusion of a world filled with warm, loving, and caring friends was too important to her. And I had challenged that illusion.

A few minutes later Ned left the room, shaking his head, wiping something off of his face.

Winton said, "There! That's better."

I remember thinking, How could anyone in his right mind call that new and heavy silence better?

Then apparently there had to be an accounting. Winton said, "Rhinehart, I want to see you in my office. You too, Dr. Levering. Come along."

I looked up to see if the invitation had included me, but apparently it hadn't. I watched as he herded his staff down the hall and out of the door. Rhinehart was the last to leave. She looked back at me, but I couldn't read her expression.

So I was alone then with the new, better silence, and the added weight of another failure, and the keen suspicion that in a short time I would be asked to leave. Grim thoughts in the new, better silence, the certainty of what I would find behind the closed door. It had happened so fast: one minute she had been grinning modestly over the fact that I had given her a bath, and the next minute she had been one single thrust of fury, rage out of control. Now she was what? Now she was nothing—silent, restrained, absent from the living.

So total was my frustration that my initial impulse was to leave then, leave right away without waiting for the inevitable—Levering, Rhinehart, someone telling me that my services were no longer needed. But it was difficult to give up a possession so easily. And Hatter Fox was mine for the moment. By right of investment.

The new, better silence seemed a din around me. Then ambivalence set in. I wanted to see her. I did not want to see her. I wanted to make a difference in the disaster that was her life. I never wanted to have anything to do with her again. She was salvageable. She was hopeless. The best thing for her would be a drugged, restrained future in the nearest mental hospital. The best thing for her would be a total reformation and the right to a decent life. Caught. I stood outside the door, listening to the mob within me. Then I went in.

In spite of what I found in the room—the mess, the disorder, the restrained though still struggling Hatter Fox on the bed—there was also a peculiar and disquieting smell of success. She had set herself a goal and had achieved it. The struggling stopped when she saw me standing there—her futile struggle against straps binding her knees and ankles, against the canvas strait jacket encasing her, and against a gag pulled tightly between her lips. She was still breathing heavily from the exertion, but she looked at me in a cold, victorious way. What she said clearly, without words, was, "See? I told you so."

I watched her from the doorway. With incredible singlemindedness she had prepared herself for punishment and restraint. Then why did the struggle continue? Why even then was she angling toward the far edge of the bed, propelling her body by the heels, hips, and the back of her head? Didn't she know? Hadn't she heard? It was over. She wasn't going anyplace for a while. Suddenly I saw the disarrayed mattress slip to one side, saw it tilt toward the floor, saw her, arms and feet bound, deliberately roll into a stunning blow, a fall from the height of the hospital bed to the floor, dead weight to a tile floor beneath. The mattress tumbled off after her.

She wasn't injured, only the wind knocked out of her. I pushed the bed to one side, returned the mattress to the bed, then lifted her up. I removed the gag from her mouth, and turned her on her side. Moving around the straps and buckles of the strait jacket, I rubbed, pounded, and massaged until I heard that first sharp intake of breath, followed rapidly by others. I listened dispassionately as she complicated the process of breathing with sobs. It was madness, crying over something you've gone out of your way to accomplish. Was an improper response the only response she was capable of making? Was insanity the only transformation of rage?

Her breathing restored, I straightened the mattress, retrieved the pillow from a far corner of the room, placed it under her head, and pulled the twisted hospital gown down over her bound legs. In all honesty, I had very little desire to remove the restraints. I think she thought I might remove them as I had done before, but I didn't.

I picked up the chair, restored the small room to a semblance of order—all the time hearing her sobs, all the time aware of her eyes on me. The stoicism of her ancestors was gone. She no longer looked regal.

There was nothing more to stay for. The sobs were deep, defying comfort; a poor outlet for rage, but better than nothing. So let her sob. Apparently sobbing was permitted. She was disturbing no one. In a way I found that I was as incapable of words as she was. With nothing to say, and nothing to stay for, I started for the door.

My hand was on the doorknob when I heard her whisper in a short, broken breath, "Help me."

Under any other circumstances, the request might have been amusing. Even then it had amusing aspects. I looked back at her, curious about just what her definition of help might be.

"How?" I asked.

The sobs subsided. I moved closer to the bed, and asked again, "How can I help you? I've tried everything I know to convince you that I want to help. But so far you haven't let me do too much. So tell me, how can I help you?"

She looked directly at me, her face not stern or masked. She said, "Kill me."

I searched for signs of melodrama, the skillful performance I knew from experience she was capable of pulling off. But unfortunately for her as well as for me, I saw and heard nothing false; instead, I heard only a simple, direct plea—for death.

"How?" I asked, trying to match her directness. "I have no gun, no razor, no knife, no poison. I'm afraid I came poorly equipped. Besides, I don't think you'd enjoy it any more than I would."

In response to this logic, she merely repeated her request. Her face was so serious, her eyes begging. Mucus ran from her nostrils down into the corners of her mouth; tears had plastered a strand of black hair across the side of her face like a black scar. But she seemed impervious to the havoc of her face, and repeated still a third time, "Kill me."

I fished for a handkerchief in my pocket and made an attempt to clean her face. "I can't kill you," I confessed. "Mainly because I have no desire to kill you. I wouldn't be very good at it anyway. I'd probably botch the job."

She turned away from my words as well as my effort to clean her face. Rebuffed, I stepped back. "Besides, it's such a coward's trick. Takes no guts to die that way. Anyway, I have a feeling I'm going to be leaving here soon. We both blew it today, Hatter. But don't worry. Sooner or later, they'll have to let you go and then you can find the right weapon and do it yourself. I hope that at least you have that much courage, to do it yourself."

An incredible stillness had settled over her face. Again I found nothing to stay for and started toward the door. Suddenly she was struggling against the restraint of the strait jacket, trying to sit up as though to raise herself. Over the effort, she cried, "I have no friends." Although it was only four words, it was a giant step forward. The confession was clear. And painful. For her, and for me.

She was sobbing openly now, without embarrassment. I went back to the bed. I lifted her and felt the awkwardness as she fell against me, her head pressing against my chest. I held her then, the entire bulk of crossed arms and straps, and listened, helpless, as she found the courage to repeat the confession, "I have no friends."

I focused on the white window curtains and the bars beyond, and noticed, to my surprise, that night had come. At the moment in which I felt I was for the first time in a position to do much for her, I also felt that my time with her was limited. Winton's face had been nothing but adamant.

In spite of the splintered thoughts, the moment was a good one, holding her, sharing her defeat, recalling her words, "I have no friends." Like all good moments, it was over too soon. I heard someone in the corridor outside the room. It was Rhinehart, but a curious Rhineheart: the body was Rhinehart's ample one, but the face was pinched, adamant, stern—the same expression I'd just seen on Dr. Winton's face. She was balancing a tray and stopped in the doorway to survey the tableau at the bed. "All sweetness and light now," she snapped.

I returned Hatter to the custody of the pillow. Rhinehart kicked the door shut with her foot and avoided eye contact with either one of us. "I suppose it's too much to ask why you couldn't have staged that tender scene about an hour ago?"

She was mad or afraid or both—I couldn't tell which. I moved back from the bed to give her plenty of room and watched as she placed the tray on the table and surveyed the messy bed. "Damn it" was all she said. But it was enough. There was not a trace of kindness in her voice as she spoke to Hatter. "Now, you've got a decision to make," she said. "I can take that thing off you and you can sit up in bed and eat like a civilized human being, or you can stay just as you are and I'll pour it down your throat. What's it going to be?"

Rather quickly, Hatter said, "I'll eat"—a model of cooperation.

Rhinehart hesitated, unbelieving. "I'm warning you," she said. "You try any of that screaming again, and I'll send you back down to Claude and recommend that they leave you there until you rot."

If it was a pose, it was a damn good one. Winton apparently had conjured up the wrath of God. I had the feeling that Rhinehart had been threatened. But I had no time to pursue that possibility. She turned Hatter roughly onto her side, and as she began unbuckling the strait jacket, she said to me, without looking up, "You'd better go get your things together in the cottage."

So! My services were no longer needed. "Is this a permanent exile?" I asked. "Or do I have visiting privileges?"

"What exile?" she snapped, still fumbling with the complication of straps and buckles. "You're moving into the infirmary. Winton's got to get his money's worth out of you somehow. That's some sort of a big deal he made with you, isn't it? Three quarters of your normal salary with room and board thrown in? Well, I'll tell you this. It's a hell of a lot better than some of them around here are getting. So earn it! Some sort of doctor, I guess," she grumbled, jerking hard on a stubborn strap. "But I figure even you can handle menstrual cramps and constipation."

I wasn't absolutely certain that I had heard correctly. But the quick light in Hatter's face suggested that I had. She smiled, all the time submitting to the roughness of Rhinehart's hands. The straps undone, the strait jacket fell away; as Hatter rubbed life back into her cramped arms, she smiled at me again. The smile was most becoming, incredibly rewarding.

There were many things about the moment that Rhinehart didn't like, and one of the main things she didn't like was Hatter's smile. She held up the strait jacket as though threatening us with it. "Now, listen, both of you. One more scene like we had here today and all three of our heads are going to roll. I really don't give a damn what happens to either one of you, but finding another job at my age would be god-awful hard. On my recommendation, you both have been given permission to stay here. That makes *me* responsible. Do I make myself clear?"

She did.

To Hatter she said, "I went to bat for you, and I want you to know it, to think about it every waking moment. Winton was ready to lock you up and throw away the key. And you—" she said to me, "you were to be given a one-way ticket not only out of this place, but out of the state as well. Now I want to see an expression of gratitude from both of you, and that gratitude is going to be demonstrated in absolute cooperation. If I come to either one of you some day and say I want you to stop breathing for a few minutes, I want you to stop breathing. Is that clear?"

It was. We were both suitably impressed by her anger. She *had* been threatened. I was sorry for that, but pleased as hell at what she had accomplished. I tried to say thanks, but it seemed inadequate. Then my chance was gone, and she was giving orders again.

"Sit up!" she said to Hatter. And Hatter sat up. She placed the tray on her lap in bed. "Now, when I come back, I want that tray empty and I want the bed made. Sheets tucked in properly, the whole thing. You messed it up. You straighten it. Understand?"

Hatter nodded.

Rhinehart gathered up the strait jacket and assorted straps, and passed me in the doorway. "Get a move on," she said. "Ned's waiting to escort you out and in. As long as we don't have an epidemic of something you can take one of the rooms here. But *you* keep it clean. I don't have time to run a maid service. And hurry. A girl just came in puking all over the place. Your first patient. See if you can treat her without turning her into a raving maniac."

She was gone, waddling down the hall and disappearing around the corner. I looked back at Hatter, sitting up in bed, studying the food on the plate. Suddenly her head fell backwards, her neck arching on the pillow. She said to the ceiling, "God, I feel like puking myself."

"I wouldn't advise it."

She looked at me, recognizing the tone of voice. She said, meekly, "But I'm not hungry."

"Think about Claude," I suggested. "And that cell in the basement."

Her eyes widened, then closed.

"Are you all right?"

She nodded, and slowly lifted the spoon and started to eat.

A very hostile Ned was waiting outside in the hall to escort me through the labyrinth of locked doors to the guest cottage outside. The cold air was good. I felt as though I had been given a second chance. The remembrance of Hatter eating was an exhilarating one.

In the cottage I gathered up the new shirts and Levering's razor, and made a mental note that soon I would have to return to Santa Fe, if only for a few hours. Ned drove with me in the jeep and directed me to a side parking lot. As we got out, he said his first words. "Lock it!" Of course. What else?

In the front hall of the administration building, he handed me a pass, a small rectangular card with my name and a stamp of some sort on it. "This will get you in and out of the front gate. Don't lose it," he said. I pocketed the pass, feeling that it was somehow closely connected to my very existence.

All the girls had gathered in the dining room and were singing: "Old MacDonald Had a Farm" in rounds, and "Jingle Bells," and "Silent Night." They were being led from the platform by the tall girl I'd seen decorating the Christmas tree. They seemed to be having fun.

To Ned's displeasure, I stopped at the door of the dining hall and listened for a moment. The room had a girls' camp atmosphere. Simple, warm-hearted female fellowship. Mendable personalities. Slightly gray sheep, not black ones. I had a disquieting moment then. I tried to fit Hatter into what I saw and heard, tried to imagine her sitting at a table surrounded by smiling faces, singing her heart out over Old MacDonald's farm. She didn't fit, didn't belong. Even in my imagination I could find no valid place for her in that large room —not at the tables, not on the platform, no place at all. Then where could I find a place for her? Above the robust singing, I heard her plea: "Kill me." Jingle bells, jingle bells, jingle all the way.

Ned stood impatiently at the next locked door. "Come on," he called. "I don't have all night."

I took the room next to Hatter's, an exact duplicate, a monk's cell painted white. I deposited my few possessions and went out to look for Rhinehart. A girl was crying out of sight at the end of the hall. I went toward the sound of distress, and just as I turned the corner, I collided with Rhinehart. She was carrying an enema bag, hands dripping. It seemed to be a standard remedy.

"She ate glue in art class," she said, jerking her head toward the girl drawn up into a knot on the bed. "What kept you?"

"It's a long walk," I said. "All those locked doors."

"Did you get settled?"

"I did." We walked back down the hall, passing my new door. "There."

She glanced at Hatter's closed door and renewed her admonitions. "Now, look, you keep her quiet or we all get axed. Winton's had it up to here. It's going to be the looney farm for her and the street for us."

"I'll do the best I can."

"You do better than that. She's your bag now. You asked for her, and you got her." She walked off down the hall toward her apartment, still talking. "You better look in on her," she called back. "There's a cold chicken in my refrigerator. Half of it's yours, if you're interested."

She closed her apartment door behind her with a slam. I stayed in the hall for a moment, trying to figure out if what I'd heard was an order or an invitation. With Rhinehart it was hard to tell.

There was no sound coming from Hatter's room. Good or bad? I opened the door a crack. She was in bed, the bed had been straightened. The tray was on the table, and from where I stood, most of the food appeared to have been eaten.

"How do you feel?"

She said nothing.

"It's better than where we were last night," I suggested.

She looked at me as though considering what I had said, and finally she nodded her head in agreement. Again, something had changed about her. The light of the recent smile was gone as though it had never been. She seemed totally lifeless, lying in a position as fixed as if she were still bound.

"You sure you're all right?" I moved closer to the bed. Her moods were so mercurial, so changeable. A word occurred to me. Schizophrenia. But I dismissed it quickly. Every sign on which I had based my new optimism was gone—the smile, the encouraging alliance, the mutual need. There seemed to be coming from the bed a clear resentment of me and my presence in the room, as though I were no better or worse than her other jailers. It was not fear now. The fear was gone. It was just indifference, total indifference.

"Did something happen while I was gone, Hatter?"

No response. Her eyelids lifted and fell as though I were keeping her from sleep. There was no connection between the still, neutral, passive figure on the bed, and the girl who had kicked and screamed her way into a strait jacket. I reached for her hand with a possessor's familiarity. She did not oject, nor did she approve. The hand was just a hand, no more hers than mine.

I realized then that I could cope with almost anything except her silences, those bleak periods of total withdrawal, when she shut herself in and shut the world and me out. "Maybe you'll feel more talkative in the morning," I said. I didn't rush to the door. I gave her plenty of time to speak up, say something, anything.

But she didn't. She closed her eyes and kept them closed, although I did not think for a moment that she had gone instantly to sleep. True, she was without a doubt exhausted. But how much energy did it take to say thank you?

I closed the door and wondered if perhaps the door shouldn't be locked. Apparently the lock-and-key syndrome was a contagious one. For some reason I wanted her to hear the door being locked. I wanted her to know that I was not as gullible and foolish as she might think. In short, I wanted to punish her, to bring her into line. *My* line.

I knocked on Rhinehart's door and went in. She stuck her head around the partition of the kitchen. "Is all well?" she asked.

"I think her door should be locked," I said. "Do you have the key?"

"You're kidding." She looked at me as though seeing something she hadn't noticed before. "You're a quick learner, Summer. Unfortunately you're learning all the wrong things."

"I just think that for her sake—"

"For *her* sake? For your sake, you mean. What happened? Didn't she fall down and kiss your feet?"

"Wait a minute—"

"Now you wait a minute. I don't have a key to that room, or any of these rooms for that matter. This is not a maximum-security ward. This is an infirmary. She's not going any place, I promise you."

"You said she was my responsibility."

"And she is. But one Claude is enough."

I resented like hell her implication. "Then I refuse to take that responsibility if I can't—"

"You're in no position to refuse a goddamn thing." She sounded like a top sergeant. Then her tone and manner softened. She smiled. "I should have warned you. Indians aren't long on gratitude. But then who is? What did she say?"

"She didn't say anything."

Rhinehart nodded. She seemed to be mellowing before my eyes. "Come on in and sit down. I didn't mean to bark." She was wearing a large red apron over her white uniform, and lifted the hem then and wiped her forehead. The odor coming from the kitchen was irresistible. Garlic bread was my guess.

"Oh, come on," she coaxed. "Anyway, it's too late to go to the dining room. If you're hungry, you're stuck with me. If you want to wash up, you go that way," and she pointed toward the bathroom. "If you want a beer, you come out and get it yourself." She disappeared behind the partition, leaving me to make the decisions.

I did both. The dinner was delicious: cold chicken, hot garlic bread, tossed salad, and an endless supply of cold beer. No talk. She ate as heartily as I did. Near the end of the meal, she commented on the lack of words. "It's catching," she said.

"What?"

"Hatter's silences. Do you know what the two most exhausting things in the world are?"

I didn't.

"Sex. And words. At least the first is reasonably pleasant. Don't worry. She'll talk again, I promise. Probably one day you'll wish she'd shut up."

In truth, it wasn't Hatter's silence which had produced my own. Rather, the small but persistent doubt that I could be of any real help to her. Rhinehart's hospitality had been warm and generous. I felt like including her in the privacy of my doubt. But I didn't know how to begin.

She seemed to sense that I wanted to talk, but didn't know how. "Where're you from, Summer?" she asked.

"Lowell, Mass."

"How did you get way down here?" She led the way to the sofa.

I settled comfortably, grateful for the question. "I've been trying to figure that one out for myself," I said.

She lit a cigarette. "You're young," she said, as though it were some sort of final pronouncement, or absolute answer.

"What's that supposed to mean?"

She shrugged. "I gave up asking questions like that years ago." The buttons on her uniform struggled to stay in the buttonholes after the added bulk of dinner. She had brought another beer with her from the table and guzzled it contentedly. I looked at her closely. There were no rings on her fingers. There was a man-sized watch on her wrist, a triple chin above the top button of her uniform, and a silent, repressed, perfectly controlled scream of loneliness coming from her eyes.

"Where are you from, Rhinehart?"

She looked up from her beer. "My turn? Already? Which do you want, the ten-minute version, or the two-hour version?"

"Suit youself."

"I don't have enough beer for the two-hour version. Besides, I can hit the high spots, both of them, in ten minutes." She propped her feet up on the coffee table, lit another cigarette, although one was still burning in the ashtray, and addressed the ceiling.

"Australia," she said, smiling. "Would you believe Dinbeck, Australia? Ever heard of it?"

"No."

"Who has? It's not even on the map. It's what they call way-y-y-outback. They raise good, savage aborigines in that part of the world, and not much else. Father. German Lutheran. Missionary. A godly man. A son of a bitch. Mother. Don't know. I have a private theory that when my father learned what he had to do to produce an offspring, he decided to do the whole thing himself. I left as soon as I was old enough to figure out which direction the ocean was in. Nineteen twenty-nine, and I was in New York. Nineteen years old and big as a barn. Guys were jumping off buildings then, and I took one look and figured that what the world needed was a good nurse. Walberg's All-Night Cafeteria put me through nursing school. Are you really interested in all this crap?"

"I am." And I was. The oldest trick in the world. Forget your problems by listening to someone else's. She seemed to be deriving a certain enjoyment from the story herself. So I listened. And she talked.

"Well, I graduated with honors, if I do say so myself, became a citizen of the United States, and joined the Army Nurse Corps."

I smiled. I had been right. She *had* been an officer. She read the smile. "Does it show?"

"Now and then."

"The army is like athlete's foot. Damn hard to get rid of. Anyway, after a long time of being an army nurse, I retired and decided to hell with nursing. I'd go all the way, be a doctor. And you know what? I got right to the front door."

"What happened?"

"They wouldn't let me in med school."

"Why?"

"Oh, come on now. Take a look. Would you let me in your med school?"

"Yes."

For a moment my vote of confidence seemed to do more harm than good, reminding her of a lost dream. She gave a small, self-deprecating laugh. "Where were you when I needed you? Well, no big loss. I signed on at a clinic in New York City that specialized in wealthy geriatric cases. An old man, rich as sin, took a shine to me and invited me to go to Arizona and watch over him while he died. So I went. He always said he'd remember me in his will. And he did. I was Lady Astor for about three months. But after I'd buried him, family popped up out of the woodwork and had the will broken. No big loss. Money makes a person mean. So I started working my way back to New York, and got as far as Albuquerque when I heard they needed a nurse out here. And here I am. You know, it's funny. I keep thinking every month I'll save enough for that bus ticket back to New York. But I never do. And I never will. These girls aren't much, but they're family. You take what you can get. Right?" She smiled. "Like Hatter."

I had a question, perhaps an indelicate one, but a question all the same. "Did you know when Hatter first came to the institution?" I asked.

She laughed outright. "Of course I knew. Everybody knew. When the water came dripping down from the flooded dormitory upstairs, I knew. When I stitched up that girl's arm, I knew. Hatter has a way of letting people know when she's around."

"Why didn't you do anything to try to help her before things got so bad?"

The amusement on her face faded and was replaced by indignation. "Oh, for God's sake, Summer," she exploded. "Look around you. Maybe you haven't noticed. This isn't Bellevue or Menninger's. This is a one-woman show, and you're looking at the one woman. It's all I can do to handle the problems that come in that door out there. Until they devise a thirty-six-hour day, there's no way that I can go out into the corridor and play Good Samaritan to three hundred girls."

"I just asked."

"Well, don't ask again. After you've been here for a while, you'll learn that we do the best we can with the materials that the state gives us, and the time and talent that God gives us. Beyond that, there's nothing more I can do except try not to think about it too much, and try not to let it keep me awake nights. Half deaf, half blind. Those are necessary conditions for survival in a place like this. For survival anyplace in this world, for that matter."

The indignation subsided. She smiled weakly. "Brace yourself, Summer, for the next announcement. This is *not* the best of all possible worlds."

I nodded and studied her, a picture of lost opportunities, missed boats, hopeless dreams. One not only takes what one can get, but learns to adjust to it as well. The mood cast by her bleak story was complete. I felt the need to say something, but couldn't think of anything worthwhile to say.

Apparently neither could she. She stood up abruptly. "Need some pajamas?" she asked.

"Huh?"

"It's late. I'm beat. Do you need some pajamas?"

"No. I have—"

"You have nothing that I could see. I snooped. I have a pair of men's flannels. They're clean. You're welcome to them."

She was all business again. I didn't really want the evening to end, but it seemed useless to continue it. Anyway, I couldn't have topped her. By the sheer act of living she'd piled up more minuses than I could dream of in my worst nightmare. I accepted her offer of pajamas and said by way of explanation, "I'll have to make a trip back to Santa Fe soon."

"But not tonight," She went to a chest of drawers and produced a pair of men's flannel pajamas. "I wish you could get the wrong idea," she said. "But I wear them myself."

At the door I said, "Thanks for the evening, Rhinehart."

"Thank you. For listening and eating my chicken. It's your turn next time. To talk. I want to hear about your scars. Then we'll be even. Friends."

"We're friends now."

"You'd better check back with me in about a month," she said. "You may change your mind."

She closed the door and left me standing outside, clutching her gift of flannel pajamas. A month from now! I had no intention of staying there for a month. It was my plan to stick around for a couple of weeks, make sure that Hatter understood what she had to do in order to avoid Claude and the dog pens, then leave, go back to the only moderately insane world. It's the degree of madness that's important.

I looked in on Hatter and found her sleeping, peacefully for a change. She was no longer lying in the rigid position of restraint, but had assumed a graceful, abandoned position—arms outflung, knees curled to one side, sleeping deeply. I kept telling myself that I had accomplished something. For the first time since I'd known her, she was in decent surroundings, in the care of a most decent woman. All threats were far away except for the most dangerous ones, those she carried within her. And until she decided to talk again, there wasn't much I could do about those.

I closed her door and entered my own white monk's cell. The hospital bed was better than the cot from the night before, but not as good as my bed back in the trailer in Santa Fe. Before sleep came, I experienced a mild wave of an ancient illness: homesickness, the child's lost feeling, and the child's certainty that everything would be solved if he could just go home. I went to sleep trying to grasp one clear mental image of where home was.

Thereupon followed a series of days which seemed to be without end. Like the refusal of minutes to pass in solitary confinement, whole blocks of hours refused to pass in Rhinehart's infirmary. I was beginning to regret like hell the deal I had made with Winton. If I could have conceived of a decent, civil exit, I would have taken it. But I couldn't. I had agreed to stay until the problem of Hatter Fox was solved. I had vowed to myself that I would not leave until the job was done. But the routine in the infirmary was enough to suffocate, and it almost did. Not even any professional excitement. I treated ingrown toenails, menstrual cramps, sore throats, and migraine headaches. Rhinehart continually pushed me in the direction I was supposed to go, and was there to redirect me at the end of each duty. For five days I saw nothing but the white walls of the infirmary, the pinched, adolescent faces of unhappy young girls, Rhinehart's triple chin, and Hatter's sullen, totally cooperative, and totally silent exterior. No Winton, no Levering, no Ned or Claude, no fresh air. Each morning, the weather check was made through barred windows; each evening, semi-relaxation with Rhinehart in her apartment, each of us telling the other the stories of our lives, variations on old themes, over and over and over again.

I began to wish that Hatter would go on another spree. Anything to break the tedium. It was a peculiar confinement. I knew that I could leave at any time, but I didn't. Every morning and every afternoon I sat with Hatter, thinking, Today she'll talk, say something, curse. But she never did. Rhinehart kept telling me that it was a new tactic, and to wait her out. And I agreed with her. But by the fifth day, I wasn't so sure. To make matters worse, it was Christmas Eve.

On the morning of the twenty-fourth, I told Rhinehart that if she didn't need me, I thought I'd drive up to Santa Fe for a while.

"How long is 'a while'?" she looked suspicious.

"Long enough to get some clean clothes, and throw the rotten stuff out of my refrigerator. A few hours."

Then she said a most un-Rhinehart-like thing. What she said was "Promise?" Not at all a professional thing to say. More like a woman who has dared to hope that Christmas would be different that year. She even dangled an additional carrot in front of my nose. She said, "Guess who said she was hungry this morning?"

"Who?"

"Hatter."

"She didn't say it to me."

"But she said it all the same. Used actual words."

I didn't know if she was telling the truth or not. I only knew that I had to get out of there, away from the white walls and Hatter's frustrating silence. The drive would be good for me, there would be mail to pick up and open, and perhaps with luck I might even find a familiar face willing to lift a glass of Christmas cheer with me. If it was convenient, I'd be back by nightfall. If it wasn't . . .

Of course. I said none of this to Rhinehart. The timetable was fixed as far as she was concerned. I'd be back in time for dinner. I looked in on Hatter before I left, the frozen image which alone was enough to infuriate me. I knew that something was going on behind those brooding eyes. That she chose not to share it with me was fast becoming a personal offense.

"I'm leaving now, Hatter," I said to the statue in bed.

Nothing.

"I'll have to skip our talk today. I'm sure that will be all right with you."

Nothing, although her eyes left the ceiling and moved to the left wall.

"See you later," I called back, not absolutely certain if I would or not. Maybe my job was done there. Maybe all that any one could do for Hatter Fox had been done. And on that note of self-comfort, I left the room and left the infirmary, counting the steps that led to the front door and freedom.

Abandoned for several days, the jeep was loath to start, but finally I coaxed the motor to turn over. Suffice it to say that my mood was not Christmas-like, although I enjoyed the drive, the sights and sounds and smell of the world preparing for the Great Celebration. There was little traffic on the road; who goes out on Christmas Eve? The stores were beginning to close. I wanted a cup of coffee, but could find nothing open. By the time I had left the last suburb, I was beginning to feel as though I were the only person in the world still moving about. Everyone else was locked into the safety of a home, fortified by family and friends.

It was about noon when I encountered traffic on the outskirts of Santa Fe. I welcomed it. I drove to the post office and picked up half a dozen letters, and asked the man to check again, but that was all. The Plaza was only partially filled with people scurrying from the cold; last-minute shoppers, and a few Indians who looked bored by the excitement. I considered going by the police station to say hello, but changed my mind. I considered shopping for Rhinehart and Hatter, but I wasn't certain that I would be going right back.

Finding nothing to keep me in town, I drove out to my cold trailer and found two loaves of green bread, three moldly oranges, an unmade bed, and a thick layer of dust. Wrapped in a couple of overcoats, I sat in the chair at midafternoon and surveyed the world. There wasn't much to survey. Christmas alone. *Does* one learn to make do? Having fled Rhinehart's infirmary, I began to think of it again. After all, she had asked me to be back in time for dinner. Still, one listened to women like Rhinehart, and commiserated with them. But to spend Christmas with them, locked inside a state institution with a silent Indian girl? Maybe Rhinehart had learned to make do, but I hadn't.

So I sat in my overcoats for several more hours, until light abandoned the windows and left me sitting in the dark, too morbidly depressed even to turn on the light. It must have been at least 7:00 P.M. when the full stupidity of what I was doing dawned on me. I got up finally, unearthed an old brown suitcase from under the bed, packed it with the essentials, and began to readjust my mind to the thought of returning to barred windows. If there was nothing there, there was less here. It was a matter of minuses. That is how one learns to make do.

The return trip was a blank. No thoughts to speak of, no feelings; just the monotony of a white stripe, hands gripping the wheel, a slow, leisurely, and voluntary return to prison. Before I knew it, and long before I was ready for it, the reformatory appeared in the night. I caught the guard in my headlights, and he waved me through the gates.

The front door of the administration building was open. Two plastic holly wreaths bounced on the doors in the cold wind. Was there no real holly left in the world? I had a hard time making anyone hear me at the first locked door. Finally a matron appeared, her face wrinkled by surprise and annoyance.

"I thought you'd left," she said.

"I came back," I replied, equally annoyed.

A party was going on in the dining hall, laughing girls pressing close to the platform and a man dressed in a Santa Claus suit. From the back of the hall I searched the crowd for Rhinehart, but couldn't find her. I proceeded to my cell in the infirmary. Most of the lights had been turned off in the hallway, and the dark passageway only added to the bleakness of my mood. I put the suitcase in my room and stopped before Hatter's door.

The door was open. She was gone. There! It probably would be all my fault, my responsibility. Maybe she had committed some new offense in my brief absence and had been sent back to spend Christmas with Claude. The only thing that mattered to me then was that at last I had found something of substance to rail against. There was light coming from beneath Rhinehart's door. I moved toward it in glorious anger, and went in without knocking. My mouth was open, the angry words were ready. But I was stunned into silence by what I found in the room.

A lovely, slender young girl dressed becomingly in a soft red robe was just lighting candles on a Christmas dinner table. Her long straight black hair had been brushed and tied at the back of her neck with a red ribbon. She looked up as I burst through the door. At first she appeared frightened; then she smiled, and went on serenely lighting the candles. At about the same moment, Rhinehart appeared from the kitchen, carrying a large wooden spoon which was dripping something. She seemed impervious to the dripping. Relief covered her face, her smile broadened; she said, "You're back." Then to the girl she said, "See? I told you he'd come back. Now the party can start."

She disappeared back into the kitchen and left me alone with my useless anger and a Hatter Fox I'd never seen before. The candles lit, she looked directly at me. "How was Santa Fe?" she asked.

Now it was my turn for silence. Words, all words failed me. She went on, covering my silence. "We were afraid you weren't coming," she said. "I was afraid anyway. Rhinehart said you'd come." She moved about the table as confidently as if she owned it, making small adjustments on the napkins, straightening a fork. "We worked all day," she announced, looking about the room. "Do you like it?"

Still in a state of shock, I forced my eyes off her and into an inspection of the room. The small green artificial tree looked neither small nor artificial. It had been decorated with strings of lights and Christmas balls, a dazzling tree. On the coffee table were a poinsettia plant and bowls of Christmas candy, and indescribably good smells were coming from the kitchen. Every place I looked I saw a new and pleasing sight, but none so pleasing as the young girl, standing upright, as regal as ever, her dark eyes shining, her face only slightly drawn and sober from recent ordeals.

I did well to shake my head in astonishment. Rhinehart yelled from the kitchen, "What the hell? I get one to talking and the other one stops. Hatter, give him some wine. No, wait. We'll all have wine while the turkey cools."

She produced three glasses and a bottle of wine, her face flushed with the heat of the stove or excitement or something. The glasses filled, she handed them out and drew me close to the center of the room. And in one of the most memorable human triangles I've ever formed, I lifted a glass with Hatter and Rhinehart, and drained it, and with the first warmth of the wine, I put my arms around both women and drew them close, encircling Rhinehart's ample shoulders and Hatter's frail ones. The moment was good. It was Christmas, more of a Christmas than any other I'd ever spent in my life.

Rhinehart rallied first. "How about that, Hatter? I guess he likes us after all. Come on, let's eat. I'm starved."

Back into the kitchen she went, and left me alone again with Hatter. She sipped at the wine, made a face, and placed the glass on the table. I tried not to stare at her, but I couldn't help it. She was aware of my gaze and not absolutely certain how she should respond to it. Timidly she smoothed down the red robe and asked, "Do you like it?"

I nodded.

"Rhinehart brought it for me, said she thought it would fit her, but it didn't. So she gave it to me. The ribbon too. See?"

She turned around so I could see the ribbon in her hair, and I nodded approvingly at everything I saw.

"We have presents for you over there." She continued to show me everything in the room, a little girl's excitement in her voice. The tree cast soft multicolored lights on her. Never had I seen such an amazing transformation. Doubt, that old dragon, reared its head. How long would this new mood last? Little-girl excitement? I had the feeling that Hatter had never been a little girl in her entire life. So what I saw then was at best a pose—a damn good one and certainly an attractive one, but a pose all the same. Still it was pleasant, Hatter pretending not to know what it was to be Indian in an all-white world. And from what I could see, her Indian-ness accounted for her loveliness, her serenity, the old regal quality, the straight lines of her shoulders and neck. Somehow she had even managed to convert the lines of a completely conventional robe into the flowing folds of an Indian ceremonial gown. She was amazing.

"Well!" Rhinehart said after the last trip to the

kitchen had been made. "I think we're ready. God, I hope you both are as hungry as I am. We have enough here to feed the entire institution. But we won't. This is a private party."

I held their chairs for them. The gesture seemed to please them. The table was filled, a bountiful Christmas dinner with all the trimmings. Someone had worked for long hours. We all ate heartily, including Hatter. Now and then we caught strains of Christmas carols coming from the dining room. The chatter at the table was light and insignificant, the kind of talk that aids good digestion, all problems forgotten, past pains merely dim memories. Hatter seemed to shed a portion of her timidity and giggled at Rhinehart's poor jokes.

About mid-meal we started playing a game. "Where were you on Christmas of——" Hatter listened as Rhinehart and I worked our way up through the sixties to 1970, 1971 and 1972. At some point, I felt an inclination to involve her in our memory game. "Do *you* remember last Christmas, Hatter?" I asked.

She ducked her head and studied the napkin in her lap. "I don't remember it very well," she replied, not looking at us.

"Where were you?"

"I don't remember." She looked at me and smiled apologetically. "I must have been somewhere." Then as though to compensate for her inability to contribute, she added, "I remember the first time I had your Christmas, though. At the mission school."

I sat up, alert to any clue. "Where was that? The mission school, I mean."

She shook her head. "Back there someplace." She bobbed her head in the general and vast direction of north.

"In this state?"

She shrugged. "I guess so. I remember there was a tree, not like that one," and she glanced at the artificial tree, "but a real one that someone had killed. And they told us it was the birthday of one of your gods who lived a long way away. I kept thinking it was going to be like a Blessing Way, but it wasn't." She smiled at the napkin in her lap. "And your god never even showed up." Suddenly she seemed to feel our intense interest and became embarrassed. "I don't remember anything more."

I saw in my mind's eye the image of a dark-skinned child trying to comprehend the greatest event in the history of Christianity, and failing to understand, substituting her own gods, her own ritual. She still didn't understand, and while her lack of understanding didn't seem important, I thought it very important that she continue to talk, to remember.

"This school, Hatter," I began, pursuing. "How did you get there? Did someone send you there?"

She was eating again, obviously enjoying the stuffing from the turkey. Her mouth full, she merely shook her head.

"How old were you? Do you remember?"

No, she didn't remember. Rhinehart tried to change the subject. "No one's touched the cranberries. Come on." She thrust a dish at me as well as a pointed look.

I took the dish of cranberries and disregarded the look. "Hatter, I'd like to hear more about this school. Do you remember who ran it?"

Her fork, en route from her plate to her mouth, stopped in midair. Her eyes met Rhinehart's, beseeching. She looked at me, obviously wanting very much to please me, but not wanting to answer the questions. She returned the fork to the plate and sat primly in her chair, hands folded. "A man," she said, in a voice no more than a whisper. "And his wife."

Her face was dead, no longer flushed with the excitement of the party. I had touched a nerve, an incredibly alive and sensitive one. At the same time, I had broken through her mask of gaiety and little-girl excitement. I never caught a clear glimpse of what was on the other side. I only saw the outline of something desolate, abandoned, terrified.

Rhinehart gave me a firm kick beneath the table,

and did nothing to hide her annoyance. "Summer, you're about as subtle as an army tank. This is a party, remember? Christmas Eve? No more third degree, you hear?"

I heard. Reprimanded, I ate in silence and watched, without appearing to watch, for Hatter to pick up the fork and resume eating. But she never did. I felt guilty then for spoiling her evening and the party in general. The end of the meal was a dreary, tense affair.

Rhinehart sulked forever over the dishes and turned down all offers for help. Hatter and I sat silently in the living room, waiting for her, I on the sofa drinking too much wine, and Hatter in the far corner, safe in shadows.

An eternity later, Rhinehart emerged from the kitchen. Apparently she'd done some regrouping. She was her old officious self. She took one look at us, sitting in our respective corners, and exploded. "Now look, this is Christmas, and I'm not letting anyone spoil it, you hear?"

She waited a moment to see if we would move of our own volition, and when we didn't, she started barking orders. "You, Hatter, come over here and hand out the presents. And you," she said to me, "—that's the last of the wine, so you'd better make it last."

There were four small gifts beneath the tree, two for me and two for Hatter. Nothing else. I felt empty-handed and embarrassed. I remembered my impulse to shop for both of them and wondered how I could go about gift-wrapping an impulse. I took the gifts from Hatter and fought a losing battle with remorse. "I'm sorry," I muttered. "I brought nothing."

"Nonsense," Rhinehart said. "You brought yourself. That's enough. For both of us."

In one package I found a dark green muffler with white stripes, and in the other package a dozen hand-kerchiefs with a card signed "Your friend, Hatter Fox." What to say? Eventually one runs out of ways in which to say thank you. I put on the muffler for them, flipping it over my shoulder, then wearing it bandanna-fashion like an old woman. They laughed at my clowning, and the party was on again.

"Now you, Hatter," I said. "It's your turn." The blush was back on her face as she unwrapped the first package. It contained a handful of multicolored ribbons similar to the one she wore in her hair. She picked them up, creating an explosion of satin rainbows as the lights caught the colors. The second box held a necklace of small terra-cotta stones. As with the ribbons, she held them up for our inspection. Rhinehart suggested that she wear the necklace. At first she didn't seem to want to do this, but there was no way to ignore a suggestion from Rhinehart. She slipped the necklace over her head and sat, frozen, as we inspected her.

"They look nice," Rhinehart said. "*You* look nice, almost human." The last was said as a joke. Rhinehart had been making poor jokes all evening, but I noticed that Hatter didn't laugh at this one. She fingered the beads, gathered up a fistful of the necklace in her hand, and turned away from our inspection.

There was a moment's silence as Rhinehart apparently realized she'd said the wrong thing. Rather quickly she offered us a choice of pecan, mince, or apple pie.

Nothing for any of us.

For about a half an hour, Rhinehart and I tried to revive the party as well as the girl sitting silently beside the tree, studying the lights. Shortly before midnight we heard footsteps outside in the corridor as the girls returned to their dormitories from the party in the dining hall. I filled the vacuum in the room with small talk, complimenting Rhinehart on the dinner, thanking her again for the muffler and Hatter for the handkerchiefs. Finally the hall outside grew quiet, and it seemed the time for all parties to come to an end. "I'm beat," I said.

Hatter took the cue willingly. She gathered up the ribbons and without a word walked to the door. In the

manner of a mechanical windup toy, she said to Rhinehart, "Thank you for the presents," and to me she said,
"Thank you for coming back."

"I wouldn't have missed it for the world. It was
a fine Christmas."

"Good night," she said, her face without expression, her voice flat.

"Sleep well," Rhinehart called after her. But she
was gone.

Rhinehart muttered, "Me and my goddamn
mouth."

I tried to console her. "I think she was tired, that's
all." I thanked her again for the party, and from the
door I said, "Don't worry. She'll survive. I think it's
probably what she does best."

Rhinehart nodded, still brooding. It wasn't an
ideal way to end a party.

"I'll look in on her before I go to bed," I said.
"Get some sleep yourself. And Merry Christmas."

She smiled weakly from the middle of the sofa. I
had the feeling that she'd still be sitting there at dawn.
I felt sorry for her. She'd tried so hard. A fitting epitaph.

I knocked on Hatter's door and, receiving no answer, went in. She was sitting on the edge of the bed,
swinging her feet back and forth in midair. She'd taken
off the red robe and put on the mussed hospital gown.
Her hair fell down over her face in customary disarray.
She looked up and smiled. "I knew you'd come," she
said.

She'd changed again, a complete transformation.
Her voice was hard and slightly overconfident, her eyes
and the whole slant of her face was one of defiance.
"You really want to hear about the son of a bitch who
ran the mission school?" she asked.

Every instinct I possessed said beware. "Sure.
Why not?"

"You'd better close the door. It's very important
around here to keep the doors closed. You should know
that by now."

I did as she suggested, closed the door, leaned

against it, and saw in the far corner of the room the red robe tossed carelessly on the floor, the beads and ribbons on top, discarded. She saw the direction of my vision. "If you know anyone who wants that crap, be my guest," she said.

"Rhinehart was only trying to please you."

"The hell she was. She's a fat, stupid bitch, and you know it."

"That's not true, Hatter." I felt anger rising. This was the same hard exterior I'd first seen in the cell in Santa Fe. "Rhinehart is probably one of the best friends you'll ever have," I added, "and don't you forget it."

She retreated with a shrug. "Did you come in here to talk about Rhinehart or listen?"

"Listen. If you want to talk."

"I thought you wanted to hear."

"And I do. Just don't knock Rhinehart. She's done everything in her power to help you."

"Forget Rhinehart," she said. "Let me tell you about Shitworth. Reverend Shitworth." She grinned. "That wasn't his real name. That's just what the kids called him behind his back. And he had a wife named Belle." She continued to sit on the edge of the bed, swinging her feet back and forth, thoroughly enjoying center stage. "Sure you don't want to sit down?" she asked, pointing to the chair.

"No, thank you. You were saying."

"About Shitworth? He and Belle ran the mission school, and they were both ten feet tall and had the ugliest white faces I've even seen. You know, you really got some ugly white faces running loose in the world."

I conceded the point, and wondered vaguely if anything I was about to hear would even remotely resemble the truth. I leaned back against the door and made myself as comfortable as possible for whatever was about to come, fact or fiction.

Again she asked, "You sure you're interested?"

I reassured her that I was, and she continued to

swing her feet back and forth, and continued to talk. "Well, old Shitworth wasn't too hard to get along with as long as you didn't wet the bed or talk back to him, or go to sleep while he was reading from that big black book. But if you did any of those things, then he had a game he played with you. Growing out back of the school was a big cottonwood tree with lots of low branches, and if you got him really mad, he made you go out under that tree, and lie down and take off your underpants while he threw a couple of ropes up over one of those low branches. Then he tied the ends of the ropes around your ankles, and tied your wrists together over your head. Then he'd get on the other end of the ropes and pull until you were hanging upside down, bare ass to the wind. The other kids got to watch, and they had to play the game too. As soon as you got strung upside down, they were supposed to line up and come along and take a good hard whack at your bare bottom. It got to where everyone in the school had been strung up so many times, it wasn't much of a game any more, for anyone except old Shitworth. But if you refused to take a whack at the bare ass, then you found yourself on the ground with your underpants off, and more ropes being tied around your ankles, and being strung up on the same branch. Once I counted nine bare asses hanging in that tree. The bare-ass tree." She laughed at this, but the laugh faded rapidly; the feet stopped swinging in midair. Her voice changed, fell.

"I remember—" and she stopped again, as though she were out of breath, as though she'd run a great distance. "I remember—I guess I was about thirteen because the bleeding had started for the first time, and I didn't know what had happened, and I got some of Belle's sheets dirty. And he made me go out to the tree one night, just him and me, and he made me take all my clothes off, and he strung me up and he—"

Again she stopped. She did not appear to be breathing at all then. Her eyes were fixed on the far wall. Watching her, I had the sick feeling that I was hearing the truth. No one could contrive such an expression, not even Hatter. She stopped speaking altogether then; her eyes lifted from the remembered horror and went toward the ceiling; in one final effort she tried to drag enough air into her lungs. She fell sideward onto the pillow and drew herself up into one tight knot, eyes open, still staring at the wall.

Someone had to apologize. For Shitworth, for the mission school, for the atrocity, for Christianity. "I'm sorry, Hatter," I said.

"Why? You weren't there. You had nothing to do with it." She was trembling, but her breathing was easier. "I used to lie awake nights, thinking up ways to kill him. Oh God, but I invented deaths for that bastard. Belle, too. I had them both strung up in that tree."

"Why didn't you tell someone?" I asked, knowing it was a foolish question even as I asked it. And it was.

"Who?" she asked. "The white cops came out there once after a kid died. They'd strung him up and left him there overnight, and he'd started bleeding from the mouth and eyes. But the cops didn't do anything. They just took the dead kid away. And old Shitworth didn't get his ropes out for about a week. But then he got them out again."

She turned on her back and stared at the ceiling. A few things had been explained, one of which was her ability to survive, to endure. Apparently she had been introduced to mindless brutality at an early age. What could Claude invent that Shitworth and others like him hadn't already tried? Looking down on her, I again had the disquieting feeling that the kindest thing I could do for her would be to kill her.

She was through remembering then and aware that I was staring at her. "Help me get away from here, Summer. Please," she whispered. "You have a car. Please help me get away."

I didn't say no, although I knew that no was the

only answer. "Where would you go?" I asked, trying to lead her to the inevitable no.

She seemed to think a minute. Her face brightened. "Alcatraz."

"That's all over, Hatter. They're not there any more." I thought of the tiny island—cold, fogged in, the abandoned prison in a hideous state of decay. We had denied them even that.

"I could go to San Francisco. There are lots of Indians in San Francisco." She seemed alive on a thread of hope.

"Do you know any of them? Anyone who would give you a place to stay, something to eat?"

She scoffed at the question. "I don't need a place to stay."

"Or anything to eat?"

"I could get a job."

"Doing what?"

Frustrated, she turned on her side and grew quiet. I tried reason, although it seemed a weak tool. "Running away would solve nothing, Hatter. They'd find us and bring us back, and it would go very hard on you, and they'd send me away and I couldn't see you again. So what would be solved?"

She seemed to study the walls, the ceiling, and her place in them. She shuddered. "God, but I hate this place."

"And with good reason," I conceded. "But the only way out is on their terms."

"What's that mean?"

"It means that I think I can help you out of here, if you'll listen to me, trust me, do everything I ask you to do without question."

It was a tall order for someone who probably had never trusted a living soul in her life, particularly not a white man. Her face on the pillow was awash with suspicion. She fingered the hem of the blanket, pleating and unpleating, considering everything I had said as though she had an alternative. Without looking at me, she asked, "What would I have to do?"

I tried to make it sound simple. "Very little, really. Cooperate, smile now and then at Winton and Levering. Help Rhinehart here in the infimary. No more screaming, no more freeze-ups, talk to me now and then about things like Shitworth—"

She grinned. "That wasn't his real name."

"I know. But it suits him."

"And that's all?"

"That's it."

"Then what happens?"

I hesitated a moment, choosing my words carefully. "I'm making no promises, but if you do everything I ask you to do, I think that by one day next spring, you can walk out of here, legally and with their blessing."

"Next spring?" She made it sound like an eternity. But she seemed to be considering carefully everything I had said. "Will I have to go back to the dormitories with the others?"

"No promises, but I'll try to arrange for you to stay here. But you'll have to work."

She wasn't pleased with anything I had said to her, but for the first time, she seemed to realize the hopelessness of her predicament. There were no alternatives. She closed her eyes, as though to prepare herself for the ordeals ahead. With her eyes closed, she said, "All right."

It was a surrender, clear and simple. Perhaps not so simple; possibly one of the most difficult things she'd ever done in her life. I said, "Get some sleep. It's late. We'll talk tomorrow."

"I need some clothes."

"I'll get you some."

"There's an army surplus store in town."

"Okay." Army surplus? Why not? This was probably the best thing to come out of all the wars. The leftovers were now clothing a whole new generation.

Then apparently the talk was over. She appeared to be drained by her surrender. On the other hand,

I had never felt so confident. I told her good night, told her not to worry, and started to leave.

As I reached the door, she asked, "Summer? When it's all over, will I be white or Indian?"

At first I thought she was joking. But she wasn't. White or Indian? I didn't know what she meant. She must have seen the confusion in my face for she lay back down on the bed, without waiting for an answer. White or Indian? Did it have to be one or the other? Acculturation took place every day. Completely painless. Survival for anyone was a matter of adjustment, of flexibility. This was just one of many lessons she would have to learn. I left the room without answering her question. White or Indian? What the hell difference did it make?

In bed, pleased with myself, thinking that it hadn't been such a bad Christmas after all, I recalled against my will her account of the mission school. I saw too clearly the image of dark-skinned children hanging by their heels from low branches—the humiliation, the pain, permanent scars, the residue of hate and outrage, old debts that someone would have to pay.

Thank you, Reverend Shitworth, in the name of the Father, the Son, and the Holy Ghost.

White or Indian? I had no answer for her.

The days following our midnight Christmas Eve talk were smooth and calm. Clothed in new bell-bottoms and an oversized navy shirt, Hatter took over the cleaning of the infirmary as though she owned it. Yet another incredible transformation. On her hands and knees, she scrubbed daily the entry hall and long corridor, yelling at both Rhinehart and me if we walked on it before it had dried. She was responsible for the laundry list and kept a meticulous inventory. She took her meals in Rhinehart's apartment, or if Rhinehart was gone, with me at the big desk in the receiving office from two trays brought to us from the dining hall by a disgruntled matron. Hatter's presence in the infirmary seemed to be a bone of contention with the others. Inmates and staff alike resented her, although I testified to both Winton and Levering that she probably worked harder than any other girl in the institution. In spite of my past differences with those two men, I was grateful for their trust in me. Hatter was mine, my responsibility. Apparently I alone knew what was best for her. Their only condition was that I was to keep her "on the mend" and as invisible as possible, the latter a condition I viewed with a certain ironic amusement because it probably had been the predominant condition of her life.

She seemed not to mind, however. In fact, her one major fear during those days was the possibility that she might be sent back with the other girls.

She wasn't bad company. It was fascinating to watch the curious and subtle ways she chose to reveal herself. There were still extremes within her; one meal spent merely discussing bad food, another meal, plunging without warning back into the past, beyond the point of pain. Incredible extremes. My weeks with her as almost sole companion were restless and confined, but they were never boring.

In a way, our world was insular and secure. Strange, the number of worlds that exist within the larger world of an institution of this nature. For example, the world of the kitchen and those who worked there was as remote from Claude's world of solitary confinement as, say, Park Avenue is from the jungles of Bolivia. The safe, structured business offices in the administration building were yet another world, the dining hall still another, and the dormitories still another. The locked doors served two purposes—to keep us out, and in. Again there was disorientation. I found myself denied a whole picture. I saw and felt and heard only to the limits of my world —in this case, the infirmary—and I wrongly began to feel that this was the only world. It's a universal failing. I found a perfect microcosm within the institution, human effort being expended in a thousand divergent ways, like horses being driven in opposite directions. How to unify human purpose? A good question. Unanswerable, but good.

So Hatter and I passed the days together, daring to reveal glimpses of ourselves to one another, confident that our world was the only world that mattered.

One night—it must have been mid-January—we were eating alone at the big desk, struggling to digest the fried canned meat. Between mouthfuls, she asked, "You ever been hungry, Summer?"

"Sure. Who hasn't?"

She looked at me, unbelieving, and smiled. "You haven't." She wiped the plate with a biscuit and appeared to swallow it whole. She said, "The old woman used to make soup of sheep's fat and grasses. Ever tried that?"

"What old woman?"

"The one I lived with."

"Your mother?"

She giggled. "No. I called her grandmother, but I don't think she was. She was nice, though. We had our own hogan, and sometimes people would bring us food or invite us to Sings, where there was always lots of food."

"Did she tell you anything about your parents?"

She looked at me as if I'd asked the most ridiculous question in the world. "I didn't have any parents," she said, as though it were something I should have known. "The old woman used to tell me that Changing Woman had given me to her."

"This old woman—is she the one who sent you to the mission school?"

"Are you kidding?" Having cleaned her plate and mine, she was eating sugar then, dipping it out of the bowl a spoonful at a time, and enjoying it. "She would never have done that," she went on. "She hated white people. Oh God, how she hated white people. She used to tell me stories—" Suddenly she laughed outright, had another spoonful of sugar, and left the table. She found a place on the floor that suited her and sat down. She leaned back against the wall, drew her knees up, and studied me closely. The laugh was over, but she was still amused by something. "She would have hated you, Summer," she said.

"Me personally?"

She seemed to think on this for a minute. "No, maybe not. Just the color of your face." She appeared then to be privately remembering the stories, ancient battles, old injustices—all carefully omitted from the history books. But I was more interested in Hatter's origins.

"How long were you with her—the old woman, I mean?"

"Not long enough," she said, breaking out of the mood of memory. "She got sick, and people came and sang over her, and I thought she was going to get better, and it was a good time because there was lots of food. And one day they moved her outside the hogan and I knew she was going to die. And I remember she wanted to talk to me, but the others wouldn't let her for some reason, and finally she just raised up and screamed my name. Then some men got me and took me to her, and she thanked me for living with her and sharing her hogan, and she told me that I was to wait there and someone would come for me. And she died."

She studied her hands as though the past were written there, examining carefully her palms and not speaking.

I tried to be patient as she pieced together the fragments of memory. She was as close to her beginnings as she'd ever come.

"And she died," she repeated, drawing a deep breath as though to fortify herself all over again. "And she died. They took her away, and I remember I cleaned up the hogan and sat in the doorway and waited for someone to come for me. I knew where the spring was so I had water, and it was summer so I didn't need fire. But oh, God, I got hungry. And no one came. I think as long as she was alive, I was okay.

They liked me because of her. But after she died, no one came. One day a couple of men rode by on horses, and I got up and got ready to go, and they stopped and looked at me, but they rode off. And that night the old woman came back and told me not to wait any longer."

"Came back? What do you mean?"

"Her ghost." She said it matter-of-factly, without hesitation or embarrassment. "She told me to start walking toward the dawn and not to wait any longer. I begged her to take me with her, but she wouldn't do that. But she walked with me until morning, and kissed me goodbye, and told me to keep walking."

She continued to stare at her palms, as though remembering the feel of the old woman's hand as she spoke of ghosts and midnight walks. The spell spread, and I saw clearly the child walking hand in hand through arroyos and canyons with the ancient ghost. I not only saw, but I believed.

She seemed disinclined to talk further, and shuddered suddenly and looked at me and made contact with this century. "It's cold in here," she said.

I found it comfortable—if anything, too warm—but then I was not the one involved in the midnight walk with the ghost. She must have seen the interest in my face, and seemed to realize for the first time where she'd been. "God, I haven't thought about her for years. That old woman."

"Don't stop now. What happened?"

"When?"

"After she left you."

She shrugged. "Who cares?"

"I do."

She looked at me as though to signify that she was doing all this only for my benefit, a "this is part of the bargain" look.

"Well, there was a kid taking a herd of sheep out to pasture," she began, no longer interested. "I followed him out to the mountain and followed him back to his hogan that night. There were about a hundred kids there already, and the woman tried to chase me away, but the man got mad at her and said no, and gave me some food, and then they had a hundred and one kids. Oh, what the hell, Summer, haven't you heard enough? Come on, let's go watch television."

She was on her feet and out of the office before I could protest. I followed her down to Rhinehart's apartment. She liked the talk shows better than anything else. There was an ancient Indian chief on one of the shows. He had written a book about the old life, the way things used to be and would never be again. I found him garrulous and fascinating, colorful in his ceremonial garb and magnificent headdress.

Hatter watched him and listened for a few minutes. She seemed annoyed. Finally she said, "Stupid old whore," said it twice under her breath, said good night to me, and went to her room.

Winton and Levering made periodical inspection tours of the infirmary, and generally they were very pleased with what they found. Not only was Hatter improving, but the health care in general of the entire institution seemed to be functioning more smoothly. Rhinehart scolded Winton in her own fashion and reminded him that she had been telling him for years that they could use a full-time doctor. With Hatter doing all of the maintenance, Rhinehart and I were free to make diagnoses and get the girls back on their feet as quickly as possible. We were quite a team, Rhinehart, Hatter and me.

In addition, there was the added bonus of watching Hatter change from a bowed, restrained, outraged thing to a reasonably calm, reasonably productive young woman. She kept her clothes in order and kept herself clean and brushed. Try as we might, neither Rhinehart nor I could get her into a pair of

shoes. But it seemed a small failure. She had two persistent fears then that I could discern. One, the fear
that she would be sent back to the dormitory with the
other girls, and two, that she would never be free
of the institution, that spring would never come. She
was eating well, and was beginning to fill out, no longer
the skeletal scarecrow I'd first seen down in solitary.
She had a dazzling smile which complemented her lovely
dark eyes; she seemed to be aware of its effect, and
used it generously on the big brass. I knew it was
phony, but they didn't. And after a visit from Winton
or Levering, after long minutes of "yes, sir" and "no,
sir" and that dazzling smile, she would make a private
face for me that resembled a gargoyle, or worse.
Only occasionally did I wonder about what was actually going on inside her head, wonder if she had digested her surrender, wonder if she was happier
now, cooperating, than she had been in the past, re-
belling. There were moments when I saw nothing at
all in her face—no light or movement or life—quiet
moments when she was waiting for dinner or relax-
ing in Rhinehart's apartment, ghost moments when
she would merely sit and stare at the floor or at a
blank wall, as if she were aware of something dying
or dead—an organism containing multiple foreign
bodies, all rejecting.

There was one incident. It was in early February, after an endless number of cold, gray, and uneventful days. Hatter had not played the memory
game with me for some time. Apparently her life
was a blank after she had found the young shepherd
and had begrudgingly been taken into his family. I had
probed, asked outright, and had been denied any
further information. We passed each other every
day, locked into the same dreary schedule of up at
six, lunch at twelve, and dinner at five. Rhinehart
was ailing with what she said was arthritis. Whatever it was, it made her grumpier than usual.
Neither of us had been into town for several weeks,

and every room in the infirmary was filled with coughing, sneezing girls as a mild flu epidemic swept through the institution.

At times Hatter, locked in this contained, sick world, looked more than ever like a caged animal. She brooded more than usual and kept to herself, and once or twice went out of her way to test me, leaving jobs undone or half done, then sulking through my reprimands. It was not a pleasant time for any of us.

One day my old friend Mango, the giant girl-guide who had tried to kill her father, checked into the infirmary. The symptoms were clear, though not serious: fever, runny nose, minor congestion in the lungs. But the real tragedy of the moment was the fact that on that weekend, Mango had been scheduled to go home. For good. Her suitcase had been packed, her cousin was coming, and only at the last minute had the matron decided she was too contagious for the outside world. So, what I received that morning was a sneezing, coughing, heartbroken, and apparently inconsolable Mango. I put her to bed, treated her, then sat with her for a while, trying to help her to understand the matron's point of view. I reassured her that in my professional judgment she would be out and on her way home in three or four days, barring complications.

Between sneezing and blowing her nose, she sobbed, "They just want to keep me here. I know how to run this place better than they do."

"I don't doubt that for a minute, Mango. But I don't think they want to keep you here. They want to see you well and healthy and on your way home. And you will be soon. I promise."

But she wasn't buying my promises. And the sobbing continued, louder and more heartbroken than ever. The time I generally spent with Hatter, I spent with Mango that day. Why not? Hatter had refused to say anything of interest for several days, and I felt that Mango needed my attentions more. So I sat with her and had lunch with her in her room, a special favor she seemed to enjoy. And by midafternoon the sobs subsided, as I finally convinced her that three days would pass rapidly, and the tears weren't really helping her, and she'd soon be free of barred windows and locked doors. She seemed so grateful for my small attentions. She told me that she was going back to school when she got out, that she wanted to be a teacher. And I congratulated her on her decision, and told her that I thought she would make a fine teacher.

"Will you eat with me again tonight?" she asked timidly, still sniffling.

I said that I would and that as soon as I'd taken the trays to the other girls, I'd bring ours into her room.

Outside her door, I encountered a very dark, very brooding Hatter Fox. I was certain that she had been eavesdropping. She moved back quickly to the far wall and assumed a position of suspect ease, hands shoved in her pockets.

When she saw me, she looked up. "You going to sleep with the Mexican tonight, Summer?"

I started to ignore her, but didn't. "Her name is Mango," I said, "and no, I'm not going to sleep with her."

"Why not?" she asked, glibly. "That's what she wants. She's a whore. A big fat Mexican whore."

I tried to match her glibness. "It takes all kinds. You want to give me a hand with the dinner trays?"

She followed me down the hall, still talking. "She's a slut, Summer. You've just spent the whole day with a first-class Mexican slut."

Her voice was loud and shrill, and I was afraid the words would carry back into Mango's room. I stopped and addressed her directly. "What she is or isn't is unimportant to me, Hatter. She was supposed to go home today, and instead she was sent in here. Naturally she is very disappointed. Surely you can understand that."

"Tough life."

"It is. Sometimes. You should know that better than anyone. Now, will you please give me a hand with the dinner trays?" I proceeded on down the hall for several steps, suddenly aware that she wasn't behind me. I looked back and saw her standing where I'd left her, in an attitude of complete defiance.

"Well?" I asked.

"I don't feel so good," she said.

I was in no mood for her theatrics. Her symptoms were clear, a severe case of jealousy. "Then maybe you'd better go to your room," I said. "And stay there until you feel better. There's work to be done out here."

She outstared me, the same smoldering rage I'd seen on her face so many times before in darker days of restraint. She called me a bastard, then took off down the hall running. She went into her room and slammed the door. So, I would have bridges to mend later. At that moment she bored me with her backlog of hate, her willingness to call other people names, her complete inability to see and respect and feel compassion for another's distress.

I distributed the dinner trays, a task made doubly hard by the fact that I was doing it alone. By way of punishment for Hatter, I spent the entire evening in Mango's room. I heard the story of her life, a grim tale which needs no elaboration here except to say that the general outline was one of human neglect and selfishness, a long procession of boyfriends for her mother and girl friends for her father, a zoo of half-sisters and half-brothers, cousins, aunts and uncles—some related, some not. Hatter had been right. Mango had been a prostitute, in order to eat when there was not enough food at home. Finally Mango talked herself out, and asked a promising question. She asked, "There's a better way, isn't there, Dr. Summer?"

I reassured her that there was, and told her that I had complete confidence in her ability to find that better way. I sat with her until she went to sleep, and left her room sometime after midnight. The other rooms were quiet, everyone had gone to sleep. I considered looking in on Hatter, but changed my mind. Let her sulk for one night. It wouldn't hurt.

I saw light coming from beneath Rhinehart's door, and found her wrapping her ankles in warm bandages in an attempt to ease the arthritic pain. She told me that Hatter had spent the evening with her, had fixed her a bowl of soup, had been a model of consideration. "I think we've won with that one, Summer," she said between groans as she doctored her ankles.

I said nothing about the incident in the hall. I asked if there was anything I could do for her. She said no unless I could find her a couple of new legs somewhere. "It's worse in winter," she groaned. "I'll be fine tomorrow."

I had my doubts, but said nothing. I told her about Mango, then said good night and went to my room.

About 2:00 A.M. I thought I heard something outside in the hall. I listened for a moment, wanting only to go back to sleep. Nothing. Just my imagination. But I couldn't go back to sleep. I lay awake listening and heard it again, a door opening somewhere, someone moving about. I left the bed, went into the hall, and found Hatter's door open, the room empty. As always, my first thought was that she had escaped, forgetting in the confusion of half sleep, the number of locked doors between the infirmary and freedom.

Hurriedly I started down the hall toward the main corridor, passing a half-dozen closed doors behind which girls lay sleeping. In front of Mango's door, I stopped. It was ajar, not closed completely, although I was certain that I had closed it earlier in the evening. There was no sound coming from within, nothing to inform me that anything was amiss. Still, it wouldn't hurt to check. I pushed the door open quietly and saw a figure standing beside the bed, only vaguely lit from the dim light in the hall. I knew by all the signs and angles that it was Hatter. She appeared to be standing by the bed, looking down on the sleeping Mango. Then suddenly she was no longer merely standing and looking. I saw her right arm lift into the air, saw her step closer to the bed, saw clearly in her upraised hand a glint of something, saw her body tense, recalled with incredible clarity her attack on me in the jail cell in Santa Fe.

I shouted one word, *"No!"* and went for the upraised hand, grabbing her wrist and jerking it down. In truth there was no battle. In fact she didn't protest in any way. Nor did she seem surprised to see me in the room. She handed me the knife, a rather pleased expression on her face, as though she had staged some complicated theatrical and was reassured to see the audience's predictable reaction. She walked smoothly to the door.

"I suppose you'll want to talk to me in my room," she said, quite calmly, as though again she had set a goal for herself and had achieved it.

For myself, I was not faring so well. The initial shock of seeing her, arm raised, knife in hand, came belatedly. Murder. That was all she needed to complete her fate. Relief replaced the shock, and anger replaced the relief. The knife, I suspected, was from Rhinehart's apartment. The "model of consideration" who had kindly fixed Rhinehart a bowl of soup had had darker motives. Had she staged it or not? Would she really have killed? I didn't know.

Incredibly, Mango had slept throughout the entire incident. So no one knew anything about it except Hatter and me.

I found her in her room, sitting on the edge of the bed, hands folded in her lap, the picture of remorse. "I'm sorry, Summer," she said, and she sounded as though she were on the verge of tears.

I didn't believe her or the tears for a minute. "You would have been," I said. "You would have been very sorry. No more five days in Claude's solitary, no more dog pens, not even a trip to the mental hospital. You would have gone all the way to the top this time, to the women's section of the federal penitentiary, with perhaps a death sentence."

Her eyes grew wide. "They don't do that any more," she said.

"Oh, don't they?"

"I wasn't going to hurt her. I just wanted to scare her. She's a whore."

Suddenly her smug, self-righteous face infuriated me. I closed the door and went directly to her. "And what are you?" I asked. "Some kind of goddamn virgin? Since when do you have the right to sit in judgment? Of anyone? If we set out to kill all the whores in the world, there wouldn't be many left, men or women. And you'd be among the first to go, so let's stop calling names, shall we?"

Standing so close to her, I could see clearly the effect of my words. I took one look and was instantly sorry for what I had said. She flinched visibly as though I had struck her. Her eyes filled with tears. But I couldn't let her off so easily. We shared a secret then, and somehow I had to be certain she knew that now I literally controlled her destiny. I grabbed her face and held it with one hand and forced her to look at me. She seemed shocked by the force in my hand, but submitted to it, tears streaming. In the other hand I held the knife inches before her eyes.

"Are you still interested in dying?" I asked. She tried to back away from the knife, but I wouldn't let her. "Here. Take it," and I shoved the knife even closer. "Whether you kill Mango or kill yourself, it amounts to the same thing. But at least do it right. Have the guts to do it yourself. Here!" The blade was touching her forehead. Fear vaulted in her eyes.

"Let me go," she pleaded.

"No, why should I? It's what you want, isn't it? It's what you've wanted for as long as I've known you. Just do it quickly, and don't waste the taxpayers' money with a long trial and an execution. Here!"

Suddenly she wrenched loose from my grip and

dragged herself, animal fashion, to the far edge of the bed. Still scrambling, she left the bed and ran to a far corner of the room. She crouched down, sobbing, both arms over her head, as though to ward off blows. An old position, left over from her time in solitary, in the dog pens.

I wasn't certain that I had accomplished anything except to terrorize her further. But I had experienced a bit of terror myself that night, and somehow I felt that the score was even. I tossed the knife onto the table. "It's there, if you change your mind," I said.

Through her crossed, locked arms, I could see her watching me, half in fear, half in curiosity. She was muttering something through the tears, but I couldn't hear.

"I can't hear you, Hatter. Stop blubbering."

She lowered her arms, and shouted directly at me. "They said I killed one of the kids, too," she sobbed.

"One of what kids?"

"Where I lived after the old woman died. They said I killed one of the kids, but I didn't. The older boy did it, I saw him, he pushed her off a cliff because she wouldn't give him his ball. But he said I did it, and they said I did it. But I didn't. I liked her. She was my friend. I wouldn't have killed her. But they said I did it. The boy told them I did it. I got blamed if I was good, and I got blamed if I was bad."

She was incoherent and still sobbing, out of control. The words tumbled out, a door opening unexpectedly on the past, without warning for her or me. Sobbing, she went on, "The woman said I was a witch, said people died when I came around. I tried to tell them, but they wouldn't listen to me. They had a Sing then, and they all took me out to that canyon at the bottom of the cliff where the kid's body was and tied me up and made me lie down next to her. Her head was broken open, and they made me lie down in the blood, and they said her ghost would come back and kill me, and then she could be alive again. And they just left me there."

She began to shake her head as though to reject the memory she had resurrected. No more words then, just a growing horror in her face as she pushed back into the corner, away from whatever it was she saw in her mind. "No," she cried out. Suddenly she began beating her head against the wall.

Quickly I went to her, pulled her away from the corner, and held her through the most racking sobs I've ever heard. What was the point? Every memory was more brutal than the one before it. What was the point in insisting that she retrace such a bloody path of agony? What in hell was the point?

She clung to me then and through the spasms of tears told me again she was sorry for what she had done. What *had* she done? Tried to kill Mango, yes. Her crimes paled after a while. The terror was lost in its own excess. The horror became relative. Which was worse? The falsely accused and convicted child lying bound in blood, or the attempt to take the life of an innocent girl?

I sat with her on the floor behind the bed and held her head in my lap, the rest of her pushed as close to me as possible, as though for protection against the ghost of the dead child.

When the sobs subsided somewhat, I asked, "Were these Indians, Hatter, the ones who accused you?"

She nodded. "Navajos. But they hated me."

"How long did they leave you in the canyon?"

No answer.

"How long, Hatter?"

"Don't remember. Someone came for me. They took me to the mission school."

So! A small circle was complete. I could then account for her existence from about the age of five to about the age of thirteen. Abandoned, and found by the old woman. Abandoned, and taken in by a large family. Abandoned, and given to the mission school. I leaned back against the side of the bed and continued to hold her. Now and then she murmured, "I wouldn't have killed her. I wouldn't have—" And I didn't know if she was talking about the dead child, or Mango. At that point, it didn't seem to make a great deal of difference.

Finally I got her on her feet and into bed. She was completely pliable to my touch. I asked her if she wanted me to stay with her; she said no and apologized again for the trouble she had caused. As I started toward the door, she said, "Take that thing away, please," and pointed to the knife on the table.

I picked up the knife. "Are you sure?"

"I want to get out of here, Summer. That's all. You won't tell anyone about what happened, will you?"

I said I wouldn't. And I didn't. I believed her.

On a cold but sunny Saturday near the end of February, Levering gave me permission to take Hatter into town for one day. Three weekends in a row, I had asked him for permission. He had weighed the request, chewed a pencil or two, studied the window and the dog pens below, and told me to check back in an hour. An hour later, a negative reply had filtered down from Winton. There had been no reason for the *no* that I could see, and I had argued valiantly, pleading her case, keeping quiet about the knife incident, and pointing out the efficient, hard-working young girl who had taken upon her shoulders the entire maintenance of the infirmary. Other girls were permitted a day's pass, released into temporary custody of a relative. Because no one had stepped forward to claim Hatter, I felt that it was unjust to penalize her. But my arguments had been notable in their lack of success, until that one Friday near the end of February when Levering had asked me to check back in an hour, and an hour later, with a pleased smile, as though he had had something to do with it, he had told me yes.

I had not told Hatter of my efforts on her behalf. Better to watch her struggle under the weight of routine than the weight of disappointment. I kept the secret to myself until that Friday evening, and I watched carefully to make sure she had done her duties: the wastebaskets emptied, the soiled linen sorted and bundled for a Saturday pickup, her own room dusted and scrubbed.

Rhinehart was in on the secret, and was only slightly jealous that she couldn't go along. I reminded her that she had had the last three weekends off, and also reminded her that this wouldn't exactly be a day off, not with Hatter in tow. In fact, between the time that I received permission from Levering and told Hatter of the plans, I had serious misgivings. Maybe I was moving too fast again. Perhaps she wasn't ready for the stimulus of the outside world. It had only been a few short months since I'd seen her totally restrained, a perfect candidate for the mental hospital. And while I had learned enough about her to begin to understand her, understanding wasn't all that important. I also knew at that point that she was as divided as ever, capable of mercurial changes. And I knew, although it was still my secret, that she was perfectly capable of homicide. Still, I had asked for her release and had finally been granted it, and I couldn't possibly back out.

So it was with a strong sense of ambivalence that I met Hatter that Friday night in Rhinehart's apartment for dinner. She was visibly fatigued, having done all of her Friday chores and most of her Saturday ones at my request, never once asking why, just doing them, holding herself with a new rigidity that I had noticed since the knife incident, as though she was afraid to release any excess energy except for what was needed for the job at hand.

She half sat, half fell into Rhinehart's sofa, her head flung back, her hands still red and wrinkled from hot scrub water. She said little or nothing throughout the meal, while Rhinehart chattered amiably about the glories of a trip into town. After coffee, I commented on Hatter's fatigue and suggested that she go right to bed. Robot-fashion, she stood up, not protesting in any way—a lifeless female machine, void of all will. The image was not a pleasant one, and I felt the proper moment had arrived to inform her of my surprise.

"Hatter, I'm going into town for the day tomorrow. How would you like to come with me?"

She stopped at the door and looked back as though I were playing a joke on her. "Sure. Why not?" she said, and turned to leave.

"I mean it. We'll leave about eight in the morning and spend the entire day."

"Good night, Summer," she said, halfway through the door.

"No, wait." I caught up with her in the hall. Rhinehart was right behind me, grinning like an idiot. I produced the pass with Hatter's name on it that Levering had given me that afternoon. "Look," I said, "if you don't believe me."

Suspicion was still there on her face, but she took the pass in her hand and studied it, held it long enough to read it a dozen times.

"I haven't done anything," she protested. Her mental processes did not know how to respond to reward, only punishment.

"Of course you haven't done anything," Rhinehart explained, "except a damn good job. And you get a holiday tomorrow, a whole day, you and Summer in town. Now, what do you think of that?"

For several long moments, no one in the hall, including Hatter, knew precisely what she thought of that. She studied the pass some more, and looked closely at both of us for signs of treachery. Finally she handed the pass back to me, shoved her hands into her pockets, and studied the floor. "Do I have to go?" she asked.

Rhinehart and I exchanged a look of pure incredulity.

"Well, no," I stammered. "We thought you'd want to go."

She shrugged. "I've got things to do here tomorrow."

Rhinehart was as baffled as I was. "What do you have to do tomorrow? You did most of the chores today. I'll finish up tomorrow."

"I'm supposed to do them myself," she said.

I was completely bewildered. I had anticipated several reactions ranging from hysterical pleasure to quiet gratitude. What I had not expected was total indifference.

"Then forget it," I snapped, and went back into Rhinehart's apartment, still smarting from the rebuff.

I heard Rhinehart whispering to her, hissing out her disapproval. Not once did I hear Hatter respond, although a few moments later, she was standing before me, still the robot obeying.

"I'll go if you want me to," she said.

"Don't do me any favors."

"I said I'd go."

Rhinehart, the peacemaker, stood in the doorway, looking very pleased with herself. "Then it's settled," she said smugly.

Nothing was settled as far as I was concerned. I said good night, walked past them both as though they didn't exist, and went to my room. I kept thinking that before the evening was over, Hatter would come and apologize, say something. But she didn't. The hall outside my door was quiet, and after midnight I went to bed, still trying to find a reason for her behavior.

The next morning over coffee, Rhinehart mentioned the "safety syndrome": even though the girls hated the institution, they did feel safe here, protected against their worst enemy, themselves.

"She'll enjoy herself, I promise," she added. "It may take awhile, but be patient with her."

Patient was about all I had ever been with Hatter, patient to a ridiculous point. I was about to run out of patience, even when she appeared a few moments later, clean and brushed, in bell-bottoms and a new shirt, and believe it or not, wearing shoes.

"Well, now," Rhinehart exclaimed, overcompensating for Hatter's expressionless face. "Don't you look nice. Doesn't she look nice, Summer?"

No, she didn't. Looking nice requires more than shoes and clean clothes. She looked as if she had been sentenced again to solitary or worse. But at that moment it occurred to me that if her mental processes didn't know how to respond to reward, neither would her emotional processes know how to respond to pleasure. Perhaps she felt more comfortable with abuse and neglect, knew thoroughly how to suffer. But tragically, she did not know how to enjoy. Pleasure was an unknown quantity in her life, and she was human enough to fear the unknown. Incredible! Hatter would have to be instructed in the art of pleasure.

Rhinehart told us to wait a minute. She went to her purse, pulled out a five-dollar bill, and handed it to Hatter.

"What's this for?" she asked, the picture of ingratitude.

"In case you want to buy something," Rhinehart replied. "Make-up, a little lipstick is good for the soul."

"I don't wear lipstick."

"Then you can take me to lunch," I snapped. "Come on, let's go."

It was not an auspicious beginning. I led the way out through the locked doors, always staying a few steps ahead of Hatter, clearly letting her know that it didn't make a damn bit of difference to me either. There were the usual number of curious females who watched our passage. I looked back once at Hatter. She was walking erect, head up, eyes straight ahead, impervious to everything.

Outside the building, I thought the first warm rays of sun or the elixir of fresh air would make a difference. But it didn't. Doggedly she walked behind me, eyes straight ahead, following obediently around to the side of the building where the jeep was parked.

I opened the door for her. She crawled in and sat, feet together, hands in her lap, still clutching Rhinehart's five-dollar bill.

Behind the wheel, I tried gentle reason. "Look, Hatter, it isn't necessary that we go today. In fact, we don't have to go at all. Ever. I just thought it would please you."

She stared at the hood of the jeep. "It does," she said.

"You don't act like it."

She shrugged.

"Are you afraid of something?"

"No," she said, rather too quickly, looking at me for the first time.

"I thought this was what you wanted. To get away.

"But I have to come back, don't I?"

"Yes."

She looked out of the window, her way of signaling the uselessness of words. My watch said 8:20 A.M. The whole day stretched ahead of us. The thought was devastating.

At the first intersection, I asked a foolish question. I asked, "Now, where would you like to go?"

She shrugged.

Patience. Rhinehart said to be patient. "All right, we'll just drive for a while," I said. "If you see anything that interests you, holler."

She never hollered, and as far as I could tell, she saw nothing that interested her. We covered all of Albuquerque from one end to the other, and still she sat in exactly the same position, feet together, hands clutching the five-dollar bill.

Around lunchtime, we were in the vicinity of the university. Here she stirred for the first time. Looking out of the window, she said, "I used to know a kid who went there. I used to go to classes with him until they found out I wasn't enrolled and kicked me out."

Miracle of miracles. It was a speech, a whole

incredible speech. I drove with one hand, and tried not to let my interest show.

"Oh? Who was the kid?"

"Someone I knew."

"Did you enjoy the classes?"

She shook her head. "They were all right. Boring."

I stopped in front of a small restaurant, a college hangout alive with kids. "Come on," I said. "I'm hungry. Let's get something to eat. You can tell me about those classes."

She seemed to hesitate for a moment and seemed on the verge of refusing, but I didn't give her a chance.

Inside we found wall-to-wall kids, all types, long-hairs, straights—all colors, sizes, and shapes. I noticed what might have been self-consciousness on Hatter's part as we entered the cafe. She made an attempt to straighten her hair and tuck in her shirt, and when we finally found an empty booth and sat down, I noticed that her hands were trembling.

I tried to reassure her. "You look nice."

"Why did we have to come in here?" she whispered, eyes down.

"Because I'm hungry. Why don't you put that money in your pocket, and let's order."

She moved as far into the corner of the booth as she could, carefully folded the five-dollar bill, and put it in the pocket of her shirt.

There was no menu, only a big board on the wall listing the varieties of hamburgers. A harried-looking waitress sloshed a wet sponge over the top of the table, and sighed, "What'll you have?"

Hatter shook her head. "I'm not hungry."

I ordered for both of us: two deluxe hamburgers, French fries, and coffee.

After the waitress had left, Hatter looked at me angrily. "I said I wasn't hungry."

I ignored her and looked about at the jammed, smoke-filled room. Acid rock was blaring on the jukebox; all the kids were totally engrossed in their own small worlds—an intense conversation there, a couple making out, shouts at a familiar face, a stag table sizing up all of the single females, and a female table sizing up the stags. I had bad news for Hatter. They didn't even know she was alive.

"Tell me about those classes," I said.

"Nothing to tell," she replied, eyes darting about the room, pulling back as kids passed too close to the booth.

"Why didn't you just enroll in school? Then they couldn't kick you out."

She had a way of looking at me now and then as if I were the world's biggest fool. "I didn't want to go to school," she said.

"What were you doing in Albuquerque?"

She wasn't listening to my questions. She was too engrossed in the faces around her, as though she were half searching for a familiar one, and half afraid she might find one.

A thought occurred to me. "Have you been here before, Hatter?"

No answer.

Coffee was served, and as she lifted the cup, I noticed that her hands were still trembling.

"There's nothing to be afraid of," I said, and touched her arm. "You have every right to be here, as much right as the rest of them. Do you hear?"

She nodded and returned the cup to its saucer, and drew a ragged breath. Still, the longer we sat there, the more agitated she became. The slightest unexpected noise caused her to jump, and she seemed to be torn constantly between her curiosity to see and her dread of being seen. The stress was incredible. I was becoming uncomfortable just watching her.

Finally I asked, "Do you want to leave?"

"Yes."

The hamburgers were served. "Let's eat them in the jeep," I suggested.

Grateful, she helped me gather up the food, and

stood close beside me while I paid the check. For the first time, she led the way through the crowds, pushing toward the door, as though toward a safe harbor. Once inside the jeep, she drew another deep, shuddering breath and closed her eyes; on that cold February day, I noticed perspiration on her forehead.

"What are you afraid of?" I asked.

"I just didn't like it in there, that's all."

It wasn't all, but I pretended to believe her, and handed her a hamburger. We ate in silence, I heartily, she less heartily, more concerned with the passing parade of people outside the window of the jeep.

For obvious reasons, it seemed foolish to continue the day. I was beginning to suspect that I was doing more harm than good. When she handed me a half-eaten hamburger, I suggested, "Let's go back to the reformatory."

"No. Not yet."

"Then what?"

"There's a candy store about two blocks up. Can we go there?"

"Sure."

"After that, I'll show you something."

"All right." At last she was making an effort. I was pleased, and signaled my pleasure with a smile. A portion of the fear had left her. Her face was more relaxed. She might have returned the smile, although it could have been only the sun in her eyes.

In the candy store, she bought a bag of black licorice sticks, a bag of lemon drops, and a gift-wrapped box of chocolates. There was no hesitancy in her shopping. She seemed to know precisely what she wanted. When she had finished making her selections, she took the bag the clerk handed her, fished in her pocket for the five-dollar bill, gave it to the clerk, and started out of the door.

The woman called after her, "Hey, you got change."

Hatter stopped at the door, embarrassed.

"Change, money back. Here." The woman gave her a handful of coins, shook her head, and looked toward the ceiling.

On the sidewalk outside the candy store, Hatter stopped two ragged little black boys. "You want this?" she asked, showing them the coins. She emptied the change into their receptive hands, then popped a lemon drop into her mouth and headed toward the jeep.

"You want some?" she asked, extending the bag of lemon drops. "The licorice is for when we go back, the chocolates are for Rhinehart. Do you think she'll like them?"

I assured her that Rhinehart would love the chocolates, took a lemon drop for myself, then asked, "Now where?"

"Just follow this street straight on to the edge of town. I'll tell you when to turn."

A good smell of lemon filled the jeep, and there was also the equally good feeling of two people at last trying to communicate. She told me she used to know a kid who worked in that candy store. "But I didn't expect to see him there today. I think he went to Canada, or somewhere. He was a real licorice freak," she smiled. "His teeth were black all the time."

"Where did you meet these kids, Hatter?"

"Around." Suddenly she sat up straight. "Now, up there, see? At the bread sign, turn there, to the right."

I turned at the appointed spot and we drove past the jagged edges of town, heading south toward the foothills, past tire shops and salvage yards, third-rate bars and dives. Hatter took it all in but did not respond to it in any way. Eventually we left town far behind and took a road which led up into the low hills. There were curves then, as the ascent grew steeper. The sparse brown stubble of desert gave way to evergreens and pines. The air was fresher and cooler; and there was no traffic. The sun was warm, and Hatter sat up eagerly, searching for something.

We must have driven about ten miles before she gave me further directions. "There," she said suddenly, pointing toward a dirt road which led to the right. "Turn there."

I followed the road to its end and stopped in the middle of nowhere. "Now what?"

"Now we walk." She smiled. "Come on, it isn't far."

I looked around. We were on a desolate mountain road with no trace of a house in sight, surrounded by high pines and fir, and buffeted by a freezing wind. It occurred to me that she might try to escape. It was the perfect spot. I had a feeling she could outrun me, and there were many hiding places in the canyons and gullys.

She saw my hesitancy and misread it. "Come on, Summer, a little walk won't hurt you. I've never taken anyone here before. You're the first."

"Lead the way. I'm right behind you."

She led the way from the end of the road down to the beginning of a thick pine forest. She walked easily across the earth, her footsteps sure and steady, her whole attitude one of eagerness, as if she had at last found something that interested her. The wind was bitter cold, and her light jacket offered only meager protection. But she seemed not to mind the wind or the cold, and led the way through the pine forest, following no discernible path, but moving always with the sureness of one who knew exactly where she was going.

We must have been walking for ten or fifteen minutes when suddenly, beyond the edge of the forest, I saw the bright unobstructed light of day. She saw it too, and ran ahead eagerly toward the sunlight; she was waiting for me on a rocky ledge high up on the side of the mountain, looking down and out over one of the most breathtaking vistas I've ever seen. The spaciousness of land meeting sky was beyond description—rainbow colors of earth and cloud, brown, dormant fields blending with patches of strange green, road ribbons, and the illusion of seeing the actual curvature of the earth—a vastness that could not be ignored, the two of us on the frail rocky ledge, the rest of the world spread out at our feet, the angle of the mountain perfect for uninterrupted and unlimited vision, an incredible, amazing sight. The only blotch was Albuquerque, slightly to our right and down, a mistake of ugliness, covered over in that one spot with the smoky haze of its own destruction.

"There!" said Hatter, as pleased as if she'd had something to do with the vista. The cold wind caught in her long black hair and blew it backwards, permitting me to see clearly the transformation in her face. She seemed to be taking actual nourishment from the wind, the sun, space. She moved out perilously close to the edge, extended her arms outward as though to embrace the wind, and laughed outright at absolutely nothing. She looked back again for my approval.

"See?" she exclaimed, still urging me toward the vista as though I had failed to see something of importance. In truth I was as fascinated by the change that had taken place in her as I was by the dazzling view. There was not a trace of the old Hatter, the sullen disaster of a girl who had led marchers through a blood bath in a dingy jail cell, the screaming, protesting, weeping girl who had been restrained in a strait jacket. That person was gone, replaced by someone so buoyant, so alive, that I would not have been too surprised had she stepped off the steep edge of the rocky ledge and taken flight.

"How did you find this place?" I asked.

"I used to ride a bike out here all the time," she said. "When I could find a bike. Once I stole one. But I didn't keep it. When I got through with it, I put it right back where I found it."

"Aren't you cold?"

"No. Are you?"

I lied. "No."

Finally she sat down and drew her knees up close to her body, and seemed more than satisfied just to sit and stare out and down on the rest of the world.

I sat slightly behind her on hard, cold rock and wondered why she didn't seem to feel the hardness or coldness. I could have initiated my customary line of questioning. In fact, several times I felt an urge to do so. But there was something in the moment which defied talk. I had the feeling that she would not have answered me. So I set for myself the task of enduring the wind, and sat behind her and bore witness to her quietness, to the new peace freshly risen within her, and wondered why science had not yet discovered the medicinal qualities in high, cold, windy places. And in silence.

We must have sat like that, without speaking, for almost an hour. I could see nothing but her profile against the vista, but I could feel what was happening to her, a release, a relaxation, a return to absolutes—sun, wind, space.

She was the one who broke the spell. "Summer," she said quietly, just when I was beginning to understand the silence. "I'm sorry about Mango."

"Mango?" I repeated, trying to make the connection.

"For what I said about her, the trouble I caused."

"It's over. Forget it."

"I wouldn't have hurt her."

"I know."

"And I'm sorry I called her what I did."

It seemed at best ancient and unimportant history. Why resurrect it? But she seemed determined. "You know that place back there?" she asked, not looking at me. "The place where we stopped to eat?"

I nodded.

"I've been there before. Lots of times. I used to stand out on the corner and try to get the college boys to take me home with them." She was talking to her hands laced tightly across her knees. She laughed suddenly. "White men think they're going to get something extra with an Indian. And I made good money. One fraternity house kept me for a whole week. Until the housemother found out about me. I had lots of money then, and if I was ever broke, all I had to do was go back and stand on that corner."

There was not a sign of embarrassment in her confession. She might as well have been telling me about some innocent childhood escapade.

She said it again, as though to make absolutely certain that I understood. "I worked all last year as a prostitute, Summer. Did you know that?"

I shook my head. "Just like Mango, then?"

She nodded broadly. "Just like Mango. And I'd still be working on that corner if it hadn't been for the Indian bastards on campus. They'd formed a club, and one night they invited me to one of their meetings, and told me if I didn't get out of town, they were going to call the police."

Her manner had altered, the breezy confidence had been dampened. Obviously the betrayal by her own people had shaken her. "I wasn't bothering them," she protested, as though I were the one who had told her to get out of town. "I didn't even know they knew about me. But they knew all right, said they'd been watching me for a long time, said they didn't want me around giving them a bad name. The bastards."

She turned away, still stung by the old reprimand. I recalled the futile intensity of the young Indian militants, the suicidal zeal with which they approached their lost cause of salvaging a dead past.

"Surely you can understand their point," I offered.

"No, I can't," she said. "What was their point? I tried to get them to tell me but they wouldn't, or couldn't. Just spouted a bunch of words I'd never heard before." She rested her forehead on her knees. "God, I felt terrible after they got through with me. I thought they wanted me to join their stupid club, but they just told me to get the hell out of town. It's rotten when you find out that people have been hating you a long time and you didn't even know about it."

There was a moment's silence as she thought about the secret hate coming from her own people. The healing vistas were lost to her then. "Oh well," she said finally, looking up. "It doesn't matter. One kid was nice, the one who took me to classes with him. He let me live in his apartment and told me how proud I should be that I was Indian. Crap. Finally he told me he knew some white kids who were going to Santa Fe, and they'd give me a ride. He told me I could find a job in Santa Fe, what with all the tourists. And that was that."

"Did you?"

"Did I what?"

"Find work?"

She laughed again. "Yes. Sleeping with the kids in their white commune. I was what they called their token Indian. I was better off with the fraternity boys. At least they had good food, and didn't treat me too bad." She stared straight ahead, miles away, seeing nothing, her face drawn. She whispered, "I've done some terrible things, Summer."

"You've had some terrible things done to you."

She looked at me. "Does that make it all right?"

"No. But everything that's happened is in the past now. It's stupid to dwell on it. There's no reason why today and tomorrow can't be different."

She smiled, as though she realized for the first time that she could call the bluff on the threat of the past. Her pleasure was contagious. I found myself grinning back at her. How many times in my association with her had I dared to think that I was at last on solid ground with her. I dared to think it again, finding in her face, her entire attitude, only complete trust. And hope for the future.

After a while, she said, "I wish I didn't have to go back. I wish I could stay here. This is a good place."

"It is. But the only way to stay here is to go back."

"That doesn't make any sense," she protested. "Look down there," and she pointed toward the smudge that was Albuquerque. "Wouldn't it be great if they'd all just go away, take all their bricks and smoke and keys and locks with them and just go away?"

"Where would you have them go?"

"I don't care. Wherever they came from. They must have come from somewhere. They weren't always here. Not like this"—she touched the rock upon which she sat—"or that," and her eyes swept the sky, a vast arc. "I wish they would go away and let the fields have it back. Let the fields and the canyons and the mountains have it all back, the empty space beneath the sky. Clear all that away, send the people packing back to where they came from. Let the fields and sky and mountains fill the empty space until it isn't empty any longer."

Her face was alive with her vision of full emptiness, her voice hushed, so quiet it seemed a part of the wind. She saw clearly the absence of Albuquerque, the beauty of virgin wilderness, and in a kind of benediction she repeated, "Wouldn't that be great?"

"Wouldn't you have to leave too?" I suggested. "You're a part of it as well."

She looked straight at me. "I've already gone," she said.

I had no reply, neither for what she said, nor the intensity with which she said it. So instead I concentrated on her vision. "Yes, it would be great," I said. "Impossible, but great."

A moment later she added, as though just realizing it. "But it's too late, isn't it? They're here to stay, and I'm the only one who has gone away, and nothing will ever change. Summer, do you ever feel like nothing in the world is ever going to be the way it should be?"

There it was again, that totally lost, desolate expression. I knew what she was describing, though perhaps not to the same degree as she knew it. But at least I knew enough to know I had no reasonable answer for her.

Apparently no answer was the best answer. "Can we come back here again sometime?" she asked.

"I'd like that."

Nothing more was said. We sat on the rocky ledge until the sun started down. I have never known the value of silence as I came to know it that day. At some point I managed to forget the wind and the hard rocks. Curious contentment, sitting on a rocky ledge, high above the rest of the world. Simple. So simple.

We watched the sun set, watched the lights come on in Albuquerque, and when it was just this side of total darkness, I suggested that perhaps we should go.

She hesitated for a moment, then reluctantly stood up and stretched the tightness out of her back. "What if I were to run away?" she asked in darkness. "You'd never find me, not here."

"Is that what you want to do?"

No answer.

"Let's come back next week, and bring a picnic."

She shrugged, as though it were totally immaterial to her what we did next week-end.

We chewed licorice all the way home. And exchanged no words. I could feel the dread settling over her, the reluctance to return voluntarily to confinement.

Once she asked, "Summer, how far could we get before they discovered we weren't coming back?"

"Not far enough."

"You sure? I know some places to hide."

"What's the difference? Locking ourselves in a hiding place, or locking ourselves inside the institution?"

When the outline of the reformatory appeared in the headlights, she said, "God," under her breath. It wasn't a prayer.

Again I wondered if perhaps I hadn't taken her out too soon. But I knew better, knew that where Hatter was concerned, there were no arbitrary divisions in time. For her, it would always be "too late," or "too soon."

Earlier that morning, I had escorted a frozen statue out of the building. And late that night I escorted a frozen statue back into the building. But there had been that one brief interval of life and grace, when she had conceived her vision of a virgin world. I wasn't absolutely certain if it was enough to build on, but it was all we had.

Inside the infirmary, she gave Rhinehart the box of chocolates, and went directly to her room. Rhinehart would not let me off so easily. She insisted that I tell her everything that had happened from start to finish. A brief recital, recounted in less than five minutes.

"And that's all?" she asked.

"That's it."

"You sat on the side of a mountain? All afternoon?"

"Right."

She shook her head. "Big day."

Early Monday morning I made a full report to Levering. His reaction differed little from Rhinehart's. He made some comment about Hatter's inability to fit into the "fabric of society." Still chewing on a pencil, he wondered if perhaps we were doing the right thing in permitting her to live in the safe isolation of the infirmary.

"You're not suggesting that she be sent back with the other girls?" I asked.

"Not totally. Perhaps just take her meals in the dining room, that's all. We'll start slowly."

"I think it would be a mistake," I said.

"Why? She has to learn to live in the world. We have to fit her for a role in society. Otherwise we've failed in everything we've done. This preferential treatment has got to stop. It isn't good for her or the other girls."

I argued with him. It seemed as if that's all I ever did with Levering. In part I had to agree with what he had said. Still, I had the feeling that it would be disastrous for Hatter.

But he was adamant. Nothing would do but that we at least try his scheme. I think I was dreading more than anything the task of having to inform Hatter that she was being fitted for a "role in society." I wondered if Levering knew precisely how much she hated that society.

Fortunately, he made it all very easy for me. "I'll send a matron for her," he offered. "You can stay out of it altogether if you wish. Her dependence on you is not a good thing either."

It was a mistake, everything, but perhaps the biggest mistake of all was my cowardice. I permitted him to send the matron and took refuge in the staff lounge on the second floor. I drank coffee and soothed my conscience with thoughts that in the long run, it would be good for Hatter, that I certainly wouldn't be available for the rest of her life to hold her hand, to make things easy for her.

About midafternoon I returned to the infirmary. Rhinehart informed me that a matron had come for Hatter at noon, and had taken her to the dining room, then brought her back after the meal. Apparently there had been no trouble. Hatter had asked for me, and the matron had told her that I was unavailable, and that was all. So. Perhaps it had worked.

I saw Hatter shortly before six that evening. She was carrying an armload of linens to the storage closet. She walked past me and said not a word. Nothing unusual in that.

About six fifteen the matron came, and Hatter went with her without a fuss. I followed a safe distance behind them and watched out of sight, from the dining-room door. Each table accommodated eight girls. Hatter sat alone at an extra table. So! That was her solution. Together, yet apart. She seemed to be the center of attraction even in her privacy. Several of the girls pointed at her and snickered. But Hatter kept her head down and ate as though it were a duty, and seemed to ignore the jeers and stares. It was not the most pleasant of scenes, but at least it was not as catastrophic as I had imagined. Perhaps Levering had been right after all.

The next few days were spent in monotonous labor. It was inventory time in the infirmary, meaning endless paper work, accounting to the state for every Band-Aid, every aspirin. Hatter moved around and through the activity like a spiritless ghost, going with the matron three times a day, returning after every meal and heading directly for the privacy of her room.

Levering had turned down my request for a pass for the following week-end, informing me that only trustees were permitted to leave every week-end. Hatter would have to be satisfied with once a month, and then only if she behaved herself.

I had not yet had the opportunity to break this news to her. No, that wasn't true. I had had the opportunity and passed it by. Her high, windy place on the side of the mountain seemed so far removed from the enclosed, confined white sterility of the infirmary. And her daily walks with the matron into the hostile atmosphere of the dining room were completely foreign to her vision of a free and unencumbered world. Still, she would have to be told.

On that Friday, Rhinehart and I worked through dinner, composing our insane lists in triplicate with one hand, and chewing on tasteless cheese sandwiches with the other. About seven thirty I told her about the denied pass and excused myself to go and tell Hatter. It occurred to me only as I knocked on Hatter's door that I had not heard her return from the dining room. Her room was empty; I assumed that dinner had gone on longer than usual, and was grateful for even a few moments' reprieve.

About eight, she still hadn't returned, and Rhinehart said, "No, something's wrong." Together we left the infirmary, walking a little faster than usual.

The dining room was empty. There were only a few girls in the kitchen finishing chores. I asked one if she had seen Hatter Fox, and received no answer.

Rhinehart found one of the matrons and reported that Hatter was missing. Suddenly the entire staff came to life. Matrons and aides appeared from all directions. We found the matron whose job it was to escort Hatter to and from the dining room—a thin, drawn, uneducated, and overworked woman in her early sixties, with missing teeth and a black mole on her chin. She told us that Hatter had sat with some other girls that evening, that she had seen a large group of them leaving the dining room after dinner. The woman was very defensive, saying it wasn't her fault, she had too much to do to "fetch and carry one spoiled Indian."

The next step was the dormitories. The girls were preparing for bed, and our entrance was greeted by squeals of modesty. Rhinehart asked them if anyone had seen Hatter Fox after dinner. The modest gigglings subsided. Slowly, one by one they turned away from the question and went quietly about their bedtime rituals. No answer. Their faces went blank when Hatter Fox was mentioned. No one seemed to know anything. Anything at all.

By then I was almost convinced that Hatter *had* escaped, although for the life of me, I couldn't figure out how. A melodramatic scene followed, something called "general alarm." A shrill, discordant bell started ringing, and a few minutes later, Ned and my old friends Claude and Clito appeared. The head matron told them to launch a general search of the entire institution. The guards on the gates outside were alerted, and during the confusion I thought that if Hatter had escaped, I knew precisely where to find her—on the rocky ledge on the side of the mountain. At the same time, I told myself that perhaps it was time for me to disentangle myself from her life. There would be no spring release for her now. At best she would be brought back and imprisoned for another year, perhaps longer. Why had she blown it? And the more practical question—how? How had she managed the locked doors? The guards? Everything?

One minute the corridor outside the dining hall was filled with at least twenty people, their faces taut and alert. The next minute they were off on their appointed searches, some muttering, "I knew it," and others, "What can you expect from that one."

Rhinehart and I, who had started the fuss, were left alone in the hall, staring blankly at one another, helpless.

"I'd better call Winton," she said, obviously dreading the call. In the distance I could still hear the muted confusion of the search—running footsteps, doors clanging open and then shut.

I followed Rhinehart back down the hall toward the infirmary, passed the supply room and the storage closet. I noticed that the door to the storage closet was not completely closed. In a gesture that was more habit than anything else, I leaned over to close it. Something was pushing against it on the other side, a stack of fallen linens, I assumed.

I opened the door, but I did not find a stack of fallen linens. "Rhinehart!" What I found was Hatter, or what was left of her. Her shirt had been ripped off and shredded; part of it had been used to tie her hands behind her back, another long strip had been used as a gag for her mouth.

Rhinehart returned quickly, alarmed by my shout. She looked down. "Oh, my God," she moaned.

Hatter had been beaten mercilessly, primarily around the head and shoulders; blood was streaming from cuts over both eyes, her lips were already swelling, and long lacerations as from fingernails started at her shoulders and moved in red lines down over her breasts.

I had been wrong. She was not on her rocky ledge. I wished then that she *had* escaped. While Rhinehart and I had been counting aspirins, someone—probably several someones—had followed her into the darkness of the corridor and launched a savage attack.

She was unconscious. I picked her up and carried her into the infirmary. Rhinehart sent a runner to the searchers. While I was examining her, I heard the confusion outside the door, as the staff gathered to find out what had happened. I cleaned the cuts and determined that only two of them required stitches. I gave her a shot to ward off infection, and another to sedate her. I dressed her in a hospital gown and applied cold compresses to her swollen face. Then there was nothing more to do. Rhinehart dispersed the curiosity seekers outside the door, and told me that she had called both Winton and Levering, that they had promised her there would be an investigation. Tomorrow.

Rhinehart sensed my mood as I stared down at the battered face. "These things happen, Summer," she said. "We have four or five gang attacks every year. There's nothing we can do about them. The girls seem to have their own system of justice."

"Justice?" I repeated, stunned by the misuse of the word.

"They don't like her. Surely that comes as no surprise to you."

"Why?"

"I don't know why. She's caused trouble here. She gets special attention. They may be afraid of her."

"Enough to do that?" Hatter's eyes were almost swollen shut, the line of her jaw lost behind purple bruised flesh.

"Maybe they're jealous," Rhinehart added, as though it might explain everything.

It explained nothing. "Jealous of what?" I demanded, "and why an investigation tomorrow? Why not tonight? If Hatter had done this to someone else, you can be damn sure where she'd be sitting at this moment. And what are they jealous of? She hasn't had a goddamn thing in her entire life, nothing. So I take her into town for one lousy day, isn't she entitled to something?" Caught hopelessly in a confusion of anger and shock, I had to settle for mere incoherency. "And where does Winton get off calling for an investigation tomorrow? Every girl in this institution should be hauled out of bed tonight, and stood up in the dining room and made to stand there until someone started calling some names. By tomorrow, they can all get organized again, their own little reign of terror—"

"Keep it down, Summer."

"The hell I'll keep it down. Every time I begin to pull her up, someone else comes along and pushes her back down again. If she goes down many more times, Rhinehart, she's not going to come up any more. And you know it as well as I do."

She nodded, agreeing, leaning over Hatter, checking for herself the seriousness of the wounds. "This probably won't make you feel any better, Summer, but I've seen worse."

"What do you mean?"

"Worse beatings. Two years ago, I had a girl blinded by a gang attack."

"And what did you do?"

"Nothing."

"Then there were no charges?"

"She was blind," Rhinehart snapped. "She couldn't identify her assailants. Her family took her home. The last I heard she was making potholders."

I turned away. Words failed me. Hatter stirred on the table and groaned; tried to open her eyes, but couldn't; tried to speak, but couldn't.

"There'll be charges this time," I vowed. "She's not blind, and in a few days, she'll be able to talk."

"But she won't," Rhinehart said flatly. Then as if to change the subject, she asked, "Do you want to take her to her room, or shall I?"

"I'll take her. What do you mean, she won't talk?"

"She just won't. They never do. You'll see. Keep those cold compresses on her. And you'd better stay with her for a while. If she manages to open an eye, I think she'd rather see you than me. If you'll excuse me, I have to file a report."

The paper world! In the face of gross injustice and brutality, the best Rhinehart could do was to file a report. She left me alone in the examining room with Hatter.

Indignation was the primary emotion then, and pity for the bruised and swollen face. And respect, for the ingenious ways in which Fate, Destiny, whatever, had managed to annihilate a whole and deserving spirit—the slowest of deaths, stretching over a period of seventeen years, every paltry interval of time, every season bringing with it a new agony. And Winton, the bastard, in effect saying that if it was convenient, and not too troublesome, and if it didn't upset the carefully oiled wheels of the institution, there might be an investigation. Tomorrow.

Hatter groaned again. One hand moved feebly up in an attempt to touch her face.

"No, don't," I soothed. "Leave it alone."

I picked her up as carefully as possible and carried her to her room. In bed she managed one word. "Thirsty." I got a glass of water and a straw and tried to find one small area on her lips where she could hold the straw. She took a sip of water and it seemed to revive her.

"Feel awful," she groaned.

"Can you tell me what happened, Hatter?"

Her eyes were closed and her words very indistinct. I leaned closer, wanting to hear everything.

"They asked me to sit with them," she began.

"Who?"

". . . said they'd walk with me back to—"

"The infirmary?"

She nodded.

"So many of them. Said they wanted to be . . . friends."

"And what happened?"

". . . the storage closet. Said they wanted to see the—" Her mind was racing ahead of her words. As though it were just happening, I could see in her face her surprise at the attack, her being overpowered by sheer numbers, the betrayal, the pain of fists beating— these girls who wanted to be good friends.

"No," she moaned, "no more."

I wasn't certain if she meant no more talk, or no more blows.

"We'll talk later," I said. "Try to rest now."

I sat with her the entire night, changing the cold compresses, giving her water when she asked for it, trying to digest for my own benefit the image of young girls inflicting such a beating. And more important than anything else, trying to imagine what effect this attack would have on Hatter. She could react in a variety of ways. She had such an impressive collection of scar tissue. Would one or two new ones make a noticeable difference? I wondered too if she would be at all interested in an explanation of why she had been beaten. I hoped not, because I wasn't certain I could tell her.

Sometime before dawn I must have fallen asleep in the chair. Rhinehart awakened me at midmorning with a hissing warning.

"Winton and Levering are on their way. Wake up."

Hatter, I noticed was propped up in bed, sipping milk, her face resembling a purple, bleeding balloon.

"Come on, wake up," Rhinehart urged, pushing me toward the basin, a fresh towel in her hand. As I splashed cold water over my face, she gave us instructions. "Just answer their questions, you hear, both of you. No more, no less. And don't start telling them how to run this place, Summer. It won't do any good. Just cooperate and get it over with. I mean it." From the door, she warned again, "Just answer their questions. Nothing else."

I dried my face and hands, tried to straighten my clothes, and asked Hatter, "How do you feel?"

She shook her head and finished the milk, and turned gingerly in bed in an attempt to place the glass on the table.

"You look like hell," I said. "Do you feel like talking?"

She shrugged, rested her head on the pillow, and said that her eyes hurt more than anything else. While we were waiting for Rhinehart's knock, I examined her again, saw that the lacerations had scabbed over. There was nothing I could do about the bruised tissue. That would just have to take its time. In a moment of perverse pleasure, I thought that she looked suitably painful. I suspected that her misshapen, multicolored face was enough to shock anyone.

Then there was Rhinehart's knock, and a moment later she escorted Winton and Levering into the room. They were dressed casually in Saturday clothes, as though they might leave the institution and head directly for the golf course. Levering, I noticed, winced visibly at the sight of Hatter. But not Winton. He moved right in on the bruised face, and asked cheerily, "And how are we this morning, young lady?"

The "young lady" responded with admirable courage, murmuring "Fine" out of the one corner of her mouth that still worked.

Rhinehart offered to bring chairs, but they said no. Obviously the visit would be as short as possible.

Winton then adopted the attitude of a friendly parson. Something about his manner seemed to say, "The world is filled with injustice. We must simply learn to live with it." "And they tell me that you found her, Dr. Summer. Is that right?"

"Yes, sir," I said. "In the storage closet. She had been bound and gagged. She was unconscious."

He made a clucking sound with his tongue and shook his head. He said to Hatter, "Do you feel like telling us about it?"

She looked at me as though for advice. I urged her to tell him everything. She took in the faces about the room, Levering standing safely by the door as though to make a quick exit, Rhinehart at the foot of the bed, Winton on one side and I on the other. Then she repeated softly exactly what she had told me the night before, no more, no less—the girls asking her to sit with them, then walking back with her to the infirmary, luring her into the storage closet, all on the pretext of friendship. No names, no accusations, nothing.

"I protested. "But Hatter, surely you saw their faces. You could identify them."

"No."

"Why not?"

"It was dark."

"In the dining room?"

Stumped, she closed her eyes. Winton came to her aid. "Don't badger her, Dr. Summer. If she says she can't remember, then she can't." He leaned over and took her hand and patted it in a paternal fashion. "You'll feel better in no time, young lady," he said. "And maybe one day soon, Dr. Summer here will take you into town again for an ice-cream sundae."

I experienced growing anger; what was worse, Hatter seemed to be responding to his fakery. She permitted him to take her hand and told him she was very sorry for all the trouble she had caused in the past.

His eyes seemed to grow misty as he continued to pat her hand. "Think no more of it," he said. "You're on the right track now. One day, and one day soon, I predict that you'll walk out of here a fine young woman. You mark my words."

I stood to one side, seeing but not believing. It was incredible. Even Rhinehart seemed taken in as she looked down with cow eyes and circumflex eyebrows on the little tableau of Winton and Hatter. Levering stood by the door, also nodding his head in consummate approval. Somehow, in the mawkishness of the moment, the fact of the crime, the beating itself had been completely forgotten, even by the victim. There had been no mention of an investigation, no effort to see that the culprits were routed out and disciplined.

In the projected image of "Hatter Fox, Fine Young Woman," the immediate purpose of the visit had been conveniently overlooked.

A few minutes later, when Winton glanced at his watch and said, "Well, it's late," I knew that nothing more was going to be said. About anything. Again he told her to get well quickly, and invited her to come to his office anytime she wished. He thanked Rhinehart and then me for all we had done on behalf of Hatter and the institution. He winked at Hatter, and she repaid him with a modest, slightly lopsided smile. To Levering he said, "Come along. I think we're finished here," and he led the way out into the hall.

I followed in rapid pursuit. When we were safely out of earshot of Hatter, I asked, "And that's all?"

He turned back, surprised. "I don't understand, Dr. Summer. Did I forget something?"

"No investigation? No attempt to find out who did this to her?"

He smiled patiently, as though he were dealing with a small child. "How do you suggest that I go about investigating three hundred girls? And what purpose would an investigation serve?"

"For starters, it might serve notice on the entire institution that these gang attacks will no longer be tolerated. And if that isn't enough, it might be educational as well as medicinal for Hatter to see that there is at least a shred of justice in the world."

He gave me that same patronizing smile that he had given to Hatter. "But she's not interested in an investigation. You heard that for yourself. You know, Dr. Summer, sometimes a good beating is just what these girls need. Punishment administered by their own peer group is frequently more effective than anything we can do to them."

I listened, stunned, to everything he was saying, and offered no rebuttal. I had none. Anyway, Rhinehart was standing behind him, slowly shaking her head from side to side.

I turned away, signaling the end of the futile conference. Dr. Winton took my arm. "If you'd been here as long as I've been here, you'd understand what I'm saying."

I nodded, conceding his superiority. He led me to one side, now adopting the manner of a very clever politician. "We *do* have a problem, though," he said. "I feel certain that we'll be able to release her very soon."

Release her? I began to understand. An early release would be the state's way of apologizing for the beating. Whether she was ready for the release or not.

Winton went on. "My problem is that as far as I can see there's no one to whom I can release her into custody. It's a state law. The girls have to be turned over to someone willing to take the responsibility. Are you interested? It wouldn't be too much of a job. All you have to do is find her a place to live and some sort of employment."

No, I wasn't interested, and said as much. Hatter Fox as a lifelong avocation did not appeal.

He took my no and ignored it. "Well, we'll talk later," he said, patting me on the back. "I'd say that your job here is about over, Dr. Summer. You've made remarkable progress with her, and I want you to know we are all very grateful." Levering nodded his head in agreement. Even Rhinehart smiled her approval, and said something about putting me on a permanent payroll. I found myself surrounded by smiling faces, and I felt like a defeated warrior who has been given the laurel wreath. For losing a battle. As they were leaving, I did manage to say that I didn't think it would be advisable for Hatter to go back into the dining room.

No. They all agreed. From now on, she could take her meals in the infirmary. One small victory. Then they were gone. I stayed in the hall until Rhinehart returned after escorting them out. "You look like hell," she said. "I'll handle things this morning. You get some sleep."

No argument from me. And there was no need

to discuss with Rhinehart what had happened. Once, a long time ago, she must have known better. But the machinery of the institution had absorbed her. I felt that at least for the time being and in order to keep peace with her boss she was in complete agreement with everything that Winton had said.

I went to my room and stretched out on the bed. I realized that I had a major task ahead of me then. Somehow I would have to figure out a way to live with the knowledge that we had changed nothing in Hatter Fox. Nothing had been solved, or healed, or cured. She was merely posing on my recommendation in order to speed her exit from the reformatory. Perhaps her last honest emotion had been the day she'd screamed "bastard" at everyone in sight. Her reward for that honesty had been a mouth gag and a strait jacket. Now I suspected that every emotion had gone underground, locked safely out of sight of polite society. God alone knew when it would surface again, and who would bear the brunt of it, and who would pay the price.

March was an uneventful month. Hatter's bruises and cuts healed—at least the visible ones. Newly meek and cooperating, she pleased everyone, a picture of normalcy, efficient, obedient, courteous. In early March she was made a trustee, a gift from Winton to soothe his conscience. Every week-end she was off someplace, either with Rhinehart or me. In comparing notes with Rhinehart, however, I found it difficult to believe that we were speaking of the same girl. Rhinehart always gave me an account of a perfectly normal female who liked to go shopping and try on clothes, who enjoyed foot-long hot dogs, grilled-cheese sandwiches, and any movie that was fit to see. She said they giggled a lot and told dirty jokes that would shock even me.

And if I disbelieved Rhinehart's account of Saturday with Hatter, she was equally as disbelieving of my accounts: the somberness of Hatter; my feeling of the changes that came over her even before we'd left the front gate; the fear, perhaps dread, of what she'd find outside; the terrible dread of the return trip. I offered repeatedly to take her any place she wanted to go. But there was only one place she ever wanted to go with me, and that was back up to the mountain and out onto the rocky ledge. There we would sit, and I would watch her, something smoldering within her, her face alternately relaxed and taut. We took a picnic once, but she ate with little appetite. And once it rained, and I suggested that we leave, but she said no. So we sat there until we were drenched, Hatter staring out over the turbulence of clouds and mist, her eyes narrowed, a strong, too-rapid, clearly perceptible pulse in her right temple.

Rhinehart's explanation of the duality was simple. "She feels like doing different things with different people," she said. "She's fine, perfectly normal. Don't study her too closely. She's not a bug under a microscope."

One evening I invited Hatter to take a walk with me outside the building, a middle-of-the-week stretch. Anything to break the monotony. She said, "Yes, sir," but I couldn't tell whether or not she really wanted to go. She had a habit then of saying yes to anything and anyone.

Outside the air was humid and damp, though still cool, the sort of chill you don't notice right off. Hatter wore her customary uniform: bell-bottoms, shirt out, a dark sweater thrown over her shoulders at my insistence. There was no moon, so we stayed on the sidewalk and circled the entire institution twice. Without speaking. Experience had taught me that generally it was more profitable to let Hatter initiate the conversation. This night, however, I had one or two things on my mind, and as we passed the administration building for the third time, I broke the silence.

"What do you plan to do when you leave here?" I asked.

She stopped walking. I looked back at her, hands shoved in her pockets, her face obscured in shadows. "What do you mean?" she asked, as innocently as though she hadn't heard the question.

I·repeated it with elaboration. "Winton says it could be any time now. Some board has to pass on it, but he says he doesn't think there will be any difficulty. He and I wonder if you have any plans."

Slowly she started walking again, head down. "Leave here? For good, you mean?"

"For good."

She seemed to think on this for a few steps farther. She shook her head slowly. "I don't know."

"You're not disappointed that you'll be leaving, are you? I thought it was what you'd wanted."

"It is."

"Then you've got to make some plans. Are there any relatives that you know of, someone who would be willing to take responsi—"

"No."

Subject closed. She walked more rapidly now, head still down. I thought of a string of possibilities, and tried them all. "School. Are you interested in going to school? You're bright. You might enjoy it."

She gave me an are-you-kidding look. I tried again. "Then a job," I suggested.

"Doing what?"

"I don't know, Hatter. You've got to help yourself. And soon. That's one of the requirements of the board. You have to have plans when you leave here, a goal, something you're going to do."

"Why?"

It seemed an incredibly stupid question, and she sounded incredibly stupid asking it. I said as much. "You shouldn't have to ask that, and I shouldn't have to answer it."

She seemed stung by the reprimand. Sulking set in. We walked in silence past the guest cottages at the rear of the institution. I remembered the night I'd spent there, the agony and humiliation I'd found the following day in the solitary-confinement cell. My attitude softened as I realized that I was as guilty as the others in viewing Hatter as whole and healed. She would never be whole, and there was still considerable doubt in my mind that we had helped her to solve any of her problems. "Look, let's sit down," I suggested, seeing the benches close by the visitor's gate.

She followed me somewhat reluctantly to a nearby bench. It was stone, cold and damp. There were halos of fog around the spotlights that encircled the institution, and ground fog was beginning to creep in around the bushes and shrubs. She stretched out her legs and leaned back and looked up at the sky.

"Clouds are moving," she said. "No stars."

"You've done very well the last few weeks," I said, trying to draw her back to the subject at hand.

"Look up there. Look how fast they're moving."

"Winton is pleased with your progress."

"Wind's from the south. Feel it?"

"Has it been difficult for you, cooperating?"

"Season of green grass. Time soon to take the sheep out to pasture."

"Do you feel changed at all?"

"Did I ever tell you about the Sing we had when the old woman died? Lasted for four days. Stupid Indians. Thought they could sing away her dying. Indians are really stupid, you know?"

"Does that include you?"

"Most of all me."

"Why?"

"I got myself put in a place like this, didn't I?"

"But you were smart enough to know what you had to do to get yourself out."

"I'll be back. Might as well stay here. I'll be back. Here, or someplace else."

"Then I can only assume that you enjoy being locked up."

"No!" Her reaction was strong and angry. She

leaned forward then, holding her head in her hands. "Summer," she asked, "what am I going to do?" Her voice was muffled coming through the confinement of hands.

"I'd say that's up to you."

She looked at me, a curious expression on her face. "I wish you weren't a white man."

"Why? What does that have to do with anything?"

"Maybe you'd understand."

"What is it that I'm not understanding? Try me."

She stood up, took a few aimless steps, came back to the bench, and sat with her legs tucked beneath her. "Who stays back there?" she asked, pointing toward the cottages, and clearly changing the subject.

"Guests, relatives, people who come to visit the inmates."

She stared over her shoulder at the outlines of the cottages. "Why do white people live in bricks?" she asked.

At best, the question seemed beside the point. "I don't know," I sighed. "To keep warm, I suppose, or cool. Whatever."

"A hogan's warmer. And cooler," she boasted.

"Then you're ahead of us. You'll have to teach us."

"Are you a Christian, Summer?"

"What do you mean?"

"Do you believe in your god?"

"In a way, I suppose."

"Old Shitworth used to tell us that anyone who didn't believe in the god would be burned in hell after he died. Is that true?"

"Depends upon what you want to believe."

"Do you believe?"

"I don't know."

She giggled. "You're not a very good white man. Old Shitworth would have strung you up right away." Her giggle faded. "I'm not a very good Indian, either. The old woman used to talk to me, and all I remember are some names: Changing Woman, Monster Slayer, Child of the Water, Reared-Within-the-Earth. The old woman believed, and those Indian kids at the university believe. But I don't. Never have."

There was a certain pride in her voice as she confessed to her disbelief. She continued, "People who believe don't like people who don't believe. I don't look very much like an Indian, do I, Summer? I used to wear real white powder and I didn't look Indian at all. Funny, sometimes it pays to look Indian, and sometimes it doesn't."

"You are what you are," I said, too patly. "Nothing can change that."

"Big joke," she laughed derisively. "Every time I act like an Indian, I get into trouble. When I act like a white person, I'm okay."

"What are you now? At this moment? White or Indian?"

She stared at her hands in her lap. "Neither. Nothing." Then she asked, "You remember that kid who cut his wrists back in Santa Fe? He was Indian. Navajo. When they arrested us that night, he cried all the way to the jail, just like a little kid. He was so scared. He threw up in the back of the police truck. He begged them not to lock the cell door. But they did. And he sat down by the back wall, and he cut one wrist, and then he cut the other. He was Indian. Navajo."

She drew a long, ragged breath as she remembered the night. "Then you came," she added. "But it was too late. I hated your guts then."

"Why? I only wanted to help."

"I thought you were going to make him live. Like you've made me live. He didn't want that. You were too late anyway."

The fog was growing thicker. I could scarcely see the back wall of the institution. Everything about us was all but obscured behind gray rolling dampness. I remembered the jail cell, the kid bleeding to death as well as she did. Also the stabbing, the penetration of the knife. I thought about mentioning it, but decided against it.

She must have been thinking about the same thing. "I was as scared as the kid," she admitted. "But not Indian enough to kill myself. And it was my knife. So I tried to kill you instead. I'm sorry."

The mood, the conversation, the fog—everything seemed so far removed from the brightness and promise of a fresh tomorrow. The purpose of the walk had been to discuss her future. But the past was too powerful. I suggested that we return to the infirmary. Obedient to the end, she followed me through the fog, back around to the front of the building. As we were going up the steps, she apologized again.

"Summer, I said I was sorry. Didn't you hear me?"

"I heard. It's over, so just forget it."

"You haven't forgotten it."

"You're the one who brought it up. I had hoped that we might talk about your future."

"What's to talk about?" she asked, her voice suddenly hard and flippant. "I'll go with you back to Santa Fe. What else? I'd be dead now if it weren't for you. You saved me. Now I'm your responsibility."

"Now wait a minute!"

She was at the top of the steps now, looking angrily down at me. "Don't worry, Summer. I won't bug you. I can find a job. I know the pueblos better than anyone. I can get a job on a sightseeing bus or in one of those stupid souvenir shops. And if that doesn't work, I can always squat in the Plaza with the other Indians and sell trinkets. You can walk by with your white friends and point to me and say, 'There! That's the one I saved.'"

"Hatter!"

But she was gone. She ran through the front door and slammed it behind her. I was left on the steps in the fog, amazed by her outburst. She was *not* my responsibility. My intention from the beginning had been

to help her, not adopt her. The thought of taking her
back to Santa Fe was a chilling one. I had my own
work to do, my own life. I could not and would not
be her keeper.

I went into the hallway and found her waiting at
the first locked door. I had keys. She had none. She
said nothing to me. I said nothing to her. What was
there to say? She was not ready to be released. And
that would be my recommendation to Winton. She went
directly to her room, and I went to Rhinehart's apartment in need of a sympathetic ear and confirmation
that I was right.

I got neither. I told her of our conversation,
and the last outburst on the front steps, the suggestion of Hatter's that she now was my responsibility.

Rhinehart listened closely. When I had finished
talking, she said, "Why not you? There's no one else."

"What do you mean, there's no one else?" I demanded. "And how long does it go on? I hoped to help
her, see her treated decently, see her settled someplace. And that's all."

Rhinehart shook her head. "You can finish things
like an inventory, Summer, and say 'There, that's
done.' But you can't do that with a human life. Besides, how would it hurt you to help her find a job, a
place to live, look in on her now and then?"

Again I demanded, "For how long?"

"For as long as she needs you."

"That's a rather one-sided arrangement, isn't
it?"

"Yes. Lots of things are one-sided. You're not as
smart as I thought you were. Besides, she's right in a
way. You *did* save her life. Now what do you have in
mind for her?"

"Anything she wants, just as long as it doesn't involve me."

"You don't mean that. Why did you bother coming down here at all, if you mean that? She could have
been safely locked up in a mental hospital by now,
drugged for life and out of your hair. But you

wouldn't permit that. Then what will you permit? I warned you a long time ago what you were getting yourself into. You seemed willing then. She's not a pet animal, Summer. She may need your care and attention for a number of years."

"Then why can't she stay here, with you? She hasn't changed, Rhinehart, not really. And you know it. She's as confused and ill as the day she entered this place."

"I know. But Winton wants her out. While she's still standing upright. That way it won't be a blotch on his record. You're stuck, Summer, whether you like it or not."

There was a finality in what she said. I couldn't explain my feelings to her. I couldn't even explain them to myself. I resented my predicament, but still, curiously, was concerned with Hatter's welfare, still stood in awe of what she had survived. But not enough to sign over my whole life in a commitment to her. Surprise. I was merely human. Clay. Self-serving. Human to the core.

Nothing was solved. Nothing was going to be solved that night. I went to bed feeling that I had dug my own grave. Hatter Fox was an albatross. I had willingly stuck out my neck and she had been dropped around it.

To the best of my recollection, we passed the month of April without saying half a dozen words to each other. The confinement of the institution was beginning to get to me, the constant company of sick and suffering females. In spite of the imprisonment and the routine, I always managed to be busy every week-end so that Rhinehart was forced to take Hatter into town. After a couple of week-ends, Hatter announced that she didn't want to go anymore, and she took to sitting in her room all day Saturday and Sunday, seeing no one, saying nothing, as withdrawn as the first day I'd seen her. I felt sorry for her, in spite of everything. But what more was I supposed to do?

Taken altogether. April was a lousy month. Several times, I considered leaving quietly, without telling her, at midnight. But I couldn't bring myself to do that. I had received a couple of letters from the Bureau of Indian Affairs, wondering when my job at the institution would be completed, the quietly hysterical letters of an overworked and understaffed governmental agency. My landlady from the trailer park tracked me down and said that I had a stack of mail and that there had been several telephone calls for me. I thought of my friends in Taos, and I missed them. There were green shoots on the trees outside the barred windows, and days of warm sun and high blue skies. At times I felt as though I were the one who had been ill and imprisoned, and now I was the one about to be released. I knew that as far as the formalities were concerned, I could leave at any time. I think Rhinehart halfway expected it of me. She was always checking my schedule, bringing coffee to my room in the morning, as though she was surprised to still see me there.

And then there was Hatter. Always Hatter. It had been over a month since I'd seen any expression at all on her face. At some point she stopped talking even to Rhinehart, although she still muttered, "Good morning, sir," to Winton or Levering if either happened to come snooping around. And it seemed as though one or the other was always there, wondering what we were going to do, informing me that the state could not support her forever. I agreed, and told them I was certain that they would work something out.

I had set myself a deadline, the first of May. That was to be the date of my exit from the world of locked doors and gang assaults, of dog pens and solitary-confinement cells, back into the world of scotch and sodas, sirloin steaks, colors and easy chairs. I had told everyone I was leaving. Everyone except Hatter.

Two days before my departure, Winton called

me into his office. He shook my hand warmly, and again thanked me for a job well done.

"I did nothing," I said, in perfect honesty.

He told me not to be modest and told me that things had worked out all the way around. He smiled broadly. "We have Hatter taken care of."

"What do you mean?"

"This morning I contacted the Good Hope Orphanage in town. As luck would have it, they have an opening. Of course they can only keep her a few months, until she's eighteen. And there's no maximum security, but I assured them that she didn't need security."

"An orphange?" I repeated.

"They'll take care of her, perhaps even help her find a job. They're coming for her on Friday."

Friday. May first. So, we'd be leaving at the same time. I was relieved to learn that she had a place to go. The state exercised certain controls over orphanages; surely it wouldn't be too bad. There would be some supervision, at least more than I could give her. Yes, it would work out for the best after all.

Winton again shook my hand, and invited me not to hesitate to call on him for personal or professional recommendations. Anything. I think the man was happy to be getting rid of both of us.

The word traveled fast. Apparently after I'd left Winton's office, he'd called Rhinehart and told her to have Hatter ready to leave on Friday. And he told her the destination.

When I returned to the infirmary, Rhinehart was standing in the doorway of her apartment, as grim as I'd ever seen her. She motioned me inside with a jerk of her head. She closed the door and seemed to be making a conscious effort to keep her voice down.

"Do you have any idea where you're sending her?" she hissed.

"Now wait a minute. I'm not sending her anyplace. Winton's doing the—"

"Do you have any idea where you're sending her?" she repeated. "That place is a cesspool of filth and disease, always overcrowded, and run by—"

"I said wait a minute. I am not sending her anyplace, and besides the state wouldn't permit conditions such as—"

"The state doesn't own it, Summer. It's run by a family, three brothers and a sister, all mentally retarded and in need of institutional care themselves. The state has been trying to close it for years. Now, you listen to me. You must not send her there."

I was trying hard to be patient. "Rhinehart, I said before, I'm not sending her anyplace. And if the state's been trying to close it, why haven't they?"

"Because it's ninety percent Mexican and Indian. No one wants those kids. There's no place else to send them. Oh, for God's sake, Summer, send her back to Claude, or put her on the streets, kill her, anything. At least give her a chance."

She was sincerely pleading. I wasn't quite ready to believe everything she had said, nor was I ready to disbelieve. "If Winton says it's all right—" I began.

"Winton wants to get rid of her, same as you."

"Damn it, Rhinehart, get off my back. If they say they've worked out a solution, that's good enough for me."

I didn't particularly like the way she looked at me. In truth, I didn't like much of anything then. But it was only a matter of time. Twenty-four hours and I'd be gone.

The night before we both were to leave, I went to Hatter's room. I had postponed it as long as possible. She was packing, if that's what you could call rolling up a couple of shirts and bell-bottoms, and stuffing them into a brown shopping bag.

I watched her for a few moments, and tried to be as gentle as possible. "This isn't the last time we'll be seeing one another, Hatter. I'll be in Santa Fe if you need me."

No answer.

"Things will work out. You'll see. This is for the best."

No answer.

She had changed again. The new neatness had faded and had been replaced with the old messy, dishevelled hair. And the old silence was back, total withdrawal, not really ignoring me, simply not hearing me. I tried again. "Hatter, there is no other way," I began, pleading. "I'm not equipped to . . . You'll be better off, I promise."

She continued to stash items in the shopping bag, not seeing, not hearing.

"Look, I'll come down and visit you. We can go back out on the side of the mountain."

Nothing. It was pointless. She was as unresponding, as uncaring as she had been the first time I'd seen her in Santa Fe. She was beyond help. Perhaps she had always been beyond help. The months I'd spent in "constructive rehabilitation" had been at best a joke, at worst a delusion.

I said good night, said I'd see her again in the morning. Then there was nothing more to say.

Rhinehart, too, was very busy. Doing nothing. "No time to talk, Summer," she snapped, swishing a mop over the floor of the examining room, a job that Hatter had done two hours earlier.

I went to my room, threw my things into the suitcase, and tried very hard to make my mind a blank. Guilt, failure—these were strong emotions. I sat on the bed and tried to examine in a precise and clinical manner my feelings, the reasons for my decision. First, how would it look for me to be responsible for a seventeen-year-old girl? The world would not know, nor would it care to know, the specifics of her painful wounds. She looked all right on the surface, nothing was visibly bleeding or bandaged. To try to convince them that it was a doctor-patient relationship would be absurd. It also would be absurd to try to convince them that it was merely a human relationship—one needing, the other giving. There would be talk, rumors, gossip. It would not be good for her. Or me. Second, there would be intervals, long intervals sometimes, when I'd be gone from Santa Fe, making the rounds of the reservations. What would she do then? She would be my responsibility. I would be held accountable for everything. Third, there was the matter of my own life, obligations to myself above and beyond the professional ones. I tried to imagine Hatter in the kinky artistic society of Taos, the all-male gatherings around the La Cocina Bar. No, it wouldn't work. It was unfair of everyone to ask me to try to make it work. So! The debate was over. The matter was closed. I would check on her periodically, do what I could for her from a distance. And that was that.

Release generally follows resolve. But it didn't that night. I heard every sound, every toilet being flushed, the ticking of the clock, the restless rumblings of my own insomnia. During the sleepless night, my mind resurrected certain images: the gray-cold, dark-haired thing battering her head against the side of the dog pen, the corpse-like body strapped down, purple bruises on a dark, smooth upper leg, lacerations on breasts, handcuffs and bleeding wrists, children hanging suspended upside down from a low branch of a cottonwood tree. The mind is clever. Ultimately sleep came—such as it was.

When I awakened, the infirmary was empty. My watch said 10:00 A.M. I'd overslept. Good. Perhaps she had already left. Fate owed me a favor. I dressed quickly and closed the suitcase, and felt my spirits lift as I discovered Rhinehart too was gone. I'd wanted to say goodbye, but maybe this was for the best. I had only to turn in my keys and I'd be finished with the place. Forever.

All the matrons gave me cheery goodbyes. Curious, how warmth is saved for the moment of departure. But I thanked them and moved on with a pronounced and buoyant feeling that I was almost home free.

I turned the corner into the front hall of the administration building. And saw them. They were seated on one of the long benches that ran parallel to the wall: Hatter, sitting erect, feet primly together, hands folded in her lap, the brown shopping bag on the floor beside her, and Rhinehart, hovering close beside Hatter and dabbing continuously at her eyes.

I handed the keys to the secretary at the front desk, took a deep breath, and walked to the bench. Rhinehart saw me and blew her nose. Hatter continued to stare straight ahead. As I stopped in front of her, her eyes seemed to be focused on my belt buckle.

"I'm glad I got to see you again," I said. "Please remember what I said. I'll call you. Next week-end, if you wish. You'll get along just fine, Hatter. Please believe me."

Nothing. The dark eyes never wavered. There was on her face only the bleakness of resignation. And abandonment. She must have looked like this when she was waiting in the doorway of the hogan for someone to come.

I asked Rhinehart, "When are they coming?"

"Any minute," she said, and turned away.

"I want to thank you for everything you've done," I said. "I don't think I could have made it without you."

"Did nothing," she said, weeping visibly then.

"Rhinehart, look, I . . ." But I had nothing to say to either of them. I said goodbye again and received no reply. I shifted the suitcase to the other hand, stepped back and away, and started toward the front door and sunlight and fresh air. And freedom.

Just as I reached the bottom of the steps, a battered station wagon of ancient vintage rattled to a stop. A thin cadaverous man dressed in soiled overalls got out. He had a toothpick between his dried colorless lips, and a gray stubble of beard.

"Hey, Mister," he called out. "I'm here to pick up an Indian. Do you know where—"

"She's in there," I said, and started off in a run

around the side of the building toward the parking
lot. The jeep was a welcome sight. I had hoped to make
it safely out of the gate, but as I drew even with the
side of the building, I looked back toward the front
steps.

Rhinehart was hugging Hatter. The old man was
standing beside the back door of the station wagon,
waiting. The embrace over, Hatter started down the
steps, head erect, clutching the shopping bag in her
hand. At the bottom step she paused, as though considering the trap of the open car door and the old
man. She looked up at the high blue sky for a moment,
and in that instant, the old man reached out and
grabbed her arm and jerked her roughly toward
the open car door with such force that she dropped
the shopping bag. As she stopped to pick it up, he
jerked her again, and then using both hands forced
her into the back seat of the car. Rhinehart started
down the steps, protesting.

I gunned the motor of the jeep with every intention in the world of driving straight toward the front
gate. Instead, I turned left, heading back toward the
station wagon, burning rubber all the way. I slammed
on the brakes, left the motor running, and pushed the
old man back against the front door of the car. I
grabbed Hatter by the wrist with one hand, retrieved
the shopping bag with the other, and yelled up at
Rhinehart, "Tell Winton I've got her. We'll figure out
something."

Rhinehart's grin covered her entire face.

I shoved Hatter into the jeep, waved back at
Rhinehart, stepped on the accelerator, and sped
through the front gate, narrowly missing a linen supply truck that was just turning in. It was all a little
melodramatic except for the persistent voice inside
my head that asked, "What in hell have you done now?"

No answers, so I concentrated on the flow of
traffic and getting into the proper lane to turn north
to Santa Fe. Hatter was true to form. She said not a
word and remained in exactly the same position she

had landed in when I'd shoved her into the jeep, clutching the shopping bag, staring straight ahead.

Once on the highway, I settled the jeep into a safe sixty miles an hour, and began to think. Maybe it wasn't hopeless. I knew of a boarding house near the Plaza, run by a Mrs. Mack. I myself had stayed there during my first week in Santa Fe. It was clean and inexpensive, and Mrs. Mack, a widow, seemed to specialize in lost souls. So I would call Mrs. Mack the minute we reached Santa Fe. Then a job. It was May, the beginning of the four months of chaos known as the tourist season. Every other shop on the Plaza was a tourist trap. They all would need extra help. Most of the tourists came "to see the Indians." A full-blooded Navajo girl might not be such a liability—*if* she behaved herself. I could see no real problem there. So, then, it might work. I would do my part. Would she do hers?

I stopped at Chief Sitting Bull's Trading Post for gas and a coke. I asked Hatter if she wanted to get out. She shook her head, and stayed glued to the seat as though she were afraid to leave it. I recalled the morning several months earlier when I had fled the reformatory and the hopeless tragedy of Hatter Fox. That morning I had made it as far as this trading post. This time I had brought the tragedy with me.

I bought her a coke. She took a sip and handed it back as though she had had her portion, and must not take more than her share.

"Go ahead, finish it," I said.

"No, thank you." Her first words.

While the jeep was being serviced, I stayed close by her window. Something should be said. By someone. She was aware that I was staring at her, waiting for more words. Finally, without looking at me, she asked simply, "Why did you do it?"

"I don't know," I said, in all honesty. "Are you disappointed?"

She looked directly at me. "Oh no. I'll do good,

Summer, I promise," she said. "I'll do everything you ask me to do."

She sounded sincere. I believed her. I had no choice.

"Then let's not be so grim." I smiled, and handed her back the coke.

During the rest of the drive to Santa Fe, I informed her of my plans for her—the boarding house, the job. She agreed to everything, said she was good at making change, and she knew now how to keep things clean. With every passing mile, my fears diminished. As she relaxed beside me, I again had that good feeling of having done the right thing. The proof was sitting beside me, the newly alert, alive face, the dark eyes searching each new turn in the highway, reading aloud now and then the silly billboards, no longer clutching the shopping bag that held all her worldly possessions. One hand now held the empty coke bottle, the other continually pointed out for my benefit a cloud formation, new green on the side of a hill, a brown dog running across a freshly plowed field. It would work. It would have to work.

When we reached Santa Fe, we went directly to my trailer. Hatter seemed curious to know where I lived. Cobwebs had taken over, and layers of dust.

"It's looked better," I apologized.

I told her to wait in the trailer while I went to the front office. I picked up my mail, renewed acquaintances with my landlady, and placed a phone call to Mrs. Mack. Yes, she remembered me, yes, she had a single room, and no, she didn't mind the fact that Hatter was Indian and a reform-school graduate.

"We are all God's children, Dr. Summer," she said. Platitude or no, I could have kissed her through the receiver.

When I returned to the trailer, Hatter was cleaning. She had the small rugs out airing, had found the broom and was using it, had made my bed, and had tied up a bundle of soiled linens and placed it by the front door, all tasks she had learned in the infirmary. I was pleased, and told her I was pleased, although I made it clear that it wasn't necessary. Apparently it *was* necessary. Even though it was past lunchtime, nothing would do but that we stay and finish the job together.

We had a late lunch in a little café downtown on the Plaza, and sat on a bench in the sun and watched the beginnings of tourists. For my benefit, Hatter recalled the night she had been arrested in the company of others with explosives and drugs.

"They were bad people," she said somberly. "I thought they were my friends, but they weren't."

"You'll meet others, Hatter, bad people and friends. You'll have to learn to tell the difference."

"How?"

"By watching them closely and listening to what they say, and remembering what got you into trouble in the first place." I had made it sound so simple. I knew it wasn't that simple, and I think she knew it too. But sitting there in the sun, in perfect freedom, observing the harmless antics of other human beings, the matter of living seemed simple. Jail cells and locked doors, strait jackets and solitary confinement seemed so far away, seemed at best the remnants of a bad dream.

At sunset we drove out to a high hill overlooking Santa Fe—not as high or as dramatic as our mountain ledge in Albuquerque, but it seemed to suit her. The day that had had such a splintered beginning had a soft, almost melancholy conclusion.

She looked down at the lights of the town for a long time. She seemed preoccupied and worried.

"What if I can't find a job, Summer?" she asked. "What if they don't want me?"

"They'll want you," I reassured her. "Why shouldn't they want you?"

"You didn't."

"It wasn't that I didn't want you, Hatter. You

should know that by now. I just wasn't certain that it—"

"What?"

"—that it would be best for you. Under the circumstances."

"What do you mean?"

She was relentless, seemed to want to know the specifics of my momentary rejection. I couldn't give them to her. She seemed to read my silence, and tried to put me at ease. She smiled. "There have been times," she said, "when I didn't want certain people. I couldn't figure out how to get rid of them, either. Don't feel bad, Summer. I've never been able to figure out how to get rid of what I don't want, either."

Guilt then. I had to make her understand, even though I didn't understand myself.

"It wasn't that I didn't want you, Hatter, believe me."

"Then what?"

"I have my job here, and it keeps me very busy. I was afraid that—"

"I'd bother you?"

"Not bother, just—"

"Well, I won't bother you, I promise. I'll do good. Did they pay you money to come down to the reformatory?"

"No, not at first."

"Then later?"

"Yes."

"And I'll get paid money when I find my job?"

"Yes."

"Navajos use buttons for money. And sheep. They're stupid."

"I'm not so sure."

"I am. Summer, I don't ever again want to be locked up. Anyplace."

"I don't think you will be."

"If I am—" Even in shadows, her face was grim. Ancient memories. Destructive. "This isn't so bad, though," she went on, looking up at the night sky.

"No."

Then slowly she got on her knees and knelt before me where I was sitting on the side of the hill. "Thank you for helping me," she said simply. "Thank you, Summer."

I touched the side of her face, which before me in the darkness was so eager. "It's been my pleasure."

She nestled in under my arm, and I thought her stillness remarkable, as though she were holding her breath. And still more remarkable was the expression of peculiar tenderness and excitement with which, as she settled down, she said, "I'm not a bit afraid." And she pressed my hand to her lips.

In silence we sat on the hill in the darkness for too long. A peace beyond description. We drove back to town in silence. I deposited her in the capable hands of Mrs. Mack, and told her I'd come for her at nine the next morning. I watched her going up the stairs of the boarding house, and hoped she'd look back at me. But she didn't. On meeting Mrs. Mack, she had become shy again and now she followed behind the ample woman, eyes straight ahead, not wanting to do anything that might "cause them not to want her."

The clean trailer was waiting for me, the fresh bed. There were only mild and conquerable feelings of uneasiness as I dropped off to sleep. No wonder. It was my first night free of locked doors in several months. That was all. No deeper darker strugglings, no other reason for uneasiness. Just the natural fear of freedom. Plus the certainty that I had been pitched into the kind of crisis that had required of me the most elemental validation of my professed decencies. And I had measured up. That, and the remembered tenderness of Hatter.

The next morning she was waiting for me, brushed and scrubbed, sitting on the front steps in front of Mrs. Mack's. I saw her while I was still a good half a block away, and I thought, watching her, of the incredible distance we had come together. Again, I was pleased.

Yes, she had slept well; yes, Mrs. Mack was nice, although there were lots of crucifixes and black books around the parlor, and in a way, it reminded Hatter of Shitworth's mission school.

She held back as I opened the door of the jeep for her, as though worried. "I did something last night, Summer," she began. "There was a picture on the wall in my room of a man with thorns stuck all over his head. He was bleeding. Is that one of your gods?"

It was too early in the morning for a lecture on the divinity of Christ. "Yes," I replied. "In a way."

She shuddered. "What I did was, I took him down off the wall and hid him in the top drawer. Do you think anyone will mind?"

I laughed and reassured her they wouldn't. We had coffee and doughnuts in a small snack shop and headed toward the east side of the Plaza and the beginning of shops. On the way we passed the Palace of Governors, where squatting on the sidewalk were a few Indians who had gathered to sell their jewelry, their blankets spread with their wares. Hatter trailed behind me, watching. Some Indians looked up as we passed and gazed with curiosity at Hatter. She walked faster then, and moved to the street side as though to put me between her and the staring Indians. At the intersection, she stole a glance back.

"That's why we wanted to blow that place up," she whispered. "They shouldn't do that."

It was fairly obvious that she didn't like what she had seen, and I had the feeling that the other Indians knew who she was and didn't like her presence among them.

In the first half a dozen shops we drew blanks. Apparently they had all the help they needed. Number seven yielded results, although poor ones. It was a mock Indian trading post, run by a puckish troll of a man named Duncan with wispy white hair and feminine hands. I had seen him before around the Plaza, and he knew of me and seemed willing to accept my recommendation. His attitude toward Hatter was a little less than amiable, and he left the distinct impression that he was doing both of us a favor. During the entire interview, Hatter hung back self-consciously, her eyes never quite lifting more than three feet off the floor.

Mr. Duncan had two conditions. One, Hatter was to wear a costume, an Indian dress and headband which he would furnish, and two, she was never to go near the cash register. She would work from nine to five, six days a week, and he would pay her thirty-five dollars a week. I didn't like the business of the costume and neither did she. But at least it was a job. The matter was settled. She was to start right away. A woman clerk took her by the arm and led her off toward the rear of the shop to assist her with the costume. I waited out front, talking with Mr. Duncan about the shortage of water, the state of the economy, and the rise in welfare cases.

"I'm glad to see one of them who wants to work," he said, obviously referring to Hatter. "I'll treat her all right if she puts in an honest day's work."

I thanked him again and assured him that she wanted to work. At that moment Hatter reappeared from the back of the shop. She was wearing a shapeless dress of brown muslin, fringed, Pocahontas-style, and a beaded headband. The woman clerk presented her to the old man with pride. "She looks good, don't she? Takes a real one to do these outfits justice."

In truth, she looked terrible, and the stricken look on her face told me that she knew she looked terrible. The old man directed her toward a collection of Papago baskets and leatherwork on the far wall.

"This will be your department," he said. "Just answer their questions and bring their money to me. And let them know you're a real Indian. They really go for that."

Obediently, Hatter took her place near the far wall among the baskets and belts. She looked totally miserable.

I started out of the door, but made the mistake of looking back. I walked over to where she stood, facing the wall. "Try to make it work, Hatter," I whispered. "At least it's a beginning. And try to remember, it's just a job."

She nodded.

"I'll try to get back at five and we'll have a hamburger together."

Again she nodded.

"Are you crying?"

She shook her head. I couldn't tell if she was or wasn't. There wasn't a great deal I could do about it one way or the other. She had to have a job.

The bureau welcomed me back with open arms and congratulated me on the job I'd done at the reformatory. Apparently Winton had submitted a glowing report. The congratulations and welcome over, they shoved a handful of cases at me, pointed me in the direction of a sixty-year-old Navajo woman who was dying of tuberculosis, and told me to get to work.

It was after five thirty before I made it back to the trading post. A young man with long hair was on duty behind the cash register. He looked blank when I asked for Hatter Fox. Then he remembered.

"The Indian? Oh, she's gone. Left at five on the button. She did good, though. Even posed for some snapshots out front."

Gone? She'd probably walked back to the boarding house. And there I found her, sitting on the front steps exactly where I'd found her that morning. She looked tired, more vacant than usual, and said nothing as I sat down beside her.

"I'm sorry I'm late," I said. "Are you hungry?"

She shook her head.

"Did you eat lunch?"

She nodded. "I found a grocery store, run by an old Navajo. He was nice. He gave me some fruit."

"Do you want to go for a ride?"

She shook her head.

"Well, how did it go. Was it too bad?"

She shrugged.

I was trying, but obviously she wasn't. I was tired too, and hungry. "Come on, let's go get something to eat."

But she didn't move.

"What is it?" I asked. "Did something happen?"

She kept her eyes down. "Do I have to work there, Summer?"

"It's a job, Hatter. It may not be the best job in the world, but it's a job."

"They hate me."

"Who?"

"That old man. Everyone."

"That's not true. If he'd hated you, would he have given you a job?"

"Yes."

She wasn't making sense, and I was too tired to explore her nonsense. "Stick with it for a week," I begged. "Promise? If at the end of the week, you're still unhappy, we'll look some more. Come on, now, let's eat."

But she refused. She stood up and walked slowly away from me into the house. I should have gone after her. But I didn't. My uneasiness returned. I recalled my words to Rhinehart. *She hasn't changed, not really . . . Nothing about her has been solved, healed, or cured.* Unfortunately I was fresh out of missionary zeal. There was a limit to how far one person could be expected to accommodate another.

For the next few days, I managed to see her at least once a day for a brief interval. She was largely silent, wholly withdrawn, looking at me now and then as if I had betrayed her. I endured her looks, although it became increasingly difficult for me to see her or spend time with her. I found myself avoiding the Plaza, and merely called late at night to check with

Mrs. Mack. Yes, Hatter was always in. No, she had caused no trouble. Yes, she had gone to work. No problems.

When three cases came up near Taos, I jumped at the opportunity for a brief respite. I called my friend, the artist who made erotic sculpture out of junk, and told him to plan on having a houseguest for a few days. I tried to phone Hatter the night before I left, but Mrs. Mack told me she had gone to bed. No, I didn't want to awaken her. I'd only be gone for a few days. In a way, it would be a good test for her. I left the message with Mrs. Mack and hung up.

I was gone from Santa Fe for three days. I can't in all honesty say they were days of rejuvenation. Suffice it to say they were different. But my mind kept wandering back to Hatter, and finally on the fourth day I gave up all hope of relaxation and started home. I had a premonition of trouble. To expect Hatter to function as a mature, responsible adult during three days without me was perhaps too much too soon.

I arrived about noon and went directly to the trading post. The old man confirmed my fears; he told me that she hadn't been to work in three days. "What can you expect?" he called after me. "Try to do them a favor and look what happens. They're no good, not one of them. Never have been. Never will be."

Mrs. Mack's was the next stop. No, Hatter wasn't in her room, hadn't been there for three nights. Mrs. Mack seemed concerned. "She's very troubled, Dr. Summer. I tried to talk to her, but she wouldn't say a word. You can't help someone if they won't talk to you."

Tell me about it, I thought.

My uneasiness mounted as I explored several other haunts around the Plaza, the café where we ate sometimes, the coffee shop, the small grocery store run by the old Navajo. No, no one had seen Hatter.

Then there was nothing else to do. I went to the police station to file a report. There was a new man

on the desk. I told him what I'd come for and started
to give him a description, when suddenly he grinned.
"Oh, that one. We got her upstairs. Picked her up
three days ago for loitering and panhandling." He
looked bewildered. "Is she yours?"

"No. She's in my custody. What do I have to do to
get her out?"

"Sign this. And you better keep a closer eye on
her. Her kind spells nothing but trouble."

I signed the form. About twenty minutes later, a
matron brought down a very dirty, but very
pleased-looking Hatter. She grinned when she saw me,
and she called out a cherry. " 'Bye," to the desk
sergeant. She followed me out of the front door, as
amiable and good-natured as I'd seen her in a long
time.

"I'm starved," she announced, as she crawled into the jeep.

But I had other things on my mind. "Why?" I
asked.

"Why what?" She was filthy, had lost her shoes
someplace, and smelled like a garbage dump.

"Why were you panhandling?"

"I was broke."

"Why did you quit the job?"

"Oh, come on, Summer, let's eat first, and talk
later."

"We'll talk now."

She slumped down in the seat and began twisting
a strand of her hair around her finger. "I told you
they hated me," she mumbled. "They fired me."

"They didn't fire you. I checked. You just quit.
Now why?"

"I don't know why." She was mad, and I was
madder.

"Since you quit," I said, "I assume you have
something else in mind. Another job?"

"I'll find something. And I don't need your help."

"Like you didn't need my help today? I can only

assume that you enjoy that jail, Hatter. You end up there with incredible regularity."

"There were other kids panhandling, Summer," she protested, "a whole damn street full of them. But the cops only picked me up. They just turned their backs on the others, the white kids. It was just me. They have it in for me."

"That's not true."

She started to get out of the jeep. But I grabbed her and pulled her back. "You're not going anyplace," I said. "Not for a while. You promised that you'd try to make it work."

"I did try."

"But not very hard."

"Summer, I couldn't wear that stupid dress. I tried to call you three nights ago, but you were gone. I looked all over for you, even walked out to your trailer. But I couldn't find you." At some point her anger and pleading had turned predictably to tears. "And I couldn't go back to that store. I did try. I'm sorry. I was panhandling to get enough money to get to Taos. I didn't think you'd want me to hitch, and I just wanted to find you. But they picked me up. I couldn't put on that dress any more. I'm sorry. I'm really sorry."

She was crying then. I couldn't tell if it was a pose or not. The image of her walking the ten miles out to the trailer and back was a sharp one. Partly it was my fault. If I had been there. But I couldn't be there for the rest of her life.

I watched her crying for a few moments, then handed her a handkerchief. I felt trapped. I envisioned a future of bailing her out, cleaning her up, making apologies, holding my breath, hoping that things would work out, knowing somehow they never would.

"Come on," I said finally. "Crying does no good." How was I to know that it did no good? It just seemed embarrassing and futile. I drove to the boarding house, told her to get cleaned up and we'd go eat.

While Hatter was upstairs, I talked with Mrs. Mack, told her what had happened. She seemed more than sympathetic, said she knew the "old coot" who ran the trading post, and said she didn't blame Hatter for walking out. She said she had a friend, a gallery owner on Canyon Road who had been looking for summer help. She wondered . . .

It was worth a try. She gave me the name and address. I thanked her, grateful for all her help. Then I looked up to see a freshly scrubbed, slightly red-eyed Hatter coming down the steps.

We celebrated my return and her release from jail with a good steak. Hatter was drearily remorseful for a while, at her submissive, martyred worst. But the meal was good—her first, I suspected, in several days—and she ate heartily and finally threw off the martyred pose and began to look eagerly around her.

"Can we come here again sometime?" she asked.

"You can pay the next time."

"When I'm with you, people look at me in a different way."

"No one's looking at you."

"The waiter was."

"How was he looking at you?"

"Like he didn't like me, but he'd like me for a while as long as I was with you."

"It's all in your mind."

"No." She might have elaborated on this, but the food was more important.

"When was the last time you ate?" I asked.

"What were you doing in Taos?" she countered, ignoring the question.

"Seeing some cases. And some friends."

"Did you have fun?"

"I guess."

"Do you have a girl friend up there?"

"No."

"Anywhere?"

"No."

"Can I have your potato?" she asked.

I scraped everything on my plate off onto hers, and tried to follow the antics of her mind.

She went on, mouth full. "You ought to have a girl friend, Summer. Even a male river needs a female river."

"I manage."

"I could be it, if you'd let me."

"All right."

She looked up, surprised, and for once stopped eating. "Do you want me to sleep with you?"

I smiled. "No."

"Why not? Because I've been a prostitute?"

"That has nothing to do with it."

"I cause you a lot of trouble, don't I?"

"Sometimes."

"Summer, I couldn't work at that store any longer."

"That's over. Tomorrow we'll find someplace else." I told her about Mrs. Mack's friend, the gallery owner. "Are you interested?"

She shrugged. "Sure. Why not? As long as I can wear my own clothes, and no one wants to take my picture."

We finished the meal and walked out to the jeep. It was dark, cool, still damp from an afternoon rain. She walked easily beside me.

"Summer," she said, "I wish I hadn't been a prostitute. I really wish I hadn't done that. That part of me was bad."

"It's over."

"I'll do better. I promise. You'll see. I just don't want to wear a costume, or have my picture taken. I'm not an animal, or a freak, or a mascot."

The gallery owner was a widow, small, birdlike, who peered at us over the rims of her glasses, disapproving. "I really wasn't expecting an Indian." She smiled. "I need someone up front to meet the patrons when I'm not here. Make a good appearance, you understand. I really don't think—"

Neither did I. I thanked her and tried not to look at Hatter's face, and wished that Mrs. Mack had somehow spread the word about God's children.

During the next two days, we must have answered twenty want ads. Nothing. Everything was against her: what she was, the fact that she was not skilled and could do nothing, and the fact that she had a police record and had spent time in the reformatory. Hatter didn't seem terribly upset over her lack of employment. With every no we received, she looked at me as though to say, "See?"

Then one day when I thought our run of bad luck would never end, it did, and in a most obvious and simple way, and due solely to Hatter's efforts. Every morning on our way to the Plaza, we had passed the small grocery store that Hatter admired so much. Every morning she had to stop to touch the fruit, exclaim over the pyramids of oranges and apples. On this morning I saw the proprietor, a Navajo, out front polishing apples. He was an old man, very dignified in his white apron. He bobbed his head and grinned at Hatter, then me. He presented Hatter with a ripe red apple. She took it, smiling, and told him directly, "This is where I'd like to work."

And he replied, as directly as though he had been waiting for her, "And I need help." They grinned at each other and included me in the grin. And Hatter was at last employed. At least for the time being.

She wore a long white apron which seemed to suit her, and every morning I met her in front of the grocery store, polishing and arranging the fresh produce of the day. She appeared to be as relaxed and contented as I'd ever seen her. No longer did she look at me as if I'd betrayed her. And she took great delight in teasing me, reminding me over and over again that she had found her own job, that she didn't need my help. Not always.

I found that again I actually looked forward to meeting her each evening in the Plaza. The sight of her running across the street, dodging tourists and traffic, her eyes focused only on me, was a good one. She fit nicely under my arm and together we made our way to the café where, laughing, she told me about the events of the day, the silliness of white customers, the way she had to scold them for pinching the fruit, the beauty of a fresh shipment of green avocados.

The attachment I felt to Hatter precluded every need of intimate relations with others. Among all my acquaintances, I had not one friend save Hatter. We shared good silences and good dinners. We shared long drives out into the desert. We shared stories of the past, mine of New England and snow, hers of hogans and arroyos.

At times it was difficult for both of us to connect and reconcile the past with this new present. There still were days when she lapsed back into the old sullen Hatter, when she thought it her duty to point out the defects in others and the world. And the future was still an immense and unanswerable question. How long would she be content merely to work in the store, sorting produce? How long before old demons and ghosts returned to haunt her?

One night we walked late around the Plaza enjoying the emptiness of the streets and sidewalks, finally selecting our bench out of all the available ones. She sat quietly beside me, talked out, content merely to focus on streetlights, and an occasional passing car. Finally with a trace of a smile of self-pity for herself, she said, "I may not be much, Summer, but I know good fruit when I see it."

"And that's something," I said. "More than I know."

She did not speak.

"What is it?" I urged.

"I'm afraid," she said, "that you'll go away. I can do more than sort oranges. I'm smarter than that. I don't want to bother you, but please don't go away."

I tried to reassure her, and declared that I had not the slightest intention of going away. "Hatter, why do you worry yourself so?" I said, taking her hand.

"Because the only time you really pay attention to me is when I'm in trouble. When I'm good, you go away."

"That's not true," I protested, "or at least I'll try not to make it true."

And instantly her despairing jealousy changed to a despairing display of tenderness. She took my arm as though she intended never to let go.

Then there was a major accomplishment ahead of us. Her first paycheck. It was a Monday. We had talked, or rather *I* had talked at length of banks and savings accounts, trying to impress upon her the need to plan for a future that included more than sorting oranges.

We were to meet beside our bench in the Plaza at noon, and together we would take her first paycheck and open a bank account in her name. It was a momentous occasion—more, I suspected, for me than for her. She looked slightly bored by my lectures on interest rates and checkbooks, the importance of having money in the bank.

At noon I was at the appointed spot. But she wasn't. I waited, paced, watched closely the grocery store across the street. Traffic was heavy, and the Plaza was crowded with milling tourists. It was unseasonably hot and the sun was directly overhead. No sign of her. I waited some more and was beginning to lose patience. At one thirty I myself had an appointment with the parents of a little Mexican boy who needed to have his tonsils out. So much effort was expended in merely convincing them that something needed to be done.

Where was she? We had only a limited time to eat and get to the bank. Why couldn't she be prompt, at least once? Finally I saw her, running too fast across the busy street, hair flying. Her appearance pleased me, in spite of my impatience, her face bright and brightening still more as she drew near. She seemed to be very excited about something, and started talking while she was still a distance away.

"Summer," she cried, "I have the day off tomorrow! The whole day. He told me so because I had done such good work. He told me that I could take anything I wanted in the store and that we could go up into the mountains and have a picnic. Like we did once at the reformatory. Remember? The whole day, Summer, and I earned it."

She danced around me, as pleased as I had ever seen her. The fact that she had worked and earned the time off was of enormous satisfaction to her. She repeated the good news in variation, recounting exactly what we would do, and what we would take, and where we would go, walking around and around me, skipping, chanting, childlike, "I have the day off, the whole day off, I have the day off."

Of course I was pleased, and told her so, and then tried to remind her of the purpose of our meeting. "I'll see if I can arrange it for tomorrow," I said. "Now what about the check?"

"*See* if you can arrange it?" she repeated, stunned. "You *have* to arrange it. I've never earned a day off before. You have to come with me. Don't say you'll see, Summer. Say yes, we'll go."

"It's not that simple, Hatter, but I said I'd try. Now the check. Do you——"

"You mean you might not——"

I was losing more patience. "I said I'd try. Now let's forget the day off and get on with——"

"Forget it?"

"Hatter, please." I raised my voice in anger. People passing by stopped and looked at us. I was embarrassed for both of us. "Your paycheck," I said again, lowering my voice, trying not to look at the hurt in her face. "Do you have it?"

She turned away and muttered something. I couldn't hear. "What did you say?"

"I said I thought you would be pleased."

"I am pleased. But we were going to the bank, remember? You were to be paid today. Were you?"

"Yes."

"Then the check. Where is it?"

She continued to look at me as though I had mortally wounded her, all the time fishing through her pockets. The search revealed exactly nothing. She looked at me, bewildered. "I had it," she explained. "He gave it to me."

"Then where is it?"

"I don't know. I was so excited when he told me about the day—"

"Oh, for God's sake, Hatter, you haven't lost it?"

"I don't know." She searched again through her pockets, looked vaguely about on the ground. She kept repeating mindlessly, "I had it. He gave it to me, but then he told me that I could have the day—"

She was making aimless circles about the bench, muttering over and over again that she had had it once, but didn't seem to have it now. She was no more concerned than if she had misplaced a package of cigarettes. She turned blithely back to me and said, "Oh well, I'll find it later. Let's talk about tomorrow."

I exploded. "We will not talk about tomorrow, Hatter. Tomorrow is off You can't go about losing a paycheck. You worked hard for that money. We were going to open an account, remember? I can't go on forever paying your rent and buying your food. You have to learn how to be independent. The job is your responsibility, and the money earned from that job is your responsibility."

She protested. "It was just a piece of paper, Summer, just a silly piece of—"

"It was more than paper. Don't be so stupid, Hatter. You know better, and I know you know better." I was yelling at her, aware but not caring about the little crowd of curious onlookers. For once she seemed to be the one feeling embarrassment.

"Don't, Summer, please."

But she had to learn, she had to understand that she was responsible for certain things. I went on, full voice. "Now, you are going to go right back to the store, and you are not going to come back until you find that check. I don't care how long it takes, or where you have to look. I don't want to see you again until you have that check in your hand. Do you understand?"

"What about lunch?"

"Forget lunch."

"What about tomorrow?"

"Forget tomorrow. We're not going anyplace until we have that check deposited in the bank."

There was a change in her face then that I'd never seen before, the change from earthly to unearthly that is seen in the face of the dead. She was fighting to keep back the tears, too proud to let the onlookers see that she was crying. I saw the tears, though, and at that moment was uncaring. She had to be taught, as a child is taught. She had to learn. She had to learn. I couldn't be there for the rest of her life.

Suddenly she turned and ran back through the crowds, crossing the busy street without looking, colliding with people, uncaring. She was hopeless. What was so difficult to understand? Why couldn't she grasp the simple conception that it takes money to live, to maintain a decent standard of living; that without money she would be forced back into panhandling, prostitution, or worse? That was all I wanted to teach her. Why was it so impossible for her to learn?

The noises around me increased as, left with the burden of my anger, I tried to calm myself, tried to remind myself that I must be patient with her. At times I had so much hope for her, and at other times nothing. Again I felt trapped. What was so difficult about holding onto a paycheck the distance of one street?

And what was so important to her about a day off? She'd had days off, hundreds of them.

All around me was shouting and talking and laughter. Down the street I heard a large tourist bus gun its motor, as though impatient. Why was the driver so annoyed? He had no job compared to my task. And where did they think they were going, the tourists, to what new and unglimpsed sight?

And where was she? She had had more than enough time to return to the store, check the counter, the floor, the boxes of apples. Either the check was there, or it wasn't.

Then I saw her, emerging from the darkness of the store, waving in her hand a small white piece of paper. The lost or misplaced check. At last she had retrieved it. She stood on the curb and waved it at me, grinning broadly, still waving the check, not looking. I heard the bus again, heard the motor turn over, heard the release of air brakes. She wasn't looking, she wasn't concerned with anything but me and the small piece of paper in her hand. I called out above the traffic noises, called her name twice, warning her. But she wasn't looking, she wasn't watching. I shouted again. The bus accelerated to full speed.

I knew before it happened that it was going to happen. With a rapid light step she went down to the curb, behind a parked car. She still wasn't looking. Look, Hatter, for God's sake.

She seemed to glance down toward the lower part of the approaching bus and the wheels rapidly moving closer, as though trying to measure the speed of the bus and her chances of making it across the street first. Look, Hatter, look, for God's sake, look!

She was struck halfway between the front wheels which drew level with her as she darted out. Too late. The huge and merciless thing struck her and dragged her down on her back. I heard screams then, the sound of air brakes too late, shouts for help. Suddenly a feeling such as I have never known before rose up within me. Suddenly a darkness covered everything.

Then I was running, screaming her name, pushing through the crowds which had gathered within the instant. And exactly at the moment I saw her, crumpled on the pavement, half under the bus, at exactly that moment her hand lifted with the small piece of paper, as though she would rise immediately. But there was no more movement. I dropped to my knees. Someone cried out for help. And the light by which she had envisioned the whole and virgin world flickered and was extinguished.

In her hand was the check. For $41.28.

She died instantly. That's what the priest told me. Father Duval. The same man who had visited me in the hospital and urged me not to press charges against Hatter Fox. He told me that he had followed both of us with interest and hope during the past year. And he was sorry, so very sorry.

He told me further that I had attacked the tourist bus, that it had taken several men to pull me away from the senseless task of pummeling steel. His first words to me, when I became aware once again of words, were that sometimes men need a blow, a blow of destiny to catch them, as with a noose, and bind them by a force from without. He told me that he had fed me and sat with me and put me to bed. He told me that I had been in the cathedral for three days and three nights.

I don't remember the days or nights. I could not admit for a while that I knew the truth, that she was dead, that I was responsible; for as soon as I began thinking calmly about it, it all fell to pieces. All I knew was that there was no escape. Anywhere. Had I desired it, willed it, the very material world a confederate, pointing the wise way?

We are bound to the dead in a way that we are never bound to the living. No affection, no loyalty, no compassion, no tie is as strong and abiding with a living person as it is with a dead one. We must learn to live with our last words, our final actions, our sins of omission and commission, our neglects and regrets. We must find a way to live with all these things because there will be nothing else, a form of dissolution that becomes more and more like one voice to a death more dead than death itself.

It is Monday. Late. Or early Tuesday. Almost dawn. I left the care and safety of the cathedral this afternoon. I am sitting on our bench in the Plaza. The streets and sidewalks are deserted.

She died one week ago today. I try to look up now and then and focus on the streetlights, neon lights, signs of life. I visited her grave this afternoon. I had a hard time finding it. The cemetery is so large, the Indian cemetery, the years between the dates of birth and dates of death so short. I discovered that someone had placed a small wooden cross near her head. I removed it. She doesn't understand the cross. She wouldn't like it there.

I know that I must make a new beginning. But something has been permanently destroyed in me. I can't stay here, making daily trips out to her grave. But I don't know where I shall go. She seemed determined to spend her days wreaking some sort of vengeance. I feel an overwhelming sadness when confronted deep in myself with the fact that I could do nothing except kill her. I feel the full weight of defeat. There are no words anywhere that can name it.

Something is wrong in me and the world, and I don't know how to fix it. It's too easy to say that the whole fault was with Hatter. Too easy. And not true. But I don't know what it is, this thing that is wrong in me and the world, or where it is, or how to curb it, or encourage it, this lack, this surplus, this something that is wrong in me and the world.

I still have the check. For $41.28. The cost of her life. I should have been content to let her be what she was. But there was no room in the world for what she was. And now there is less room for me.

I hear from our bench the chiming of bells for matins coming furiously from the cathedral. The hour before the dawn. The last hour of the condemned. How many more are waiting for death? Does everyone know that when they die, we die?

Now is my night upon me. I still wait for her. But she doesn't come. It is the silence that frightens me.

I miss her . . . I miss her . . .
I miss her . . .

ABOUT THE AUTHOR

MARILYN HARRIS is an Oklahoman by birth. She first gained public attention with a collection of short stories, published in American and European periodicals, and later in a book, *Kings Ex. In the Midst of Earth* was her first novel. European editions of her books have been published in France, Germany and England. In addition, she has published two novels for young people: *The Peppersalt Land* and *The Runaway's Diary*. Miss Harris is married to E. V. Springer, a professor at Central State University in Edmond, Oklahoma. They have two children and reside in Norman, Oklahoma. Miss Harris received her B.A. and M.A. degrees from the University of Oklahoma.

The
Best Modern Fiction
from
BALLANTINE